Please return/renew this item by the last date shown on this label, or on your self-service receipt.

To renew this item, visit **www.librarieswest.org.uk** or contact your library

Your borrower number and PIN are required.

LibrariesWest

The Maltese Herring

By L. C. Tyler

The Maltese Herring

L. C. TYLER

Allison & Busby Limited
11 Wardour Mews
London W1F 8AN
allisonandbusby.com

First published in Great Britain by Allison & Busby in 2019.

A CIP catalogue record for this book is available from
the British Library.

First Edition

ISBN 978-0-7490-2445-1

Typeset in 11/16 pt Sabon LT Pro by
Allison & Busby Ltd.

The paper used for this Allison & Busby publication
has been produced from trees that have been legally sourced
from well-managed and credibly certified forests.

Printed and bound by
CPI Group (UK) Ltd, Croydon, CR0 4YY

To good neighbours

CHAPTER ONE

Ethelred

Dr Hilary Joyner was still alive only because God did not always answer the prayers of his colleagues, however fervent and frequently uttered.

There was, however, little about Dr Joyner to suggest he cared much for his colleagues or their prayers. Early in his academic career, he had successfully cultivated a look of amused contempt – originally ironic and occasional, but now permanent and largely discounted. His dinner jacket was a monument to the many evenings that would have been more enjoyable without him. It bore a number of very visible stains, some much fresher than others. On this particular evening, he had clearly been distracted while tying his bow tie, which was neither symmetrical nor secure. And there was also something about him – it was difficult to say precisely what – that suggested he had run out of deodorant.

For the first half of the meal, he said nothing to me at

all, and I was obliged to converse with the deaf old lady that they had placed on the other side of me. She was the wife of some Fellow of the College, long dead, out of respect for whom she was invited back to dinner whenever the Principal remembered. They always sat her, she said, at High Table but next to the least distinguished of the other guests. If the person beside her was more than usually boring, she added, she would show them pictures of her grandchildren. She paused, then glanced downwards, as if looking for her handbag.

To be honest, I shared her view that photographs of a family that I had never met would enliven my evening. And, like her, I wasn't sure why I had been placed in this position of eminence, seated in one of the comfortable chairs on the raised dais, a highly significant foot or so above the rest of the dining hall. My natural place at this reunion of alumni was at one of the long, improbably shiny oak tables that ran the length of the room, whose hard benches were occupied in term time by the undergraduates and tonight by the majority of the grey-haired, balding former students. But somebody had decided that I should join High Table with, amongst others, the College Principal, a junior government minister, a moderately well-known actor and the College's only Nobel Prize winner. I did not need to be told that I was the least distinguished of the diners seated there. That would have been apparent to everyone in the room. Many would have been wondering, as they awkwardly shifted their middle-aged weight on the unpadded surface of their allotted bench, why I rather than they had been so honoured.

I turned from the deaf lady to Dr Joyner, but he was still delivering a monologue to his other neighbour, leaving me to contemplate the hall, which I knew so well from my student days. I'd forgotten how gloomy it was.

It is seldom that I return to dine at my old College without my thoughts turning to death. It is not the coffin-dark panelling. Nor is it the faces of former Principals, staring down, gowned, laced and bewigged, from the walls. It is not even the letters from the development office, which often accompany the invitations and which remind me of the possibility of remembering the College in my will. Rather it is the myriad ghosts of past Fellows, who, in spite of a shared and lifelong loathing of each other, were nevertheless obliged to eat a communal breakfast, luncheon and dinner here, seven days a week, fifty-two weeks of the year, with the possible merciful exception of Christmas Day. Dr Joyner had not been placed next to or directly opposite any of the other Fellows. They happily relinquished that pleasure to others.

Finally, Joyner pushed back his dessert plate, stretched out his legs, ran his fingers through his bristly ginger-grey hair and turned to face me.

'Not your sort of thing?' he asked.

'Why do you say that?'

'You just look bored out of your mind. And these dinners are tedious – especially if you don't get out much and aren't used to them.'

'I dine out quite often,' I lied.

'Really? Do you?'

'Yes,' I said. 'More than enough, I assure you.'

As a writer, I occasionally get asked to make after-dinner

speeches – as good a way to spoil a meal as any – though this evening there were, thankfully, to be none, other than a brief welcome from the new Principal. He seemed a nice man and, depressingly, much younger than I was.

Dr Joyner smiled a smile that was both private and at my expense, then picked up his wine glass. It contained just one or two lonely beads of red liquid. His eyes searched for a waiter. There wasn't one. The thought occurred to me, I don't know why, that it was no accident that a limit was being placed on his consumption of alcohol. The same idea may have occurred to him, because he put the glass down, more or less where it had been before, and sighed. He looked again at me but without any visible enthusiasm. We'd clearly both had better evenings.

'It's a while since I dined at the College, of course,' I conceded.

'When were you an undergraduate here?'

I told him.

'Not before that?'

'No,' I said.

'Are you certain? You look quite a lot older.'

'I came up just after they made you a Fellow,' I said.

'Ah . . .' he said, running his fingers again through the sparse bristles that now comprised his hairstyle. 'When I was made a Fellow. *Then.*'

Then indeed.

In my days as an undergraduate, Dr Joyner had been one of the more striking of the younger dons. His subject was history and mine geography. Our paths did not cross in a tutorial sense, but I did know him well. Everyone knew him well. It was difficult to ignore him. His three-piece suits, then, were never less than immaculate. His hair flowed in strawberry blonde waves. His silk ties, always a single dazzling hue, were the envy of every male student. They were made, the rumour said, by Jim Thompson in Bangkok, and flown to Oxford a dozen at a time – rich, heavy, textured Thai silk in midnight-blue, scarlet, emerald, golden-yellow, slate-grey, Imperial purple, moss green, pale lilac – each costing more than we spent on clothes in a term. More perhaps, the rumour went on, than we had ever spent on anything in our entire lives. That seemed unlikely but there is, after all, little point in a half-hearted rumour.

His ties on their own would have generated nothing more than silent envy; it was the way he combined them with a rigid Marxist orthodoxy that demanded our absolute respect. The only history, he assured us, was the history of the proletariat. Nothing else was worthy of centre stage. Wars, kings, queens, literature, art and architecture were just noises off. The elegant sarabande of courtly politics would not have interested the average mediaeval serf, even if rumour of it had travelled down the muddy lanes to his remote village in Northumberland or Devon or Carmarthenshire. Joyner was, in those days, researching the lives of a family of peasants in Norfolk and intended to publish a comprehensive history of the fifteenth century based entirely on their class perspective and likely knowledge of events. The Battle of Bosworth, for example, was to appear only as a footnote to a chapter on the birth of a two-headed calf in the next village. As for the present day, he assured us of the imminent demise of late capitalist society in general and the University of Oxford in particular. There was no point in any of us working on academic topics that did not interest us for their own sake. The chance of the university still existing when we were due to take finals was slim. The coming revolution would sweep it away, along with the House of Lords, fox hunting and the Henley Royal Regatta.

His views on the irrelevance of Oxford University did not, however, extend to his own career. He accepted with alacrity the History Fellowship offered to him by my College. He contemptuously rebuffed the northern red-brick universities that courted him with professorships while he was still in his twenties. Later, I learnt, he had declined to go even to London or Edinburgh. Perhaps they were insufficiently proletarian. His aim was to run the history department at Oxford on rigid and uncompromising Marxist lines. Nothing else would satisfy him.

Maybe, even now, he still hoped that would be possible. But more recent events had not been propitious. His magnum opus, *1485 – The Year of the Two-Headed Calf*, had been rejected by every major publisher in the country. Times were changing, and a Thatcherite Britain had been sceptical of its basic premise. A smaller and more conventional work on Richard III (entitled *Dickon, Thy Master*) made it into print but was trumped by another biography of the King, inconveniently published two months beforehand. His book had not gone to a second edition. After a while he became Tutor for Admissions at the College. His colleagues sensed he had time to take these things on.

There were of course other projects – many other projects – but publishers had looked at his sales figures and shaken their heads regretfully. He was now said to be working on a book about the English monasteries immediately before their dissolution by Henry VIII, but a work in progress was unlikely, on its own, to win him a chair. Indeed, one of his former tutees, Anthony Cox, had recently been appointed to a history professorship and to a second, newly created, history fellowship at the College. Joyner was no longer the biggest history fish, even in this small, comfortable pond.

'I read geography, of course,' I said to him. 'Not history.'

'So what do you do now?' he said. 'Teaching? Town planning? There's not much else you can do with a degree like that, is there? I'm assuming you've managed to find work of some sort by now? Unless they've already retired you.'

'I write crime novels,' I said. 'One series is set in the late fourteenth century. A bit before your period perhaps.'

'I expect that's why they put you on High Table,' he said. 'As a historical writer?'

'No, because the Principal's secretary drew up the seating plan. She reads trashy crime novels. She might well have heard of you. What's your name again?'

'Ethelred Tressider,' I said. 'I write as Peter Fielding and as J. R. Elliot.'

'I'm afraid she buys all sorts of stuff, even romantic fiction,' he said, as if apologising for something particularly shameful to the College.

I've written that too, but for some reason it didn't seem worth mentioning it, or that some readers knew me best as Amanda Collins.

'I was told you were working on a book on monasteries in the sixteenth century,' I said, carefully steering the conversation elsewhere.

Some people might have been mildly flattered that a relative stranger had followed their career to that extent, but Joyner did not seem to be one of them. He took it for granted that I would, all through the long years since my graduation, have kept up to date with his work, both published and unpublished.

'Yes, that's right . . .' He looked thoughtful. 'The dissolution of the monasteries. I was advised by a publisher I approached to find a new angle. So, I've focused on a single incident that somehow encapsulated the whole thing: an alleged dispute between two monastic houses in Sussex. Wittering Priory and Sidlesham Abbey.'

'The buried treasure story?' I said.

Dr Joyner looked surprised. Still not exactly impressed, but I'd managed surprised. 'You've heard of it?' he said suspiciously. Perhaps the angle was not as new as he'd hoped.

'I live down there. It's quite well known locally. On the eve of the dissolution of both houses, Sidlesham Abbey accused the Priory of having stolen some valuable items from them. But, after the buildings and their land were sold off by the King, nobody was able to locate the missing treasure in either place. Subsequent owners of both sites have dug for it over the years, but nobody has ever found any trace of it. It was probably quietly stolen by the Royal Commissioners sent to close the Abbey and Priory down. There was another dig at Sidlesham a few years ago, but I don't think they found anything other than some broken pots and a few coins – rather like the time before and the time before that. Iris Munnings won't allow any sort of access to the Priory, of course. That's off limits to archaeologists. She's never wavered on that point. I can see that, if something really valuable was found there, then that might provide the sort of publicity that publishers like.'

Joyner looked at me with an interest that had been absent all evening. 'You *know* Iris Munnings?' he asked.

'Reasonably well,' I said, cautiously. 'I see her from time to time.'

To be absolutely clear, what I meant by this was that I sometimes ran into her in Horrocks Greengrocers in East Wittering or in the Co-op, or when she walked her dogs on West Wittering beach. But I'd only ever visited the Priory, her family home, as a paying customer, on days when she opened the gardens for charity. I'd never been inside the house itself, though I'd glanced enviously into the hallway once when the door was half-open. By no reasonable definition of the word could I claim we were friends. It was as I said: I saw her occasionally. She didn't necessarily see me.

'So you could introduce me to her?' said Joyner.

'Possibly,' I said. I was regretting claiming any sort of acquaintance. Still, her views on opening her garden up to archaeologists were well known in the village. I could speak with authority there. 'I have to warn you that she's a bit suspicious, for obvious reasons, of anyone who might want to search for buried treasure on her land. You wouldn't be the first to want to try. She won't have her lawns dug up. It's as simple as that.'

'But she doesn't know that's what I want to do.'

'I think she'll guess.'

'Really?'

'Yes. She's pretty sharp.'

I didn't add 'for her age', as I once might have done. I was aware how soon I would be her age and admired for being able to remember my own name.

'Obviously I could come down to West Wittering in person to reassure her,' Joyner said. 'I'm a serious academic from a respectable university. Not some random oik from Billericay with a white van and a metal detector.'

There seemed very little that was strictly Marxist in this last statement. He clearly spoke Iris's language these days. There were few people that she did not feel entitled to look down on. Perhaps, after all, he would get on with her quite well. But not well enough for what he wanted.

'She still won't let you dig there,' I said. 'Whatever colour your van is.'

Joyner did not smile. This was not a joking matter. 'Oh, I think she will. When I tell her what I have to tell her. The story as previously related is wrong in a number of ways.' His voice was suddenly lower and more urgent. 'It is most fortuitous that we have met and that you can explain things to her. Much better than a letter from me on history department paper. She'll listen to you when you explain what I've found out.'

'And what would that be?' asked a voice behind us.

We both turned to see Professor Cox, who had elected to tour the table in a proprietorial manner now that the serious work of eating was done. He looked, disconcertingly, like a younger, taller, more hygienic version of Joyner. His pristine black evening suit was brightened by a red silk bow tie. His face had a healthy glow. A haze of aftershave hung around him like a summer morning. He smiled at us in a convivial manner.

'None of your bloody business, Anthony,' snapped Joyner.

'I never said it was, Hilary. I never said it was. Is Dr Joyner telling you about his latest project, Ethelred? The OUP are annoyingly dithering over whether to accept his new book. I have to say I've always found them most reasonable, but they are proving inexplicably indecisive in this case. Still, it's good that Hilary has a little research interest to occupy the regrettably brief time that remains to him here. If the OUP do turn it down, it should at least provide material for a short article for one of the popular history journals.'

Joyner said nothing. I think we both knew that Professor Cox had not intended 'popular' as a compliment.

'It sounds very interesting to me,' I said. 'Since I live down that way myself, it's a story I know quite well.'

'I'm sure you do,' said Professor Cox. 'Local historians have been writing about it since the nineteenth century. I've pointed Hilary to one or two of the better papers. But I'm sure he will be able to find his new angle. A Marxist reinterpretation, quite possibly, though Hilary is less of a Marxist than he once was.'

Joyner still remained silent. His face did not appear to register Cox's remarks in any way. But this was perhaps the response that Cox had been hoping for. He smiled softly. 'So you live in Sussex, Ethelred?'

'Yes, in West Wittering. Quite close to Wittering Priory. Walking distance, in fact.'

Cox nodded. 'We have port in the Senior Common

Room afterwards, if you would like it. We could have a little chat. I've no doubt Hilary will be joining us. You can't keep Hilary away from port. Or sherry. Or brandy. Or gin. Or cheap, high-strength cider.' Cox finally turned back to Joyner. 'Eh, Hilary?' he said.

Joyner muttered something under his breath that I didn't quite catch.

Cox winked at me and moved on. He did not trouble my deaf neighbour, though she looked hopefully in his direction, but he stopped again beside a rather pretty girl in a red silk dress; she was, somebody had said, a junior research fellow, newly appointed. They seemed to know each other well. Cox's head was very close to hers. I heard her laugh. She glanced in my direction, smiled, and turned away again.

Joyner's eyes had followed Cox down the table, like a battle-scarred tomcat watching a passing terrier. He, too, now turned back to me.

'I'd be grateful if you told him nothing, Ethelred,' he said. 'Nothing at all. He is not well disposed towards the project.'

'I got that impression,' I said.

'He thinks I stole his idea.'

'And did you?'

'I'd have had every right. He's merely dabbled in the topic, as he does. I was the one who first took it seriously. I was the one who, long ago, discovered certain papers that he has most certainly never read – and never will, if I can help it. Now, a little too late, he's realised that he doesn't know as much as he thought he did. Well, let him continue to dabble, if he wishes. It won't hurt me. I'm a good ten or eleven months ahead of him.'

'I didn't think it was his period,' I said. 'The sixteenth century. Didn't he write the book on . . .'

'. . . Peel. Yes, everyone's read that. It was on the *Sunday Times* bestseller lists for months. No bestseller can be accounted a serious scholarly work. As I say, he dabbles. Can't stick to anything. A paper on the Corn Laws here, another on the destruction of mediaeval church silver there. The man is a total—'

But at that the Principal announced that coffee and port were available in the Senior Common Room for those who did not wish to repair immediately to the bar. We rose, individually or in small groups, and, at a leisurely pace, proceeded to one destination or the other.

Joyner must have been detained, because it was Professor Cox who approached me as I took a glass of port from the tray.

'You've had a tedious evening,' he said, 'with Hilary on one side of you and dear Mrs Fosdike on the other – neither, in their respective ways, able to listen to anything you might have to say. There are none so deaf as those who can't stop talking, eh? Did you like the pictures of Mrs Fosdike's grandchildren?'

'She didn't get round to showing them to me, though she may have been considering it.'

'Ah – that is a success of a sort. I must ensure that, when you next dine here, you are better seated. Really, I owe you that much.'

I was unaware he owed me anything. Or not yet, anyway.

'I was flattered to be on High Table at all,' I said cautiously.

'A writer of your distinction?' His eyes opened wide

with nicely judged incredulity. 'Where else would we put you, Ethelred? You are far too modest.'

'You've read some of my books?' I asked, in the way that I so often do before being cruelly disappointed.

'I saw a very good review of your Master Thomas series recently,' he said silkily. 'The one in the *Sunday Times*. And I liked the piece you did for the College magazine last term. Most amusing.'

'Thank you,' I said. I noticed he had still not said that he'd actually read the books. On the other hand, he had quite possibly taken the trouble to google me on his iPhone as he progressed the short distance across the quadrangle, on a warm summer's evening, from the hall to the Senior Common Room. That was more than I might have reasonably expected.

'Do you think this project of Hilary's is going anywhere?' he asked, lowering his voice. 'I mean, the topic seems to have been thoroughly raked over already – a bit like the grounds of the Abbey, wouldn't you agree?'

I nodded. From what I knew of it there had been a great deal of speculation and little hard evidence. 'The Abbey treasure? It's just one of those gothic folk tales, really.'

'Not the dissolution of the monasteries in microcosm, as Hilary would like us to believe?'

'Well, we have the rivalry between the houses, the King's intervention, the monastery needlessly hastening its own end . . .'

'Therein lies my objection,' he said. He smiled, inviting my agreement.

'You mean it adds nothing to what we know about the period?' I said.

Cox gave me a smug grin, and I immediately felt I had been disloyal to Hilary Joyner, though, God knows, I owed him no loyalty of any sort whatsoever.

'That's Hilary for you,' Cox said. 'He's never pursued a conventional academic path. He went from being a red to being . . . what you see today, almost overnight. All the more credit to him, I say. Follow your love of history without any regard to fame . . . or money . . . or your career . . . or the respect of your colleagues.'

He shrugged, as if to say that the definitive list of Dr Joyner's sacrifices for his love of history was somewhat longer even than that. But we both knew, and he knew I knew, that obscurity had never been Hilary Joyner's game plan. Cox possessed the very things that Joyner had always coveted, and that possession was made the sweeter by the knowledge that Joyner would have murdered to gain just a small part of what Cox had now.

'Of course, he may have found something new,' I said.

Cox permitted himself a dry, academic chuckle.

'That's very charitable of you, Ethelred, but I don't think either of us really believes that, do we? I am aware, of course, that he has documents that he is withholding from me in a most unprofessional manner. That is a pity, because I in my turn have solid evidence that he would find interesting. Indeed, I have something in my room that would show him he was very, very wrong in one of his suppositions.' Cox, aware that he might have said more than he should, looked over his shoulder. Joyner was a little way off, but possibly not entirely out of hearing range. Cox studied him for a moment, but nothing in Joyner's expression suggested that he had just gained some

21

unexpected scholarly advantage. Cox turned back to me, relieved. 'But you've done some research on this yourself, Ethelred? You seem very knowledgeable.'

Again, there was a conspiratorial smile of encouragement that I did not trust at all.

'Not especially,' I said. 'I just live there and have found one or two references to it in books on the area.'

'You apparently know Iris Munnings. You might have discussed it with her?' He raised an eyebrow.

If he'd heard of Iris Munnings for the first time tonight, then he had a very good memory for names.

'I don't know her well,' I said.

'I see,' he replied. 'Then you will lack the very necessary influence with our friend Iris that Hilary was hoping for. It would make so much difference to his chances of publication if he could unearth some treasure. Something glittery and newsworthy that would persuade his publisher that he had finally hit upon a bestselling subject. But you should not feel too badly about it, Ethelred. It will be one of the smaller disappointments in Hilary's life.'

I nodded. Again, there had been more than a suggestion that Iris's name was already known to Professor Cox and that he perhaps knew her much better than I did – that he could have effected the much-desired introduction for Dr Joyner, had he chosen to do so. It seemed likely that Cox was, in fact, some way ahead of Joyner. It just wasn't clear why he was interested at all.

'But the Reformation . . . I thought your interests were nineteenth century?'

'I've written one or two well-received books on Peel

and Melbourne,' he said with carefully honed modesty. 'But the true historian limits himself to no period. His delight and happiness is the past in its entirety.'

'Including 1536 to 1541?'

'Precisely. When Henry VIII was appropriating the wealth of the church for the greater good of the kingdom. When the national character was taking shape around a dislike of foreigners and a desire to grab any free stuff that was going. Who could not be interested in those years?'

'Of course,' I said.

'You think perhaps I should just leave it to Hilary? He would certainly have the leisure to do it justice in a way that I do not. My publisher is anxious I turn my attention to Gladstone. I'm not sure the world is ready for another study of the Grand Old Man, but I'm embarrassed to admit that the advance I have been offered is very tempting. Advances are ridiculously large these days, don't you find?'

I didn't find anything of the sort but, before I could think of a face-saving reply, Professor Cox simply smiled and moved on, a fact that became more understandable when I noticed that Dr Joyner was marching over to join us.

'What was Cox saying?' he demanded, much as Macbeth might have asked Macduff if he'd caught exactly what the third witch had just prophesied.

'We were talking about the Sidlesham Abbey treasure,' I said.

'So, is he going off the idea of meddling in matters that don't concern him?'

'He thinks he may continue with it. But I'm not sure why.'

'I am,' he said. 'Malice, spite and envy. But he's not going to get to this one first. He may have stolen my professorship, he may have appropriated my rooms in College, but he's not stealing my research. Or anything else. I'm coming straight down to Sussex, just as soon as you can arrange for me to see Iris Munnings.'

I still couldn't decide whether Cox knew Iris Munnings, but I tended to agree with his assessment of my chances of success. There was no reason why she should do anything just because I said so. As I've said, she looked down on most people in the village and I had every reason to believe that she looked down on me too.

'I'm not sure that will be possible . . .' I said.

'I may as well stay with you,' Joyner said, ignoring any reservations I might have. 'It will save time if I'm there in West Wittering.'

This proposal raised the stakes somewhat. I could see that it might save him time, but that didn't mean it would be at all convenient for me to have a guest over the weekend. I'd already fended off one prospective visitor. I proposed to be equally firm with this one.

'I'm very busy at the moment,' I said. 'Very busy indeed.'

'As a crime writer? Really?'

'I have a book to finish. I've had to tell my agent that she can't come down and stay next weekend. I've just sent her an email saying that a visit is out of the question. It's not you personally, Dr Joyner. I'd love to have you visit. Nothing could please me more. It's just that having even one person staying with me will prevent my doing any writing at all.

And I cannot afford that. Not with my current deadline. I'm really so very sorry . . .'

He looked at me as if trying to decide whether what I said was in any way possible.

Then a beep announced a text. I took the phone out of my pocket. The message was from my agent.

SORRY. DIDN'T GET YOUR LATEST EMAIL SO I AM COMING AS PLANNED FRIDAY. PICK ME UP AT THE STATION AT 8.30. WITH LUCK I MAY BE ABLE TO STAY UNTIL TUESDAY. GOOD, EH? ELSIE XXX

Dr Joyner, looking over my shoulder, nodded. 'It appears that your weekend is ruined anyway, then,' he said. 'You're not going to get any work done. So, fortunately for us both, my coming down won't make any difference. Since you'd love to have me staying with you, I wouldn't think of going anywhere else. I doubt there's anywhere much to stay in West Wittering anyway.'

'Yes, there is,' I said.

'But I'd hate to disappoint you,' he said. 'And they'll probably be booked up at this time of year.'

'I could phone and check,' I said.

'I wouldn't put you to so much trouble,' he said generously. 'I'll try to arrive on the same train as your agent, to save you having to go to the station twice. It looks as if she's planning to be on the one that arrives at eight-thirty – but, just to be sure, email me and I'll make absolutely certain I'm on board the right one. I'd be most grateful if you could confirm the arrangements promptly.'

'Thank you,' I said. 'That's very thoughtful of you. Very thoughtful indeed.'

In all honesty, his strange death, a few days later, came as no surprise to me at all.

CHAPTER TWO

Elsie

It is a truth, universally acknowledged, that an author in possession of a bestseller must be in want of a literary agent.

Though, obviously, a crap author selling four or five thousand books a year is in even greater need of somebody to keep their career afloat. In Ethelred's case, preventing his writing from going down with all hands had been a constant challenge ever since I signed him up many years ago, when I was a younger and more trusting agent. It had been, if you are still enjoying the nautical analogy, like steering a badly constructed ship with no lifeboats through a sea full of literary icebergs. Honestly, if I'd been captain of the *Titanic*, I'd have got that boat safely into New York and sold the Latvian audiobook rights before we'd even docked.

It is completely untrue that the opportunity for free weekends by the sea had played any part at all in my decision to retain Ethelred at the agency, when I'd quietly dropped several better selling authors who lived in Clapham or Pinner. I'd have probably kept him on if he'd merely had a cottage in the Lake District or (better still) a small but well-appointed chateau in the Dordogne, close to a Michelin-starred restaurant and a mainline railway station. But, until I found an author with exactly that, West Wittering would have to do. A hard-working agent deserves to get away from London from time to time and go somewhere where nobody mentions the word 'diet'.

Thus, I found myself at Victoria Station, one sunny evening in July, on the seven o'clock train to Chichester. I knew that it was likely to be crowded so I'd made sure I was on board at the first opportunity in order to secure sufficient room to allow me to work on the journey. I had accordingly taken four vacant seats, with my handbag on the space beside me, my suitcase opposite me, my coat draped firmly over the remaining seat, and my laptop, doughnut, coffee, emergency reserve doughnut and notebook spread over most of the table. Several commuters looked towards the area I was occupying as they passed through the carriage, but I smiled apologetically, as if my three large and possibly psychopathic companions were about to return at any moment, and the weary travellers and their briefcases thankfully all passed on, moving ever southwards.

I had just started on my emails when a middle-aged man with ginger hair, a white-ish linen jacket and grubby tie entered the carriage and started walking down the aisle, looking for any seat that had not yet been taken. He had foolishly boarded the train late and had nobody to blame but himself. Eventually he stopped opposite me and said something. I smiled. He said something else. I took the earphones out of my ears and said: 'Good evening. Can I be of assistance to you in any way, shape or form?'

'Could you just move one of your bags, madam?' he said. 'I'd very much like to sit down. You're not the only person on this train who would like a seat. Not by a long way.'

I sighed. Other people can be so difficult.

'Look,' I said, indicating the rest of the carriage. There were still half a dozen spaces free, some not next to babies or old people with poor bladder control. 'See all of the lovely seats that nobody is yet occupying. Why don't you sit in one of those?'

'Because you can't possibly be occupying all four seats here.'

I checked. He was wrong. I was.

'Sorry,' I said. 'You are clearly making the mistake that so many people have made in the past – that is to say that you think I give a shit one way or the other. I am very comfortable here. You could soon be equally comfortable yourself. Why don't you go to that table over there, or that table there, or that table . . .'

'Because there are three seats here that are not actually occupied,' he said. 'It's bad enough you've got sugar all over the table . . .'

I licked a finger and dealt with the sugar-on-the-table problem. Hopefully spit on my table wouldn't offend him quite as much.

'You do not need a seat for your suitcase,' he said. 'It can go up on the rack.'

'Mr Suitcase,' I said very seriously, 'doesn't like it on the rack. It makes him feel ill. So I've given him his own seat. As you can see, he's cheered up a lot, haven't you, Mr Suitcase? Yes, he says, I *have*.'

Normally I find that, once I've made Mr Suitcase's preferences known, people edge away down the aisle, watching me very carefully. They're happy to let me have as many seats as I can use.

'If you don't move your bags, I shall call the guard,' he said.

I thought about this. There are, I reflected, times when you have to graciously accept defeat. To admit that you were wrong. To laugh off life's little difficulties. To move on. But he unfortunately showed no sign of doing any of these things.

'All right,' I said.

'You'll move your bags?'

'With the greatest pleasure.'

'Thank you,' he said.

I picked up Mrs Handbag and put her on the table next to Professor Doughnut, then shuffled my bottom sideways, about two feet, most of the way onto the next seat. I invitingly patted the one I had almost vacated. It was nice and warm for him.

'Come and join me,' I said, with an excruciating wink.

He did not immediately sit down.

'Don't be shy,' I said. 'I'm sure we're going to be very good friends. You know, like in the romantic novels where the hero and heroine get off to a bad start – *Pride and Prejudice*, say, if you've ever read that one – but later they get on like nobody's business. Who knows what might happen in between here and Chichester? Are you married, by the way? I'm not. You'd be surprised to learn that I don't even have a boyfriend at the moment.'

'I'm going to report you to the guard,' he said. 'Unless you move your bags . . . not stupidly like that, but actually, properly move them . . .'

I smiled sweetly. If you'd seen me and a cute baby squirrel side by side, you'd have had difficulty saying which of us was a leading London literary agent.

'Very well, I'm reporting you now,' he said. 'Don't say I didn't give you fair warning.'

He seemed to think these words would magically move Mr Suitcase onto the rack, in spite of his vertigo. Obviously, if we looked at it like adults (always an option) we could each have two seats and share the glaring-at-commuters thing. But matters had passed the point where either of us was prepared to give way. Anyway, I *needed* all four. He didn't.

'You wouldn't like this table,' I said, giving the surface another wipe with my slimy finger. 'There's still wet sugar on it. You don't like sugar. Or do you?' I gave him my unblinking gaze and ran my tongue over my finger, very, very slowly.

He swallowed hard, then visibly folded. I watched him go, a small rucksack over his shoulder and awkwardly dragging his suitcase behind him. It kept jamming against the seats. He hit one or two random legs. He did not apologise. He seemed quite cross with the world in general. So, perhaps it wasn't anything I'd said, after all. It would take him a while to get to the other end of the train and with luck he might not come back. Nine times out of ten that was what happened in cases like this – at least in my experience.

Mr Suitcase and I settled down again in our seats. I'd save the second jam doughnut until we got to Horsham, I decided. It was definitely too soon to eat an emergency reserve jam doughnut now, or no more than I had already. Wrong in every possible way. I opened my laptop. There were two emails from Ethelred that I thought I wouldn't open just yet. He could tell me when I got there. There was also an email from Ethelred's editor that needed some thought and carefully judged sarcasm.

I licked some jam off my fingers and took a sip of coffee. Then I looked up and saw a linen jacket in front of me.

He said something. I smiled sweetly. He said something else. I took the earphones out of my ears.

'I've reported you to the guard,' he said.

'Is he married?' I asked.

I noticed genuine fear in his eyes this time. He went straight to the nearest empty seat and sat down, but he didn't take out a computer or magazine or book. He just kept glancing at me, as if worried that I might follow him the length of the train until he suddenly found himself engaged to me, like Mrs Bardell and Mr Pickwick. Obviously, I had no plans for that until I'd finished both doughnuts, but the journey after Horsham can be dull, especially the flat bit round Arundel, so it was nice to have it as an option for later. After a while he took a can of premixed gin and tonic out of his bag and poured it into a plastic glass. Shortly after that he opened another.

When the guard came round to check our tickets, he

stopped by linen jacket first and they had a nice little whispered chat. Linen jacket pointed to me several times during their discussion. He was probably still pressing for me to be ejected from the train in some embarrassing way – maybe marooned at Three Bridges with just a bottle of rum, some sea biscuits and a parrot. I winked at them and undid the top button of my blouse in what I hoped was a sultry manner. The guard said nothing to me at all when I handed him my ticket and moved on very quickly. He did not raise the topic of the ownership of my table. That seemed to be a done deal.

In the end, I did some reading after Horsham and completely forgot the possibility of having fun with linen jacket. When I did glance at him, I noticed a whole collection of cans in front of him. His gaze had become vacant. There was a slight smile on his lips. I was happy for him. Bit by bit the train emptied as it approached the coast. My needing four seats became less and less of an issue, even for the most unreasonable of my fellow passengers. Eventually, I noticed, linen jacket had four seats too. His larger bag was on the rack, but he now had his rucksack beside him, his arm round it in a protective manner, which Mr Suitcase and I thought was sweet.

We had just come into Barnham when I looked up and observed that he was now on his feet, peering anxiously through the window. We'd stopped at a point, as sometimes happens, where you couldn't easily see a station sign, which is fine if you've listened to the guard's announcements or realised there was a computerised sign in the carriage saying 'Barnham, next stop Chichester'. But he clearly hadn't. He had, as an alternative, drunk six cans of gin and tonic and then started to panic. He glanced around. But, by this time, he and I were the only people in the carriage.

He appealed to me in desperation. 'Did they say this was Chichester?' he asked, his speech slightly slurred. 'I think they mentioned Chichester in the last announcement, but I wasn't really listening.'

'Hmm,' I said very slowly. You could almost hear the precious seconds slipping by before the doors closed. '*Did* they say Chichester?'

He turned quickly to the window again then back to me. 'We definitely should be there now.' He looked at his watch.

As usual we were running about ten minutes late, so his premise that we ought to be in Chichester was totally justified.

'It certainly *should* be Chichester,' I said.

He hesitated, then quickly shouldered his rucksack, grabbed his other bag from the rack and made a bolt for the door. Just as it closed behind him, he heard two things: a guard's whistle ringing through the air and a voice saying, 'No, silly me, Chichester's the next stop.'

The train moved off, at first in that slow, patient, almost imperceptible way that only trains know how to do. I had plenty of time to observe him standing there, staring open-mouthed at the sign saying 'Barnham'. He turned and, down the line and across the tracks, he would have been able to inspect a pub, a few houses, lots of fields, some cows and no cathedral. I reckoned that, even with half a dozen gin and tonics on board, he'd worked out for himself that this probably wasn't the county town of West Sussex. We were now picking up speed, but he managed to flash me one final look of hatred before his face and the rest of the station became a blur.

'Don't worry,' I said to Mr Suitcase. 'The horrid man's gone now.'

I got out my phone and gave Ethelred a call to say I'd had an enjoyable journey but was running slightly late. I wasn't expecting him to have his phone turned on and he did not disappoint me. Ten minutes later the train pulled into Chichester Station. I walked down the platform and found Ethelred waiting for me by the exit, fretting that the train might have taken a wrong turning or something.

'So sweet of you to meet me,' I said, stretching up and kissing him on the cheek.

'You ordered me to,' he said, taking my suitcase from me. 'What on earth have you got in here?'

'Just one or two outfits for the weekend,' I said. 'I like to be smart. We're not all writers, you know – some of us don't get to slop around in pyjamas until it's time to take our agent out to a nice expensive lunch.'

Ethelred did not attempt to contradict any part of this. 'Did you see Dr Joyner?' he asked.

'Who's that?' I asked.

'I emailed you to look out for him on the train. He's also staying with me this weekend and said he'd be on the one you were catching.'

'And how would I recognise him?'

'Oh, a middle-aged academic. A bit prickly. Stubbly ginger hair.'

We looked back along the platform. It was very empty. There were clearly no academics in sight. Maybe there was one in Barnham with a bit of foam round his mouth, but there were none right here on the platform in Chichester.

'Perhaps he got off too soon,' I said. 'He was probably deep in thought, about some academic thing, then he suddenly realised he'd arrived at a station, jumped off and found he was in the wrong place. Maybe he'd also had a gin and tonic too many. It must happen all the time.'

'Not really,' said Ethelred. 'That actually sounds very improbable. You'd hardly mistake Barnham for Chichester, however many drinks you'd had. More likely he just missed the train. Well, we're not waiting for the next one.'

I got the impression that Ethelred was not totally displeased. At least, not for the moment.

'Absolutely,' I said. 'He could be anywhere at all, when you think about it. A bit like the Scarlet Pimpernel. Or Heisenberg. Let's just go back to yours and you can make me a cappuccino. Three sugars. Chocolate biscuits. You can stop and buy some at the village store if you've run out. I tried calling you to put my order in, but your phone was turned off.'

'Was it?' he said. It's always a surprise to Ethelred that phones don't work if they are switched off.

He fiddled with it, fifteen minutes too late, then stuffed it firmly in his pocket to punish it. A phone rang loudly just after he'd started driving me to West Wittering. It was the everyday ringtone of somebody who didn't know or care that you can have other ringtones. I told him to keep his eyes on the road and not grope in his pocket to locate the phone amongst his collection of old receipts, bus tickets and fluff. There were several more incoming calls, eventually at thirty-second intervals, as we drove along.

'Sounds like a nuisance caller.' I said. 'You get them all the time. They probably want to know if you've been in an accident lately, which, the way you're driving, is not an entirely unfair question. Still, it's best to ignore them until you do actually crash into somebody. And don't forget to stop for biscuits.'

It was sometime later that Ethelred checked who had been calling him and phoned back. There was a brief conversation.

'You did *what*?' said Ethelred. 'Why? . . . Really? . . . That seems very unlikely. I've never encountered anyone who was deliberately as rude and selfish as that. What did she look like? . . . How fat exactly? . . . I suppose so. No, I'm not coming back into Chichester to collect you. You can get the 52 or 53 bus from the railway station. Yes, opposite the pub you are in. Tell the driver you want the Old House at Home in the centre of the village. Or get a taxi if you don't want to wait. It's about twenty pounds . . . Fine, whichever you prefer. I'll see you later.'

He switched off the phone. For a moment he looked at me suspiciously, but his very best suspicions were no match for my total indifference.

'The man's an idiot,' he said eventually. 'Or he's been drinking. Got off at Barnham. Can you believe it? Had to wait for the next train. Trying to blame some poor woman who seems only to have been trying to help him. It sounds as if she wasn't quite right in the head, to be fair, but he can sort himself out now he's finally reached Chichester. Did you see a short, fat madwoman on the train?'

'Not from where I was sitting,' I said.

CHAPTER THREE

Ethelred

Dr Joyner arrived hot and not in the best of tempers. His breath smelt somewhat of gin. I fear I was not as sympathetic as I should have been.

'Well, at least you didn't have to wait long at Barnham for another train,' I said.

'Twenty minutes,' he said. 'Then the guard was awkward about my ticket having already been stamped by the previous guard.'

'It could have been worse.'

'Then another forty minutes waiting for the bus.'

'They are less frequent in the evening. Still, we're lucky to have a regular service seven days a week. Many villages round here don't. I've put you in the small bedroom at the front. My agent, Elsie, has already taken the much larger one overlooking the garden, having arrived somewhat before you.'

It was at that point that Elsie made her entrance. She had

changed into her seaside attire – a blue-and-white-striped dress, with a wide skirt supported by stiff petticoats, deep-red lipstick and sunglasses. She might have been dressing for a fashion shoot for a firm specialising in clothes for the shorter, fatter woman who wanted to be on trend without spending more than was absolutely necessary.

Dr Joyner's reaction largely confirmed what I had begun to suspect. He stared at her with a mixture of disbelief and contempt – understandable in many respects but never advisable. He was about to make his feelings clear in some way when Elsie tilted back her sunglasses and smiled.

'I don't think we've met,' she said, holding out a small, white-gloved hand. 'Elsie Thirkettle. I'm Ethelred's literary agent.'

Joyner ignored both hand and glove.

'I know who you are. You were on the train,' he said. 'You and your bloody suitcase.' His speech was blurred at the edges but his recollections were painfully clear.

Elsie looked puzzled and slightly hurt, though, if Joyner had known her better, he would have realised that proved nothing.

'I was certainly on a train,' she said. 'That's how I got here.'

'You were on the same train as me,' he spluttered. 'At least, as far as Barnham. As you know very well, madam.'

It would have been difficult not to detect Joyner's rage. I could only admire Elsie's response.

'Oh, did you also travel down by train this evening, then?' she asked conversationally.

Joyner looked like a man who, descending a staircase,

had missed not just the last, but the last three stairs.

'Yes,' he said. He frowned. After a bit, he remembered to close his mouth.

'But you clearly arrived on a later one than I did?' said Elsie, ignoring the dribble on his chin. 'Otherwise we'd have seen you at the station. Ethelred very sweetly came to meet me. So much easier than the bus. I'm sure he'd have given you a lift too, if you'd arrived on the same train. What a pity you didn't.'

'Yes,' Joyner repeated. 'But that's my point, you see, you told me—'

'Trains can be so tiresome, can't they? And they can be crowded, at this time of year. Did you manage to get a nice seat? I do so hope that you did.'

Joyner stared at Elsie, as if questioning his own sanity rather than hers. It was a feeling that I knew well. He had been about to say something to her. Something deeply felt. Something he really wanted to say. But suddenly he had a suspicion that the rules of logic, if not the laws of gravity, had been changed without anyone telling him.

'So, we didn't have a conversation on the train . . . ?' His voice tailed off as if it had nowhere left to go.

'If we had, I'm sure I'd remember it.'

'There was somebody on the train who looked almost identical . . . you might be twins . . .'

Elsie smiled sweetly, in a way that she never did if she was merely sticking to the truth.

'I'll go and unpack,' he said to me. 'I'm suddenly feeling quite tired.'

When he had gone, I said to Elsie, 'What exactly was all that about?'

'Oh, he thought I was some woman on the train who'd made him look like a total dickhead.'

'If you didn't see him at all, how could you possibly know that?'

'Woman's intuition. And, yes, there is such a thing. And, no, men are not allowed to question it in any way.'

'So, *did* you make him look like a total dickhead?'

'No need,' said Elsie. 'I just sat there and watched.'

Dinner was a simple affair. Cold chicken, simply cooked. A green salad without dressing. Some peaches. Half a dozen Mars bars. Two or three Wall's Cornettos.

'Are you sure you two don't want a Mars bar?' said Elsie, opening the last one. 'I think I've possibly had more than my share.'

'I'm good,' I said.

'All that salad isn't healthy,' said Elsie. 'It's mainly water. Probably full of plastic. Did you see that David Attenborough programme? *All* water, *everywhere*, is about ninety per cent plastic bags. Fact. Really frightening.'

'I'm not sure it applies to lettuce,' I said.

'I bet it does.'

'Except, in real life, nobody has ever found any plastic bags in lettuce.'

'They sure as hell haven't found any in Mars bars,' said Elsie. 'If they had, David Attenborough would have told us all to eat Twix. And I honestly don't think he did. I watched one episode and recorded the rest, so I couldn't possibly have missed it.'

Fine, Mars bars were healthier than lettuce. I'd just have to remember that if I didn't want this conversation again.

'What is the plan for tomorrow?' asked Joyner. 'When do we see Mrs Munnings?'

He had been relatively subdued at dinner, concentrating on his food, drinking only water and occasionally casting suspicious glances in Elsie's direction.

'Iris won't see us until the afternoon,' I said, 'so I thought we could take a run over to Sidlesham first and look at the Abbey. Elsie's curious to see it.'

'Why not?' said Joyner. 'I'd like to take another look anyway. And maybe have a word with the idiot who runs it. He's not being as cooperative as I'd like.'

I was, in fact, a very good friend of the idiot who ran it, but I decided to let this go.

'We are due at the Priory at two o'clock,' I continued. 'And not a moment before. Iris will be happy to talk about the house and the story of the theft back in the sixteenth century. Tell her as much or as little as you wish about your own project. But please don't mention any possibility of excavations.'

Joyner grunted non-committally. Well, if he raised the subject of digging, it might as well be for his own grave. Or for his book's own grave.

'I mean it,' I said.

'There's been a new development,' said Joyner. 'Iris Munnings is no longer in the position of strength that she imagined she was. She will have to cooperate. I can make her do it.' He looked at me as if wondering how much he could trust us with this information. Then he looked at Elsie and decided. He took a sip of coffee. Personally, I doubted he could influence Iris in any way at all, whatever he'd just found out. But I'd leave him to discover that for himself.

'So, what *is* your new book about, Dr Joyner?' asked Elsie.

Joyner frowned as if fearing some new trick, but Elsie's gaze seemed to convey nothing but genuine interest and admiration. 'It's a story of intrigue and deception,' he said, cautiously, 'dating back to the sixteenth century, but continuing today. Oh, yes, continuing up to this very minute. It is the story of death and hypocrisy and of how gold can corrupt.'

'Does it have sadomasochism in it?' she asked.

'What?'

'Handcuffs? Whips?'

'No.'

'Nazis?'

'No.'

'Wizards?'

'No.'

'Could you put some in?'

'They wouldn't be relevant in any way whatsoever. If you'd allow me to—'

'You could call the book "The Nazi Wizard",' Elsie continued. 'Big swastika on the front of it. Or a riding crop and velvet-covered handcuffs.'

'It's about the dissolution of the monasteries.'

'Of course it is. But nobody will know that until *after* they've bought it. It's all about the cover.'

'The words count for something,' I said.

'But not as much as the cover,' said Elsie.

'Well, my book's to be published by Oxford University Press,' said Joyner. 'I doubt they'd have gratuitous swastikas all over it.'

'If I was representing you,' said Elsie, 'I promise you they would.'

Joyner paused thoughtfully. Was he willing to sacrifice the integrity of his book to boost sales? Probably. Did he want an agent as ruthless and lacking in moral principle as Elsie clearly was? Yes, obviously. Still, there were limits.

'There weren't any Nazis then,' he said firmly. 'Not even for marketing purposes. But the story is nonetheless full of trickery and deceit. It concerns the Maltese Madonna – or rather, the Maltese Virgin – and Christ, because there were originally two statues, each about eighteen inches high and, so the story relates, formed out of solid gold and richly encrusted with gems.'

'Also – though I'm just guessing here – maybe made in Malta?' Elsie asked.

Joyner smiled. 'On the contrary,' he said, 'they were Byzantine – immensely valuable in their own right, but priceless as objects of veneration.'

'I thought it was just one statue that the Abbey possessed,' I said.

'Yes, according to the traditional version of the story,' said Joyner. 'Which may be wrong in a number of respects. But originally there were certainly two of them. They were seen as guardians of the church in which they resided and of the city of Constantinople as a whole. When the Turks laid siege to Constantinople in April 1453, both statues were paraded around the city to reassure everyone that it could not fall to the invader. But fall it did. Legend has it that the statues were stolen by a Knight of St John, who was present in the encircled and increasingly desperate community. He escaped through the Turkish lines, but at a price. The Turks wanted payment for his safe passage. He kept the Virgin but handed over the statue of Christ. Thus, he escaped unharmed and returned to the knights' stronghold in Rhodes but, like Judas, he had sold his saviour. That's when the story of the curse begins. After that betrayal, the remaining statue brought only misfortune on its owners. The Knights of St John were, in their turn, expelled by the Turks from Rhodes and obliged, homeless, to wander from place to place until granted the island of Malta by the Emperor in 1530. Then the statue vanished again. Stolen, according to one account, by "an English friar".'

'That must have pissed the Knights of St John off,' said Elsie.

'I think they were pleased to have seen the back of it. Relieved of the curse, they remained happily on Malta, seeing off a major Turkish siege in 1565 and taking part in the naval victory over the Turks at Lepanto in 1571. They did OK.'

'And it then shows up in Sussex?' she asked.

'The same year, by some remarkable coincidence, Sidlesham Abbey announced that pilgrims would shortly have the opportunity to venerate a wonderfully bejewelled image of the Virgin. People flocked in large numbers and paid well to see the statue, which the Abbey claimed to have had in its possession for many centuries, but which, tellingly, became known in these parts as the Maltese Madonna. So the locals apparently knew something about its origins.'

'Well, at least somebody finally benefited,' she said.

'Far from it,' said Joyner. 'The curse continued to do

its work. Word got back to London of this valuable relic and the King took an interest in it. A great interest. When, a few years later, the visitations of the monasteries began, with an eye to dissolving them and appropriating their wealth, Sidlesham Abbey was amongst the first to receive the King's commissioners. They demanded to inspect the famous gold Virgin.'

'And the commissioners took it away?' she asked.

'They never got to see it. The Abbot had claimed that, yet again, it had been stolen. The commissioners did not believe him, but a week of questioning, no sleep and a diet of bread and water did nothing to change his story. Then a local resident, an employee of the Abbey, let slip that a wagon belonging to the Prior of West Wittering had been seen leaving Sidlesham late at night.'

'Yes,' I said. 'That's the part of the story that is well known here. The Abbot accused the Prior of having stolen some treasure from him and having concealed it at the Priory. The Prior stole it and buried it – or the Abbot was lying and had already buried it at the Abbey to stop the King getting it. In which case the tale of the Prior's wagon was a carefully constructed red herring to get the commissioners to search in the wrong place. It's clear that the King wasn't sure himself which was true. When the two institutions were dissolved, and the buildings and land were sold off to new lay owners, the transfer documents specifically excluded any items of gold found buried on either site. The King wasn't going to be deprived of the treasure, wherever it was.'

'So who would own the Madonna, if it was found?' asked Elsie. 'Legally, I mean.'

'I've no idea,' said Joyner. 'The Knights of St John? The Catholic Church? The Church of England? The Crown? Istanbul City Council? Possession is unlikely to be obtained by anyone who is unprepared for a long legal battle. The person who found the statue might well decide to keep quiet about it. They might also be well advised to unload it as quickly as they could in view of the curse.'

'So, you think it is there to be found?' I asked.

Joyner again looked at Elsie and me as if still unsure how much to trust us. 'In the last few days I have come to believe that it has been discovered already – or something very much like it. I have what you might describe as concrete evidence.'

'So where is it? At Sidlesham or West Wittering?' I asked.

Joyner laughed, slightly uneasily. 'For very obvious reasons, I prefer not to say exactly where it is at this moment.'

'But one or the other,' said Elsie. 'After all, you've come to Sussex. So that must be a bit of a giveaway, no? If it's not down here, your visit would seem to be a waste of time.'

'I've come to confirm certain things,' he said.

'All right,' said Elsie, cutting as usual to the chase, 'if it's in the possession of somebody down here, all you'd have to do is wait and see who dies a horrible death in the next few days, then move in and search their house.'

Joyner's reaction was a sudden coughing fit. He reached out instinctively for his water glass then, on mature reflection, seized an opened bottle by the neck and finally poured himself a glass of wine. His hand trembled slightly as he lifted it to his lips but was steadier by the time he placed the glass back on the table. 'I couldn't have put it better myself, dear lady,' he said. 'You don't get to keep the statue without something happening to you. Something deeply unpleasant and probably fatal. The Maltese Madonna and death go hand in hand.'

CHAPTER FOUR

Elsie

When you lead an innocent and blameless life, you are rarely troubled by bad dreams, but I had a very strange one that night. Ethelred had come to me, clutching a gold statue of some female, and announced that, since he was now cursed and might shortly meet a horrible end, he wouldn't be able to complete his next book on time. I immediately got straight onto his publisher, who was very reasonable (this was a dream) and said he could have an extra millennium if he needed it, but only if he abjured the Antichrist. I amended this to 'take all reasonable steps to abjure the Antichrist', and said to put it in the contract. But when I went to give Ethelred the good news, he had vanished. The Madonna was still there, tap-dancing on the table, as they so often do in dreams. I awoke to find that the noise was actually a blue tit frantically pecking at its reflection in the window. I told it to piss off back to its nest box and turned over, but sleep evaded me. Even though it was scarcely nine o'clock, I got up. Ethelred was in the garden having breakfast. I told him about my very interesting dream.

'I'll make you some toast,' he said.

'Doesn't it worry you?' I asked, as he sliced bread in the traditional manner. 'You finding the Madonna, then vanishing?'

'No, because it was a dream. Your dream. In my dream I went to the cupboard and there were still some biscuits in it.'

'I couldn't sleep,' I said. 'I got up and made myself a snack.'

'In what sense is eating a packet of biscuits making yourself something?'

'Whatever,' I said. Everyone knows that opening a packet is cooking.

'Can you manage some toast, then, or are you too full?' He waved a couple of untoasted slices of bread at me.

'I might be able to squeeze a slice or two down, if you have some Nutella.'

'I'll check whether you've eaten that too, shall I?'

I paused. Had I eaten his Nutella last night? I didn't think so. Not all of it, anyway.

'It's the sea air,' I said. 'It makes Nutella evaporate. That's why you may find you've got less than you thought. Not that I know how much you've got now. Or had before.'

Ethelred looked at me with unfounded, or at least unprovable, suspicion. Time to change the subject.

'Where's Dr Joyner?' I added. 'Still asleep? Unlike us early risers.'

51

'He was up at six,' he said. 'Or so he told me when I saw him at seven-thirty. He took a stroll round the garden while it was still cool.'

I looked at the garden. It was green and had flowers in it. I could see that from here. No need to go round anything to confirm it. And certainly not in the middle of the night. Still, maybe I could pin the Nutella thing on him.

'Early morning walks make you hungry,' I said with great subtlety.

Ethelred silently placed a couple of slices of toast in front of me. He wasn't buying the story. I wondered whether to point out that the toast was slightly charred at the edges.

'You'll notice a few changes to the garden since you were last in West Wittering,' he said. There was a hint of pride there that needed some attention before it became an irritating habit.

'It all looks much the same to me,' I said.

'I planted those roses this spring,' said Ethelred, pointing at a nearby bed.

'That rose?' I asked, pointing randomly.

'That's a peony.'

'So, basically a rose, when you think about it,' I said.

'They're nothing like roses,' said Ethelred. 'I planted the roses over there. In that new bed.'

He looked at me in a discontented way. He knew my father had run a fruit and veg stall, and suspected that he had also sold flowers and that I sometimes helped him sell them, all of which was true, but he couldn't prove it, or not beyond reasonable doubt.

'I like next door's garden better,' I said.

His little face dropped. 'Phoenix?' he asked.

'Is that the house next door? The one with the rather glamorous owner?'

'Yes.'

'*Much* better,' I said. 'It looks as if they must have spent a lot of time on it, and know a lot about flowers, and are generally very good at gardening as well as at being glamorous. That's the sort of garden you should be aiming for.'

'I thought my garden was OK,' said Ethelred. He wisely didn't even open discussions on the glamour issue.

'It *is*,' I said, reassuringly. 'Just not as good as Phoenix. It's like your books, Ethelred. They're OK, but not as good as Ann Cleeves.'

'She writes a different sort of book from mine,' he said.

'Not really,' I said. 'She writes the same thing, only much, much better, so it *seems* very different.'

'I'll put some more toast on,' he said.

'Make sure you don't burn it this time,' I said.

'Shall I get Ann Cleeves to make it?' he asked, with what he may have intended to be sarcasm.

I shook my head. 'It would be a complete waste of her time,' I said.

Sidlesham Abbey was a bit of a disappointment. I'd hoped for rose windows and flying buttresses, and at least one creepy moment where I felt that the eyes of long-dead monks were watching me in a sinister manner and, obviously, admiring my new shoes. But it was mainly low walls and paths marking where things had once been. Any dead monks would have had difficulty in finding their way around unless they stopped and read the laminated boards showing where the refectory and cloisters had been. They would have found the flower beds a bit naff. It was, in fact, a slightly untidy municipal park with a bit of historic celibacy thrown in as an afterthought.

'The monastery was almost completely demolished in the seventeenth century for building stone,' said Ethelred. 'It was given to one of Charles II's mistresses, who had it knocked down and sold off by the cartload.'

His friend nodded. 'Exactly,' he said. 'A lot of houses round this way have got stones in their walls taken from the Abbey.'

The friend was called Henry Polgreen and he was chair of some obscure committee that looked after the site, and probably the guy that Joyner had previously found unsatisfactory. Ethelred had run into Polgreen shortly after we arrived. They were buddies of sorts. Polgreen was tall and thin, with short grey hair. You'd have said he looked a bit dull and pedantic, had he been standing beside anyone except Ethelred. It was too hot for anything but a T-shirt, but he, like Dr Joyner, was wearing a linen jacket. Ethelred had toyed with the idea of a jacket to keep himself cool, but I'd told him not to be such a dick. I'm always there for my authors, even at the weekend. It's what he pays me fifteen per cent of gross earnings for. I hadn't been able to stop him putting on a tie, though.

Joyner, over on the far side of the site, was pottering around, sweating and carrying the small rucksack I had seen on the train. The rucksack looked quite heavy, but he seemed to think he required it, in the same way Ethelred needed a college tie. It probably contained his ruler, pencil case, and prized collection of conkers. I really felt like a schoolteacher with a party of boys in uniform. Fortunately, I was able to add a little tone to the gathering in a vintage peach linen frock, white straw sunhat and the white patent leather sandals that the dead monks so much envied. I was sure that Ethelred already saw how unreasonable he'd been to complain at the weight of my suitcase. Style like this normally came in a steamer trunk with labels from hotels in Palm Springs and Singapore.

'I think you may have already met my other house guest, Dr Joyner?' said Ethelred to Polgreen.

'Several times,' said Polgreen, without enthusiasm. He looked over at the far side of the site, where Joyner was removing his jacket. The day was hotting up. 'He's been here a lot, poking around. He must have sent me half a dozen emails about all the things we're doing wrong. In his view.'

'I think he'd like to excavate here,' said Ethelred.

'Oh, he would,' said Polgreen bitterly. 'He'd like it very much indeed. I can promise you that. And he'd like any new discoveries timed to coincide with the publication of his bloody book.'

'Do you, in fact, have any plans for another dig?' I asked.

'No point, Elsie. The site's been turned over more times than I can count, starting back in the 1820s. One of the local vicars – the Reverend Sabine Barclay-Wood – managed to do all sorts of damage early last century, with random and largely undocumented trenches and holes.

We did find a few interesting bits and pieces last time we dug – mainly things that the workmen had dropped during the nineteenth-century excavations. There's a little exhibition of them in the museum hut over there. Some clay pipes and a rusty trowel and some coins and a tin box with a picture of Queen Victoria's diamond jubilee on it. Take my word for it, there's nothing left to find – or not buried treasure, anyway.'

'No Maltese Madonna, so far at least?' I said, peering over my sunglasses.

Polgreen sighed wearily. 'I know more about this site, probably, than anyone in the world. Yes, of course . . . the Knights of St John, the monks, the theft. But there's no evidence that the statue venerated here in the 1530s is the same one that was stolen from Malta. The Abbey claimed it was something that they had possessed for years. Unfortunately, the relevant records, carefully preserved by the later owners of the site, all vanished around 1900. They might have shown when and how the statue was acquired, but they're gone, so we'll never know how much the Abbot was lying. Sabine Barclay-Wood again, I fear – he was chairman of the preservation committee for a while and transferred most of the paperwork, along with a number of body parts and small items of jewellery, to his vicarage in Selsey, all never to be seen again. As for the statue, whatever it was, its disappearance can be explained in a number of ways. I'm sure all sorts of stuff was taken by the commissioners or by local landowners or by the monks who had been thrown out of the Abbey.'

'I suppose it was tough on the monks,' I said. 'Wandering

around all day in itchy robes and *very* unfashionable footwear. Praying, fasting, illuminating. Not having sex. Except possibly with each other. They weren't trained to do much else. A bit like writers today.'

Ethelred nodded thoughtfully.

'They did OK,' said Polgreen. 'When their house was closed down, the deal was that they got a pension or were transferred elsewhere. But, like I say, it would have been easy for them to pocket the odd relic, before they left, to supplement their pension fund. There would have been a stage, towards the end, when nobody much cared about guarding things and everyone was looking to put something aside for a rainy day. In the confusion of closing down a place this size, there must have been all sorts of opportunities to stuff a chalice or crucifix under your robe and head off down the road to whatever the future held for them. It's not just the Madonna that vanished. The inventory of the Abbey in 1530, one of the many documents we know existed before Barclay-Wood's time, was published in a history journal in the 1880s, and it records a gold chalice, silver candlesticks, a large silver bowl, an enamelled pyx and numerous smaller items. Most of it went missing at about the time the Abbey was sold off. All of the excavations over the years to find treasure would have been no more and no less than harmless fun, if they hadn't destroyed a lot of important archaeological evidence in the process. There aren't many places you can dig now where the soil hasn't been disturbed and sifted over by somebody. Bits of pottery from one dig thrown on top of bits of pottery from another – twelfth-century material mixed with sixteenth and no clue as to which part of the site it originally came from. So, I've said – no more digs. Not that Tertius Sly takes much notice. He'd have the bulldozers in tomorrow, he would. He thinks a big find would turn us into a major tourist attraction.'

'Secretary of the committee,' said Ethelred to me, as if providing scholarly footnotes.

'Ah,' I said. He didn't need to add that Polgreen and Sly hated each other. Some things don't need subtitles. 'So, if the Maltese Madonna may never have been here, why do so many people think it was?'

Polgreen rolled his eyes. 'Don't get me started on that,' he said. 'The story, as we know it, also comes from the Reverend Sabine Barclay-Wood, in a book he wrote on Sussex legends. He enjoyed off-the-wall gothic tales. He collected some locally, stole some from other parts of the country, often just changing the name of the village in which it took place, and made up the rest himself. He was an evangelical and not favourably inclined towards religious images of any sort. He liked the idea that a statue of the Virgin might be cursed, and that it could bring death and destruction to anyone who touched it. But it's just a story. Nobody's going to die here.'

I vaguely remembered the book in question, because Ethelred had a copy. I was about to agree it was crap, because it was, but at that point we all saw a small man in shorts, T-shirt and floppy hat advancing on us. He had a determined look on his face.

'Talk of the devil. Bloody Tertius Sly,' Polgreen muttered. 'I wonder what he wants now.'

I looked at Ethelred, who showed as little enthusiasm for Mr Sly as Polgreen had.

'A friend of yours?' I asked.

'Not exactly,' said Ethelred.

CHAPTER FIVE

Ethelred

'A friend of yours?' asked Elsie in a voice that was intended to carry far enough to cause embarrassment.

'Not exactly,' I replied at a slightly lower volume.

Elsie nodded and took in Sly's baggy lower garments and the T-shirt that he had probably bought from a charity shop for 50p. She approved of frugality, but felt he had still overpaid.

I knew Sly a little, though much less well than Polgreen. I often saw him around the village. I rarely spoke to him if I could help it. His conversations were peppered with casual disclosures of anything he knew that was to the discredit of his neighbours and acquaintances. Sly regarded it as an added attraction if he had received the facts in strict confidence before divulging them to the listener. I never told him anything that I would not have been happy for the whole county to know.

Sly was one of those people who have a nervous tic

when agitated, which he was much of the time. He had overcome these minor afflictions well enough to be elected a councillor – though whether that was county, district or parish I had never felt the need to enquire – and, as we had been informed, he was the secretary of the Abbey preservation committee. These were, one suspected, the highest offices he would ever hold, but they at least spoke of his diligence and willingness to serve without payment or gratitude. Polgreen had once told me that Sly aspired to succeed him as chairman, but that the committee would never elect him. Though Sly had devoted many years to the committee and would do any job diligently for as long as he was permitted to work many unremunerated hours, I believed Polgreen. The committee would elect somebody who was less well qualified but who (on the credit side) wasn't Tertius Sly.

'Hello, Henry,' he said. 'Hello, Ethelred.' Sly looked at Elsie and twitched.

'Elsie Thirkettle,' said Elsie. 'I'm Ethelred's agent. Pleased to meet you.'

'Oh yes, you write books or something, don't you, Ethelred?' He made it sound as if writing books was the last resort of the otherwise unemployable.

Elsie nodded sympathetically. 'Yes, he does write books. It's a great shame more people don't read them – or at least buy them. And you work for Mr Polgreen, I believe?' It had taken her a very short time to work out that this was the most annoying question she could ask Sly. But she'd had a lot of practice at that sort of thing and was good at it.

'We both serve on the committee,' he said, scowling at her. 'As one of the three senior officers. And that's what

I want a word with you about, Henry. In private, if you don't mind.'

'I'm talking to Ethelred,' said Polgreen. 'He has brought his friends to see the site. Elsie and a historian—'

'Dr Hilary Joyner,' said Sly. 'A very distinguished professor from Oxford University.'

'That's more or less right,' I said. 'He's a Fellow of my old college.'

'I've met him,' he said. 'Just now. We had an interesting chat, Dr Joyner and I. He seemed very much in favour of further excavations here and at the Priory. As I am myself. An extremely clever and well-informed man, I'd have said. Unlike some here, even if they do have university degrees.'

There was a great deal about the way he said 'university degrees' that indicated he thought all academic qualifications, except possibly Hilary Joyner's, were mere ostentation.

'It's still not a good idea,' said Polgreen. 'Whatever Dr Joyner may think. Not at the Abbey. And Iris will never allow it at the Priory – you know that.'

'But she would allow it *here*.'

This seemed a slightly odd concession on Iris's part, then I remembered that she was also on the Abbey preservation committee in some capacity.

'Even if that were true, the whole committee would have to approve it,' said Polgreen. 'Not just you and she.'

'As it happens, I've checked the rules and under certain circumstances the approval of two of the three senior officers is sufficient authority. For example, you and I, and Iris as treasurer, can take whatever action we deem necessary, if we have reason to believe that a committee member has acted improperly . . .'

He left this accusation hanging in the air in front of us.

'Sadly, I don't carry the rule book with me at all times,' snapped Polgreen.

'Fortunately, I have a copy with me,' said Sly.

'For some reason, that comes as no surprise. And you are suggesting that I have behaved improperly and that you and Iris can therefore approve further excavation to prove it?'

Sly smiled the smile of one who knows they have finally been understood. 'It wouldn't be appropriate to discuss that here and now, would it? Not with your friends here. I wouldn't want to embarrass you.'

'No, it wouldn't be appropriate,' said Polgreen. 'Or convenient. I'll come and find you later. We can discuss it then.'

For a moment, he and Sly faced each other down across the geraniums and snapdragons.

'I'll be in the office,' said Sly, pointing to the small green shack that served as a museum and, apparently, the administrative hub of the operation. 'I've got some important work to do there, anyway.'

Polgreen watched him depart.

'Dr Joyner seems to have impressed Tertius Sly,' I said.

'Anyone who favoured digging here would have his vote,' said Polgreen. 'Tertius Sly's easily pleased in that respect. Dr Joyner wants to promote his book. Sly wants to add to the fame of the Abbey – and hence of himself. The discovery of a gold statue would do nicely in each case. Well, I'm very sorry that you had to witness that little scene, Ethelred. Sly's determined to have me out and replace me as chair of the committee. He's got a bee in his bonnet that I've been searching privately for the Madonna, for my own

63

gain, and he thinks a new investigation here will reveal that. He knows the committee won't support him, so he's come up with this obscure rule, that he probably drafted himself this morning. I've no idea why Sly thinks Iris is on his side, though. She actually thinks he's a tedious little shit, as he'll find out if he decides to descend on her at the Priory and demand action.'

I nodded. In spite of our invitation to the Priory, I was still unsure that Iris necessarily thought any more highly of me than she did of Tertius Sly. 'I must bring Dr Joyner over before you go off and have your chat with Tertius,' I said. 'I know he's got some questions he'd like to ask you, if you can spare a moment.'

Polgreen nodded unenthusiastically. I was sorry to impose this burden on him, but it would possibly save him a visit from Joyner to his home later on. There was, as I had already discovered, no avoiding Dr Hilary Joyner if he was determined to see you.

It was at that point that we saw Joyner striding across the site to join us, panama hat firmly on his head, awkwardly juggling his now discarded coat and his rucksack. He was breathless, either from his speed of travel or from his indignation.

'You will *never* guess who I've just seen,' he announced.

We knew he'd seen his new admirer, Mr Sly, but it seemed unlikely that that was what was troubling him.

'Brian Aldridge?' said Elsie. 'Eddie Grundy? Linda Snell?' She'd always liked guessing games, especially when other people took them seriously and might get annoyed if she didn't.

'Anthony Cox!' he announced, without waiting for her

to go through the rest of the cast of *The Archers* and move on to *EastEnders*. 'What is he doing here?'

'Where is he exactly?' I asked.

'Over there,' said Joyner.

We looked in the direction Joyner had come from and where he was now pointing to, but there was no sign of anyone.

'He must have gone,' said Joyner. 'But he *was* there.'

'A brief visit, then,' I said.

'You treat his intrusion remarkably casually, if you don't mind my saying so.'

'He has as much right as we do to be here. I'm sure there's a perfectly innocent reason for his visit.'

'Innocent?' said Joyner. '*Innocent?* You think so? I swear to you, Ethelred, I'll kill that man. One day, I really will murder him. If he doesn't get me first, of course.'

'But are you sure it was Professor Cox?' I asked, as we drove at an even pace through the narrow Sussex lanes. Tall, dark-green hedges hemmed us in on both sides, but there was always just room for two cars to pass each other, if driven with care. You just had to hope that you didn't meet a combine harvester coming the other way. In places, the trees arched right over the road, making a dappled tunnel for us to travel through.

'Of course. I've seen him from most angles over the past twenty years. If you'd just been a bit quicker off the mark, Ethelred, we might have caught him and confronted him.'

I wasn't aware that I'd ever offered to do that. More to the point, I hadn't stopped Joyner doing anything. Anyway, as I'd said, Cox had as much right as Joyner to view the Abbey in the course of his research.

'Well, you saw him first and could have confronted him there and then if you wished,' I said. 'I was never informed of any plan to chase him across West Sussex. You'll presumably see him back in College next week. There should be plenty of opportunity to confront him then, if that's what you'd like.'

'It's what he'll do in the meantime that worries me. It wouldn't surprise me if he went straight round to the Priory. Now I think it, that must be his plan. We should drive there without delay. We must be very close. And by good fortune we have your car available to us.' He fiddled with his phone, trying to work out directions from Google Maps.

'I've booked a table for lunch at The Lamb,' I said. 'And Iris Munnings isn't expecting us until two o'clock. She's not the sort of person who would take kindly to our arriving out of the blue, when she's probably having lunch herself. She'll simply send us away and I'll have wasted the time I spent on persuading her to see you.'

Actually, fixing the appointment had been easier than I had feared. I'd phoned and dutifully explained the problem. She'd said she'd think about it, and then called me back five minutes later to say yes. I was pleasantly surprised at how persuasive I'd been. But she was notoriously touchy on matters of etiquette, and I wasn't sure that I could charm her twice in one week. There was no advantage, from my point of view, in upsetting her for the sake of an hour or so.

Joyner was still protesting, though largely to himself, when I swung the car slowly but firmly into The Lamb car park. He condescended to eat a hearty lunch – as did Elsie –

but he sulked all the way through it and looked at his watch at every opportunity. Seeing Cox like that had completely unsettled him. Eventually, at one-thirty, I conceded that we might pay the bill and leave. Fifteen minutes early was probably forgivable.

In fact, we were twenty minutes early when I parked outside the Priory. I sighed and prepared to be admonished for my inconsiderate timeliness.

The Priory was a mellow red-brick building, for the most part just two storeys high, but with a Tudor gatehouse that had long offered a distinctive landmark for sailors navigating the coastline to and from Chichester Harbour. It had never possessed the grandeur of Sidlesham Abbey – no Cathedral-like church, no vast monks' refectory, no gothic cloisters – everything had always been on a cosy and domestic scale. The very modest priory church had been demolished soon after the cluster of buildings ceased to be a religious house, and a new kitchen wing, also in red brick, had been added in the early 1800s. Its grounds had once stretched all the way down to the pebbly beach. They were now slightly more curtailed but still extensive enough to be worth opening to the public a few days a year, for the benefit of various local charities. From where we stood, rhododendrons blocked the view of most of the garden, but I knew well their damp, mysterious woodland paths, sunny lawns and bright flower beds. At this time of year, they would be full of roses, peonies, verbena, lavender, stocks and geraniums. There were some pink elders that would be in flower. I was looking forward to seeing it all again. Once I had apologised sufficiently.

'That is outrageous!' Joyner exclaimed.

I was about to lock the car but, instead, I turned, following the line of Joyner's trembling finger. He was pointing to a white Mercedes convertible that was also parked outside the house.

'The sports car?' I asked. It was a pretty little thing – low, sleek and well-cared-for. Not a saloon car lacking a roof, but a proper two-seater, designed to be driven fast on an open road, down towards the glistening blue Mediterranean or along the rugged, winding coast of the Adriatic. It was perhaps not everyone's cup of tea – it lacked proper luggage space – but it seemed unlikely to arouse the sort of distaste that Joyner was exhibiting.

'*Cox*,' said Joyner. 'That's bloody Cox's bloody car! He must have driven straight here from the Abbey. It is precisely as I feared. He has come here and turned Mrs Munnings against us. You should have listened to me, Ethelred. I hold you personally responsible for any damage he has done through your neglect.'

I looked at Joyner's face. He was genuinely worried, though I doubted the hour or so Cox had had with Iris would persuade her to do anything she didn't want to do. If anyone in the village knew her own mind, then Iris Munnings did.

'Well, it's partly as you feared,' I said. 'His car is here. There's no evidence that Professor Cox has done anything yet except park it under that tree. It's a lime, and he'll be sorry when he sees the sticky mess that drips from it at this time of year.'

Joyner surveyed the pristine leather seats and allowed the merest glimmer of a smile to pass across his lips, then he recollected that greater matters were at stake. 'Ring the bell at once!' he commanded. 'The only dripping that's going on at this moment is Cox dripping poison into her ear.'

That, too, seemed unlikely, but I pocketed my car keys, rang the bell and prepared myself for Iris's recriminations.

There was, in fact, a long pause and a slow tread of feet, then Iris opened the door. She was dressed in a short white jacket, white T-shirt and black jeans, rather than one of her usual knee-length summer frocks. It wasn't clear if that was in some way in our honour or because she needed to do something for which jeans were more appropriate than a skirt. Her short grey hair was also neat and practical. Perhaps she envisaged a hand-to-hand struggle with Joyner to prevent his digging up her garden. The white jacket would show the blood, though. In that respect it was not a good choice. She looked at me and swallowed hard. Her gaze was normally firm, aristocratic and thoroughly entitled. But, for once, she appeared ill at ease, even on her own doorstep.

'Ethelred!' she exclaimed more enthusiastically than I had any reason to expect. 'You're a little more prompt than you said but . . .'

'Yes, I'm sorry, Iris,' I said. 'We finished lunch early. If you like, we can go away for ten minutes and take a stroll along the beach—'

'Don't be so silly,' she interrupted. 'It's not important. Not important at all. You must all come in and . . .' She paused, hearing footsteps behind her.

'Hello, Ethelred,' said Professor Cox, emerging from the sitting room and into the hall. He stood there as if he rather than Iris owned it. 'Good to see you. Hello, Hilary. And this is . . .'

'You can call me "Hello Elsie",' said Elsie. 'You must be Hello Professor Cox. Nice motor. Must have cost a bit.'

'Yes, it did,' said Cox, not taking his eyes off Joyner.

'I bet you got here from Sidlesham in no time at all,' said Elsie. 'Speeding along the narrow lanes, in a way that Ethelred doesn't, or possibly can't.'

'Absolutely,' he said, still without looking at her. He was enjoying watching Joyner far too much for that. It seemed to be one of his hobbies.

Iris looked from one to the other, then swallowed again. 'Maybe you'd all like to come through into the garden. Dr Tomlinson, Professor Cox's . . . er . . . colleague, is also here. We were having coffee. I'll get Pia to make some more.'

Elsie noted the 'er' and raised her eyebrows at me. I shrugged. Whatever the reservation was, we would soon see whether we shared it or not.

Coffee was duly served by Pia, Iris's new Filipina housekeeper. We drank it on a terrace, overlooking the main lawn, in sunshine that would have been far too hot had it not been for the gentle breeze off the sea. Croquet hoops adorned the short grass. The mallets and balls were piled up close by, but nobody appeared anxious to play. Cox leant back in his chair and, for the most part, silently contemplated the view. Joyner scowled at him and said even less. Dr Tomlinson proved to be Fay Tomlinson, the junior research fellow whom I had seen at the College dinner, then looking rather elegant in her scarlet silk dress. This afternoon, she wore a simple pale-blue linen blouse and a dark-blue cotton skirt. Both she and Iris were better attired for practical tasks than Elsie was in her bouncing retro petticoats and improbable white lace gloves. Fay checked emails constantly on her phone, her long legs stretched out in front of her. She was in her late twenties, blonde and with redder lipstick than most historians I had met. Her sunglasses, like Elsie's, were perched on her head. She wore a gold bracelet and a necklace of a simple but probably very expensive design. Beauty is perhaps a subjective thing, but whenever Cox turned in her direction, he undoubtedly appreciated what he saw. This perhaps accounted for Iris's 'er'. But, other than the occasional shrug or single-word response, Dr Tomlinson chose largely to ignore Cox. It was reasonably clear to us all why Cox might have chosen to bring her in the white convertible, less clear why she had elected to come. Once or twice I noticed she tried to catch Hilary Joyner's eye, but he declined to talk to this ally of his most bitter rival. If her role was to bring about any sort of rapprochement between the two warring camps, then she had failed miserably. But I wasn't sure, to be honest, why most of us needed to be there.

Indeed, on reflection, we were not the jolliest of parties. Elsie alone made lively, one-sided small talk with Iris, who still seemed unusually ill at ease for somebody who was often grudgingly accorded, within the village, the status of Lady of the Manor. Everyone was aware that an almighty row was brewing and only Elsie was genuinely looking forward to it.

'It's very kind of you to see us, Iris,' I said to her for the fourth or fifth time.

'*As I've told you*, Ethelred, it's always a pleasure to share the house and garden with others. You might say it

71

is a duty. In some ways, I've been very fortunate in my life. I have to remind myself of that. Very lucky. In some ways, at least.'

Her hand stretched out for the coffee pot, then she recalled that she had only just offered us more coffee and she sat back again with an involuntary sigh.

'Do you know West Wittering at all, Dr Joyner?' she asked.

Joyner blinked twice and turned to her.

'I had an aunt who lived round here,' he said. 'Dead now. I used to visit.'

'Really? What was her name?'

'Harriet Joyner. She lived in Bracklesham.'

'Ah,' said Iris. 'It's a while since I had any reason to go to Bracklesham. The beach is so much nicer here. What did you and your aunt find to do there?'

'Trips to boot fairs, mainly. That was what she liked doing in her old age. She collected novelty teapots. You'd be amazed how many different ones there are out there. Cottages. Castles. Houses. Lighthouses. Postboxes. Phone boxes. Big Ben. Buckingham Palace. Cats. Dogs. Frogs. Mickey Mouse. Donald Duck. And she seemed determined to have them all. I took the whole lot to the tip the day after she died. Threw the black plastic sacks into the skip and listened to the sound of breaking china. They had to be destroyed. I didn't want other lives blighted the way hers was.'

Joyner looked round the group, as if wondering if he had revealed something – some small weakness – that Cox might, in due course, be able to exploit. But Cox appeared not to have heard him. Joyner relapsed into an uneasy silence.

Perhaps, after all, he regretted the Mickey Mouse one.

'Has your family owned the house here for long?' I asked Iris.

'The Priory? My grandfather bought it. He was a banker in London. He wanted to move his family closer to the sea. His wife, my grandmother, was suffering from . . . well, she was ill. He thought it might benefit her.'

'Did it help?' I asked.

'I don't think it can have done. She died shortly after they arrived. That would have been in 1959 or '60 – '59, probably. Nobody's really sure exactly. My grandfather passed away himself at about the same time.' She sighed again and fiddled with her pearl necklace, as if it were a neat and expensive rosary.

The sun continued to shine down on us. Perhaps Iris felt it was a gloomy conversation to be having on a bright, cloudless afternoon, the hottest of the year so far. I was curious to know more, if she'd tell us, but felt that it was indelicate to enquire. Fortunately, Elsie did not feel in any way constrained.

'Your grandfather never got the chance to search for the famous buried treasure, then?' she said.

Iris looked at Elsie vaguely as if only half taking in what she'd said. 'I was still quite young when he died. It's not necessarily the sort of conversation you have with a child.'

'And your parents?' she asked.

'Not really. They never mentioned it. I didn't get much chance to discuss it with them either, of course. Under the circumstances.'

'Perhaps they didn't believe in it all?' Elsie persisted. 'The treasure. The curse.'

'Oh no. They believed in it all right. They'd seen it in action.'

'You mean you know that the Madonna is probably here somewhere?' she enquired.

Iris, who had had a distant look in her eyes for a while, suddenly focused on Elsie with the intensity I remembered from her admonitions to dog walkers who failed to carry enough poop bags with them on the beach.

'I've no idea what could be buried here, Elsie. But there's no way I'm having this garden dug up. My grandfather created it for my grandmother, you see. I wouldn't have it destroyed just to find some mediaeval trinkets that are likely to be of no possible value to me.'

'Metal detectors,' said Joyner, every bit as impervious to questions of delicacy as Elsie was. 'I've been thinking about it. Metal detectors. And spades. Five or six of us could do it in a couple of days. There'd be no need to dig up more than was absolutely necessary. Just a flower bed or two. Then we could let things rest.'

'Well . . .' said Iris, as if suddenly uncertain of herself. She half turned to Cox.

'There's no hard evidence that anything of any value was ever buried here,' said Cox quickly. 'None at all. We know that one of the statues – the Virgin – was in Malta in the 1520s. And then it disappeared. But there's nothing to connect that with the so-called Maltese Madonna that appeared here shortly after. There are no pictures of the statue. There aren't any good descriptions in contemporary accounts. Even the name can't be traced back further than the early twentieth century. A book on Sussex by some obscure clergyman just says that was what people called it in the olden days.'

'Sabine Barclay-Wood,' I said. 'It's difficult to discuss the Madonna without his name cropping up. In a sense he created the whole mythology around it. I have a copy of the book in question, but I've done no more than glance at that particular story, to be fair. I find his style of writing somewhat mannered at the best – rather irritating at the worst. But he would have known about it, if anyone did. He was the one who set up the trust to preserve what remained of the Abbey. He was chairman of the committee for about forty years.'

Cox nodded. 'All of that may be true, but I can assure you he offers no proof for any part of the narrative. Most of the book, as you know, is just a jumble of folk tales and gossip, and the tale of the Sidlesham or so-called Maltese Madonna is very much of the same type – picturesque, unsubstantiated twaddle. The stories of treasure possibly being buried here are, at best, merely apocryphal.'

'Which is, of course, what I meant to say myself,' said Iris to nobody in particular.

She again picked up the coffee pot and scanned the state of our cups, and then put it back down.

'You're the treasurer of the Abbey preservation committee?' I asked Iris.

'Yes. That doesn't make me an expert on the Abbey, of course. Still less on things like the inventory. I just about know how to do spreadsheets – that's all that's required. The Abbey did possess a lot of documents at one stage, but they were all lost about sixty or seventy years ago.'

'Henry Polgreen says they were taken to Selsey,' I said.

'Well, he'd know. The Abbey is pretty much his life. I'm unsure what he'd do without it.'

Then I, and the others, heard raised voices from inside the house – one high-pitched and querulous, one annoyed but resigned. It was part of a heated argument that had clearly begun some time before and looked set to continue for a while yet. Then Sly strode through the French doors into the garden, followed by Polgreen and a slightly agitated Pia.

'Miss Munnings, these two gentlemen—' she began.

'We need to talk, Iris,' Sly announced. 'There have been irregularities in the management of the site. Rule forty-seven states quite clearly . . .' Then, for the first time, he became aware of the rest of us sitting round the terrace, gazing at him in his charity-shop T-shirt and shorts, and he paused thoughtfully.

'I'm very sorry that we've interrupted you, Iris,' said Polgreen. 'I told Tertius that this was not appropriate. I see it's also very badly timed. We'll go away, and I'll phone you and make a proper appointment, unless I can persuade him that we can deal with the matter at the next committee meeting. God knows, we have enough of them and very little to do there.'

Iris looked round the group. Her afternoon had been ruined long ago but her duties as hostess were clear and overriding.

'Well, you're here now,' she said to Polgreen. 'Why don't you both stay for coffee?'

Sly was unfolding a small typed and stapled booklet, rather grubby along its edges and possibly the rule book that he had referred to. He had not quite given up hope that Iris's frosty tone really concealed a genuine affection for him and a deep and lasting respect for the constitution of the committee. He turned uncertainly to see what Henry Polgreen would say.

Polgreen, in fact, hesitated for a moment then said, 'That's very kind of you, Iris, under the circumstances.'

Sly's mind was now also made up. He certainly wasn't leaving them alone together. 'Thank you, Iris,' he said. 'A spot of coffee, you say? I don't mind if I do. Very, very kind of you.'

And so they entered fully into the spirit of our little party.

For a while Sly scowled silently at Polgreen, Joyner scowled at Cox and continued to ignore Fay Tomlinson, who tapped her foot impatiently. Joyner said very little to Iris. No doubt he'd hoped to talk to her alone and found this motley gathering inconvenient. Iris poured the fresh coffee that Pia had brought to the table in the hope that somebody would drink it. Eventually she sighed for about the tenth time that afternoon and said, 'Why don't I show you all round the garden. I think that's what some of you at least have come for?'

'I'd like that,' I said, getting quickly to my feet.

'A tour of the garden would be very pleasant, Iris,' said Elsie.

'Lead on,' said Joyner with some enthusiasm.

'Just the ticket,' said Sly. 'Just the ticket, eh?'

Pia appeared, almost magically, with Iris's sunhat, white, broad-brimmed and not unlike Elsie's. Joyner clapped his own panama on his head. I regretted that I had left my old folding hat in the car. The heat was becoming oppressive.

We set off in a gaggle, more or less following Iris's white jacket. Joyner had produced a slightly yellowed map from his pocket, which he had unfolded and now glanced at surreptitiously whenever he thought Iris was not looking.

'There's a well somewhere in the garden?' he asked, as we paused to admire some azaleas.

Iris froze for a moment, then turned and gave Joyner a very stiff smile.

'Yes, just over there,' she said. 'Under the trees.'

'Ah,' said Joyner slowly. 'Yes, of course. Under the trees. I didn't see it for a moment.'

We all squinted into the shadows. We'd have to take her word for it. It was very dark in there. Layer upon layer of leafy branches filtered the sunlight, leaving a twilight world of ferns and damp brick.

'Everything has grown so much since the well was last used for drinking water,' said Iris. 'It was originally in an open space. You wouldn't want too many leaves dropping into it, I imagine. But since the well has been abandoned for all practical purposes, the trees and shrubs have been left to grow round it – especially in the last fifty years. But the old well looks rather romantic in its shady little grove.'

'You don't mind if I take a closer look?' asked Joyner.

'A look? I suppose not. Be careful, though! The well has an iron grill over it, but I'm always afraid somebody could still fall in – especially with it being so gloomy. Originally there would have been some sort of wooden cover but, after they stopped using the well, that was just left to rot, I'm afraid. So, my grandfather had the present grill made in its place. To ensure there wasn't another—that is to say, to prevent an accident.'

'Can you remove the grill?' asked Joyner.

Iris looked doubtful. 'I have the key on my key ring,

as it happens, but I don't think it's a good idea. The wall round it is a bit crumbly now. You can see reasonably well through the grill.'

'Have you looked recently, then?'

'I've felt no need to do so. But I'd much rather the grill stayed in place.'

'I want to get a proper look down there with my torch,' said Joyner.

'One of the previous owners apparently searched the well,' said Iris. 'Some years ago. A small boy, carrying a lantern, was lowered on a rope, one summer when the water level was very low. I can promise you there's nothing down there. No treasure, Dr Joyner.'

'When was this?'

'I don't know. A long time ago. Certainly before the last war. Maybe before the one before that. I'm not sure you're allowed to do that to small boys these days. But, whenever it was, the point is that if the Prior had concealed anything there, it would have been found.'

Joyner smiled. He seemed relieved at some part of this answer.

Fay Tomlinson, who had said almost nothing all afternoon, finally spoke up. 'I really don't see the point, Hilary,' she said. 'What exactly do you think you're after?'

'I am merely curious to examine it,' Joyner said to her. 'It would have been the original source of water for the Priory.'

'Water's water,' said Fay. 'You can see that anywhere. I think we are just wasting time.'

'You must let me decide what's worth investigating,' he said.

'Even so . . .' said Iris. 'It's not really safe.'

'Precisely,' said Fay. 'Let's all move on, shall we? I thought that was the plan? That we all see the garden?'

'Oh, let Hilary fall down the shaft if he wants to,' said Cox. 'What harm can it possibly do, if the well's no longer in use? Iris has the key.'

Iris looked at Cox, then knelt down carefully and unlocked the grill. Working like a practised team, she and Cox lifted it off. The old ironwork clattered ominously onto the surrounding stone path. Iris instinctively stepped back from the deep shaft with evident distaste. She brushed the pale dust from the knees of her black jeans and examined a white sleeve for possible rust marks. Perhaps neither the jacket nor the trousers had been such a good idea after all.

'We'd better stay while you do it, Dr Joyner,' she said. 'I really don't like the thought of your leaning over that well alone. It must be fifty- or sixty-feet deep. It makes me quite ill just thinking about that drop.'

'You go on. I'll be fine,' said Joyner. 'I may be a while, though not as long as Anthony would like me to be.'

'Very well, Dr Joyner,' she said. 'I'll lock it again later, when you've finished. Just *please* don't fall in.'

'I'll stay with you,' said Fay Tomlinson, somewhat unexpectedly.

'No, I'll stay with Hilary,' said Cox. 'I'd hate it if we lost him, so soon before his retirement. Everyone's been looking forward to the party for longer than I can remember.'

'I'm sure they have,' said Joyner. 'But I'm also sure you'd like to see the garden, Anthony, having somehow gained admission to the place. And you, Fay. Don't worry about me. I know what I'm doing.'

'Really?' said Fay.

'Yes, really,' said Joyner.

Professor Cox hesitated, clearly unsure whether a tour of the garden or Joyner falling to his death would be more diverting on a hot summer afternoon. 'Come on, Fay,' he said. 'We'll leave Hilary to it, shall we?'

'Please do,' said Joyner. 'I'll be dining at the College for a while yet, Professor Cox. Maybe longer than you will be.'

They set off together, with Iris and Elsie following just behind, but Fay flashed Joyner a final look of – what was it? Curiosity? Irritation? Warning? Whatever it was, she and Cox vanished into the trees together.

Sly had also been observing the well with interest, but Polgreen seemed inclined to follow the others, and Sly did not wish that Polgreen and Iris should have the chance to talk alone, with the many opportunities that doubtless offered for subverting the committee rule book, as lately amended.

That left just me and Joyner. I leant over the top of the well as far as I dared. One of the bricks that I was clutching moved slightly but did not actually come away. I noticed one or two others were already missing. I looked down. The well, in this half-light, seemed very deep and very green. Ferns grew out of the brickwork that lined the shaft, light green near the top, then dark green, then almost black, then invisible. Even without the trees blocking out most of the light, I doubted Dr Joyner would be able to discern much of interest. Of course, he had come prepared: he took his torch from a jacket pocket.

'I said, don't worry about me,' said Joyner rather irritably. 'Why don't you catch the others up, Ethelred, and enjoy the garden?'

'As you wish,' I said.

It was with some foreboding that I set off to join the others as they meandered through the main woodland area, still colourful with purple rhododendron flowers. When I looked back, Joyner was already hidden by the trees, presumably kneeling in the gloom by the vertiginous well shaft, making whatever observations he wished to make by torchlight.

Iris treated us to a leisurely tour. There was a seventeenth-century ice house: a domed brick structure, half set into the ground and almost entirely covered in ivy. Its entrance was also protected by a strong iron grill against intruders.

'My grandfather added that too,' she said. 'He was worried that somebody might harm themselves in there. You can see how the mortar is crumbling away. I need to get it all repaired. But everything costs so much money now. And there's always something that needs doing at the main house. It's the roof at the moment, but the gatehouse will need repointing before too long. We had a lot of work done fifteen years ago, but you never manage to do everything that needs fixing. You always have to stop somewhere. And, sooner or later, it all needs fixing again. The expense of maintaining these buildings is horrendous.'

'Indeed,' said Sly, shaking his head sadly. He was rumoured to rent a small flat somewhere near Chichester, but that didn't mean he had no idea what it cost to repoint a mediaeval tower.

We were allowed to disperse and pursue our own interests: architectural, horticultural or idle curiosity. Everyone proceeded at their own speed, small groups forming and re-forming. I was sufficiently worried that I found myself constantly watching out for Joyner. For a moment I thought I saw his linen jacket in the distance, through the trees, then I lost sight of it again. Hurrying after him, I came out into some sort of sunken winter garden, on the far side of which Iris, in her white jacket, was in deep conversation with Sly. I was mildly annoyed at my mistake, but I was also curious to see how Sly got on – I was not optimistic for him. For some time they stood there, oblivious to my gaze: Sly, in his baggy shorts, speaking in an agitated manner; Iris, in her well-cut jacket, motionless. I could hear the faint buzz of their conversation but could not make out what they were saying. Finally, I saw Iris shake her head and walk away from him, towards the house. Sly stood rooted to the spot for some time, his fists clenching and unclenching, then he went after her. I quickly lost sight of him but, if he had a second attempt to lobby her, it was unlikely it would have been any more successful than the first.

Later I noticed that Polgreen, Cox and Elsie had formed a little group together and were laughing at something. Then I saw Fay on her own, checking her phone. Worryingly, I did not see Joyner at all. After a while, by pure chance, I arrived back at the well. There was no sign of him there amongst the trees either, but perhaps that was not entirely surprising. He had long since finished his investigations and moved on.

In due course, we each completed our tour of the garden and found ourselves back at the terrace one by one. Iris and I were the first to arrive. I gave her a sympathetic smile.

'I noticed that Mr Sly cornered you,' I said.

'Yes,' she said with feeling. 'He had some ridiculous scheme for unseating Henry Polgreen as chair of the committee and getting himself elected in Henry's place. Well, I set him right on that, I can tell you. "I trust Henry Polgreen completely," I told him. "As for electing you in his place, Mr Sly, I don't believe you hold any relevant academic qualifications, nor am I aware of other skills that might commend you to the committee." He didn't like that at all. He accused me of snobbery, which may not have been entirely unfair, then of being in league with Henry to steal property belonging to the Abbey, which was ridiculous. That was, however, the last straw. I gave him a proper dressing-down, I can tell you. He just stared at me open-mouthed. Well, there's nothing he can do about it. Let him resign as secretary if he doesn't like things as they are. We won't miss him.'

Her comment about Sly's lack of academic qualifications echoed what Sly had said to Polgreen earlier about not having a degree. It was clearly a sore point with him and Iris would have known that. She seemed to be every bit as willing as Elsie to speak her mind.

Later, Elsie returned alone, then Polgreen, then Cox and Fay together, strolling in a leisurely manner. Finally, Sly appeared. He sat down without saying anything to the rest of us. He looked very unhappy indeed. Perhaps he had finally realised that his ambitions to chair the committee, nurtured over many years, were out of his reach. For most of us there comes a day when we suddenly see ourselves as others see us, though with Elsie as my agent I was apparently contractually entitled to a running commentary. Iris called for tea. After a while, Pia appeared with a large tray. But there was still no sign of Joyner.

'I'm slightly worried about your colleague,' I said to Professor Cox.

'I'm not,' he said, selecting a yellow-iced cake from the plate. 'I have lost sleep over many things, but never over Dr Hilary Joyner.'

'I should have checked the well when I passed it on the way here.'

'To what possible end?'

'He might have fallen in.'

'Then in due course somebody would have to retrieve him. Fortunately, the house now has mains water, so it would not be an urgent matter.'

'He could be anywhere in the garden,' said Iris. 'We've no reason to believe he's fallen into the well.'

'I think we should go and look for him,' I said.

'Can't I finish my tea first?' asked Cox.

'No,' I said. 'You can't.'

We all set off again. Of course, what Iris had said was right. There were explanations for Joyner's absence that had nothing to do with the well, but they worried me almost as much. It was a large garden and there were plenty of places where Joyner could have decided to lurk. It had occurred to me that the well was no more than a feint and that Joyner's real purpose was to dig in some obscure part of the garden while we were all otherwise engaged. The longer his absence, the more likely that became. I remembered he had had a rucksack back at the Abbey, though I had no idea what could possibly be in it. I was now concerned that it might contain a trowel, or even (at a pinch) a lightweight metal detector. If that was his plan, I wished to stop him.

Iris might forgive me for arriving early, but it would be some time before she forgot that I had introduced an uncontrolled archaeologist to the house.

As I searched behind bushes and trees, I could hear calls from other, more distant parts of the estate. That Joyner was unaware we were looking for him was very unlikely. Once we had given him more than enough time to refill a hole and conceal his trowel, his failure to appear looked more ominous. My thoughts returned to where we had last seen him.

I was not the only one. By the time I arrived almost everybody was already at the spot – or at least a few cautious yards away.

'Have you checked the well, Ethelred?' asked Henry Polgreen, motioning towards the trees.

'No,' I said.

'Nor have I,' he replied.

'How about you?' I asked Cox.

'Not yet,' he said. 'I'd assumed one of you had gone there first. I thought it would be more useful if I looked elsewhere.'

'So, which of us is going to check the well?' I said. 'I mean actually go over and look down it.'

'Be my guest,' said Cox.

'It's fairly dark under the trees – it will be tricky to see all the way to the bottom,' I said.

'I've already fetched a torch from the house,' said Iris. She gave me a pat on the arm.

As I stepped into the grove, I had to pause. Coming out of the strong sunlight into the shadows, it took a moment or two for my eyes to adjust, and I didn't want to fall into the well myself. Just for a moment, I could see almost nothing, then the well and the surrounding vegetation started to take shape. I advanced on the low red wall, and I knelt beside it. I was worried to see that some bricks at the top had been freshly dislodged – definitely more than when I'd last looked. There were some loose lumps of mortar on the ground. I peered cautiously inside. All I could make out in the damp green depths was one circular course of bricks after another, fading into the blackness. Then, with some trepidation I took Iris's torch and directed the strong beam downwards, trying to get some light on the very bottom. The shape I saw was indistinct, but there was clearly something that didn't quite belong there. It floated, sort of doubled up, face down, and it did not move.

I stood up and quickly retraced my steps.

'I'm sorry, Iris. We're going to need to call the police. And probably the fire brigade to retrieve the body. I think it's much too late to call an ambulance.'

She looked at me, her face white. 'Oh God,' she said. 'It's just like last time.'

CHAPTER SIX

Ethelred

'So, then you discovered the body?' asked Joe.

'Yes,' I said.

The police were using two of the many rooms in Iris's house in order to take statements from us. This one was panelled in a pale-coloured wood and contained faded but very comfortable sofas. The curtains were a William Morris pattern, originally chocolate brown, now distinctly milk chocolate, with flashes of faded green and red. It was like being taken back forty or fifty years – which was quite possibly when the room had last been decorated. I knew Joe, the policeman interviewing me, very well – I had consulted him many times on police procedure for my books and very occasionally I had been able to proffer advice on some real cases. In terms of who owed whom any favours, he had a lot of credit remaining. This time, as one of a number of witnesses, I felt that I didn't have much to offer him in his official investigation into the death of an Oxford don in deepest Sussex.

I'd volunteered to be one of the last to give a statement to the police. Professor Cox and Fay Tomlinson had pleaded a need to return to Oxford as soon as possible. Sly had, he said, important council business, wherever it was he was a councillor. Polgreen claimed a social engagement that his wife had imposed on him with more than usual cunning. I'd strolled round the garden while I waited my turn, avoiding the now-cordoned-off well, where the forensic team was still at work under floodlights.

I'd already described to Joe, as best I could, the events leading up to Joyner's death. Joe knew what had followed – the arrival of all three emergency services, the recovery of the body, the sealing off and searching of a potential crime scene. We now knew that Joyner had fallen into the well, then struck his head somehow on the brickwork as he plummeted into the icy water at the bottom. Or been struck on the head and then fallen, of course. One or the other. The pathologists might be able to tell us which in due course.

'He was a close friend?'

'Not at all. He was one of the tutors when I was at university. I'd had no contact with him for years – then we met again at a dinner.'

'He never mentioned that his life might be in danger?'

'No,' I said. 'Not seriously. He talked about the curse of the Madonna, but that would have applied only after he'd found it.'

'And you think Dr Joyner was hunting for the Madonna statue in the well?'

'I assume so. He implied he knew where it was. And that maybe others did too. He asked Iris where the well was located. But he never took me into his confidence. When he asked me to arrange the visit, he'd told me he just wanted to talk to Iris about the legend that treasure from Sidlesham Abbey might be buried at the Priory.'

Joe nodded. 'We all know that story,' he said. 'At least, those of us who grew up round here do. Dr Joyner insisted on being left alone?'

'Yes. Iris warned him of the dangers and several of us volunteered to stay with him.'

'Who?'

'I'm trying to recall. Iris said she'd stay. So did Professor Cox. So did Dr Tomlinson – I think she was quite keen to stay. And I offered too. Dr Joyner was adamant that he would rather we left him.'

'Did he say why?'

'No, but I did wonder, later, if he planned to look at the well at all – Iris was very certain he was wasting his time. She said it had been checked very thoroughly years ago, but that didn't seem to bother Dr Joyner. The thought occurred to me that perhaps he had plans to search elsewhere in the garden and just wanted us out of the way so nobody saw where he went. He had a map with him. That might give us a clue.'

Joe nodded. 'We did recover a piece of paper from his pocket. It looked quite old, but after its immersion in the well, you couldn't make a lot out. We'll see if anything can be done with it, but I'm not optimistic. Did you see Dr Joyner at all after you left him at the well?'

'I thought I did for a moment – through the trees – but I mistook Iris's white jacket for his.'

'You're sure? You don't sound convinced.'

I thought about it. Whether Joyner had moved away from the well, then returned, might be an important point. 'I saw a white jacket, lost sight of it again, then came across Iris Munnings and Tertius Sly together.'

'And Dr Joyner and Mrs Munnings would be about the same height and build?'

'Pretty much. I can see what you're getting at, Joe, but I really don't think it was Joyner that I saw. Yes, you might mistake one for the other, at least just for a moment from behind – similar jackets, similar build, broad-brimmed hats. But surely Iris and Sly would have also seen Joyner if he had been so close to them? And they haven't said that, have they? It must have been Iris that I saw.'

'No, they haven't said that,' said Joe. He made a note or two in his book. 'Actually, what you say fits in pretty well with what the others have told me. After you all set out round the garden, nobody admits to seeing Dr Joyner alive. It seems likely that he just fell, accidentally – possibly shortly after you all left him.'

'Is there anything else I can tell you?' I asked.

'Officially, you have been very helpful and I have no more questions. Officially.' He closed his notebook and put it on the table. 'But I wouldn't mind your view unofficially. You see, Ethelred, this looks very much like an accident. Everyone agrees that the well was unsafe but that Dr Joyner insisted on examining it, against the advice of Mrs Munnings. The light wasn't good under the trees. The brickwork was not in great condition. He could have tripped on something and fallen, striking his head on the brick parapet or the wall of the shaft as he fell. Or perhaps he leant over and the brick he was holding gave way. The one thing we do know already is that there were small traces of red brick in the wound on the back of his head, consistent with striking his head on the way down the shaft. Of course, somebody could have returned to the well, after you all left, crept up behind him and either hit him with a brick or just pushed him in. The poor light would have made that easier too. The problem would be saying who that was. Just as nobody saw Joyner, nobody saw anyone else heading for the well. More sophisticated techniques won't help us much, either. I have no doubt we'll find everyone's DNA on him, but that's because you were all sitting together, passing cups to each other, and many of you doubtless shook hands as you arrived. Same with the odd thread from any of your clothes on his or vice versa. And there's no CCTV anywhere here – Mrs Munnings says she couldn't afford it. Unless somebody unexpectedly confesses, I can't honestly see where the evidence would come from to show that this was anything but misadventure. And yet, I'm uneasy about it all, for reasons I can't quite understand. Perhaps I read too many crime novels. You know all of the people who were here today. If this was fiction – if this was one of your own stories – what would have happened?'

'You mean who had a motive for killing him?'

'If you like. You know all of the parties involved.'

'Nobody,' I said. 'As a crime writer, I've obviously been thinking along exactly the same lines. I can't help myself. There was a mutual antipathy between him and Professor Cox, but Cox held all the cards, as it were. He already had a chair in modern history, a whole raft of publications, including some bestsellers and, last but not least, Joyner's old rooms in College. Joyner was no threat to him and was about to retire. I don't know much about Fay Tomlinson . . .'

'The one who was very keen to stay with him? She's a junior research fellow. Professor Cox appointed her. She and Cox seem very . . . close, you might say. She stood to get Joyner's fellowship when he retired – only so long as Cox backed her, but she seems to have Cox exactly where she needs him. With Joyner about to retire, there was no need for her to bump him off to speed things up – even if she'd been that way inclined. She says she and Professor Cox were together in the garden the whole time. Never left his side. He says that too, which is very nice for both of them.'

'OK,' I said, slowly. I thought that I'd seen Fay Tomlinson on her own at some point, but they'd certainly gone out and returned together. I had no reason to doubt they'd been in each other's sight almost all the time. If that's what they both said. Anyway, I agreed with Joe that neither of them had much of a motive. If Joyner had killed Cox, that would have been different. But he hadn't.

'How well do you know Tertius Sly?' Joe said.

'Not that well. I don't much like him, but I can't see why he'd kill Joyner, either. They'd only just met. More to the point, Joyner was the only one who supported, albeit for his own reasons, Sly's wish to reopen the excavations. Sly would have seen Joyner as a friend and ally. He seemed genuinely upset at his death. Logically, Joyner's death was not to his advantage, and Sly is nothing if not logical in his reasoning. I think he spends his spare time planning his next move. He's not one for impulsive acts of any sort.'

'He's a county councillor? He gave his name as Councillor Sly.'

'I thought he was just a parish councillor, which technically wouldn't entitle him to that prefix. If it is parish, then it's wherever he lives – somewhere near Chichester. I think he's genuinely public-spirited. I also think he really wants to be liked and accepted.'

'But he's not?'

'No.'

Joe nodded. He flicked back through his notebook and put a question mark against the word 'councillor'.

'I see two sides forming here,' he said. 'Joyner and Sly on one side, favouring another dig – Professor Cox, Dr Tomlinson, Mrs Munnings and Mr Polgreen on the other. You might say that's four possible suspects.'

'Really? Actual suspects? I thought you reckoned it was an accident.'

'Bear with me for a moment, Ethelred. I'm still talking hypothetically.'

'Fine. But you've ruled out two of those suspects already. That only leaves Henry Polgreen and Iris Munnings. You're surely not suggesting that Iris would invite Joyner here and kill him to stop him digging for the Madonna?'

'This Madonna, if it exists, must be quite valuable. That's a clear motive for somebody. Hypothetically. Iris isn't as rich as people think. Look at this room. It could do with a lick of paint, couldn't it? And there's plenty of work to do on the exterior of the building. She could use the money if the Madonna was found.'

'If Joyner had found the statue in the garden, Iris might have to prove her claim to it, but she'd certainly have a greater claim than Joyner possibly could. She didn't need to kill him – just ask him politely to hand it over.'

Joe nodded. 'Of course, we've ruled out Professor Cox killing Dr Joyner out of professional jealousy. But no doubt he could use a few hundred thousand?'

'I would think that his professorship, his books and his television work would have made him the richest person at the Priory this afternoon. It's more likely that Cox killed Joyner because his paper on the causes of the Pilgrimage of Grace was insufficiently nuanced.'

Joe's face was completely deadpan. 'That's a no, then?' he said.

'I can't say exactly the same for Dr Tomlinson,' I said. 'Maybe she could do with the money. But how would you dispose of a gem-encrusted gold statue, even if you did steal it?'

'There's always somebody who'll buy anything,' said Joe. 'That's why we have boot fairs. And there's a market for stolen antiques of all sorts and all prices. Anyway, Cox and Tomlinson were together the whole time, so it would have to be both of them working together. If Cox is beyond suspicion, then so is Tomlinson.'

Again, the memory of seeing Fay without Anthony Cox flashed across my mind, but I just nodded. I couldn't imagine the elegant Fay Tomlinson in hand-to-hand combat with Joyner.

'So, what about Henry Polgreen?' Joe asked.

'He might be after the Madonna on behalf of the Abbey. He wouldn't think of selling it for his own profit.'

'You know that?'

'I know Henry as well as I know anybody here.'

'A good friend?'

'Yes.'

'He'd been in contact with Joyner before. They hadn't quite seen eye to eye.' Joe tapped a pencil against his lower lip thoughtfully. 'Did Henry Polgreen ever show any animosity towards Joyner?'

'Mild irritation,' I said.

'No more than that?'

'Definitely no more than that.'

'Fine,' said Joe. 'In the absence of other evidence, your mate's probably in the clear. Even hypothetically. Your agent doesn't seem to have had a high opinion of Dr Joyner, though.'

'She doesn't have a high opinion of anyone. She hadn't met him until yesterday. I think she may have seen him as a potential client, if he'd been happy to make one or two inconsequential changes to his book.'

'Mrs Munnings' housekeeper?' asked Joe. 'She's from the Philippines, apparently – arrived quite recently.'

'Yes, that's right. I think she was in the house most of the time, making coffee and slicing cake.'

'That's what she told me. When I questioned her, she was slightly confused even as to which one was Dr Joyner. Said she'd met Professor Cox before – several times – but nobody else. I've no reason to believe that Iris doesn't keep her every bit as busy making coffee as she claimed. Neither motive nor opportunity, I think.'

'There you are, then,' I said. 'Nobody had any good reason for pushing Hilary Joyner into the well – or none we know of.'

'Of course, let's not forget that almost anyone from the village could have got into the garden. There's a wall round it, but the gate was wide open this afternoon and there's no security to speak of.'

96

'As you said, Iris can't afford CCTV. For what it's worth, I didn't see anyone, other than the people we've mentioned.'

'No. Nor did anyone else,' said Joe. 'Joyner wasn't popular, though. There's no getting away from that.'

'No,' I said. 'He was pushy, rude and self-centred. But I can't see why anyone who was here today would have wanted to shove him down the well. It was perfectly possible, but it wasn't remotely necessary. Anyway, the risks of being caught with so many people around were pretty high.'

'That's right,' said Joe. 'It's not something you would do if you'd had time to consider the consequences. Wrong time, wrong place. Still, it seemed worth running it all past somebody with an overheated imagination, just to see if I was missing the obvious. It happens.'

'One thing that puzzled me,' I said. 'When the body was found, Iris said, "Just like last time." I don't know what she meant by that.'

'Somebody else drowned in the well, apparently, back in her grandfather's day. Iris would have only been a child then, of course. It would seem it was her grandfather's gardener who died. That's why they had the iron grill fitted. Shame Iris left it off this afternoon, but there you are. And you're right: she did warn him. Everyone's agreed on that.'

Elsie and I stayed with Iris Munnings until the police left. I reckoned she could do with the support.

'Thank you, Mrs Munnings,' said Joe as they departed. 'I'm very grateful for your cooperation and the use of your drawing room.'

'Miss,' she said. 'Everyone calls me Mrs Munnings, but

it's Miss Munnings, actually. I never married. There was a young man but . . . well, things didn't quite work out for us. I'm very fortunate in some ways. Just not so lucky in others.'

Later, as we drove back, Elsie asked, 'So what's Cox's relationship with Fay Tomlinson, then?'

'Officially she's a postdoctoral research fellow,' I said. 'I couldn't say what she was unofficially.'

'Still, a bestselling book, a Mercedes convertible and a blonde with legs that go on for ever – Cox isn't doing that badly. Eh, Ethelred?'

'How would I know?' I said. 'I'm only a crime writer.'

Elsie patted me on the knee. 'I'm sure you could pick up a cheap, high-mileage Mercedes convertible,' she said. 'It's just a shame you'd have nobody to impress with it.'

Much later, long after we had returned to my own house, I said to Elsie, 'That really isn't a lucky family. Not in any respect.'

'No,' said Elsie. 'The grandfather and grandmother dying like that.'

'And the gardener,' I said.

'And the boyfriend?' asked Elsie.

'It certainly sounds as if something happened to him too.'

'What about her parents?'

'She's never mentioned them to me before,' I said. 'And didn't say much this time. Just that she never really got a chance to ask them about the Madonna. But they apparently believed in the curse.'

'You're not suggesting . . .'

'No, no, of course not,' I said. 'Just coincidence, so many people dying in a short space of time.'

'Still, they haven't had much luck.'

'No,' I said. 'In spite of what Iris says about being fortunate in some ways, I'd have said they'd had no luck in any way whatsoever.'

CHAPTER SEVEN

Ethelred

Then, for some days, nothing much happened at all, good or bad.

I would occasionally go into the small bedroom and see Joyner's bag, still sitting there by the bed, a forlorn object, a lost dog waiting for its master's return. I had not opened it, but I'd lifted it experimentally. It was very light. I had emailed the College to say it was there. The College had replied that his next of kin was his ex-wife, and that they would let me know what, if anything, she wanted me to do with it. She had so far expressed no final view on the matter. I seemed to remember, from something somebody had said at the dinner, that she lived in Spain. It was unlikely that she wanted her former husband's overnight case. After a week or so, I put it up in the attic, with many other things that I had not looked at since I moved to West Wittering. To be honest, it gave me the creeps. I preferred it out of sight. It had nothing at all to do with the curse.

It was over a week after Joyner's death when I ran into Tertius Sly at the village stores in West Wittering. Though he lived elsewhere, he worked locally. We normally just nodded at each other or said a brief 'hello' but something more than that seemed required this time. We had stood side by side in the presence of death.

'Terrible business about your friend,' he said, as if discussing the weather. 'I didn't really express my condolences at the time. I was a bit stunned, to tell you the truth – properly shook up, as you may have noticed – but I'm all right now, you'll be pleased to know. And I'm very sorry for your loss, of course, Ethelred.'

'My loss? Dr Joyner wasn't really a friend,' I said. 'He was just staying with me. But thank you anyway.'

'The police haven't questioned you again?'

'Is there any reason why they should?'

'If they found fresh evidence. A new lead. Forensics.'

'I suppose so,' I said. I looked towards the chilled cabinets to see if they had any semi-skimmed milk left. There appeared to be one bottle, if I could grab it before anyone else did.

'But they haven't?'

'Haven't what?' I asked.

Haven't said anything to you.'

'No.'

I watched as a woman opened the cabinet, took my milk and departed towards the till. I'd need to drive to the Co-op at East Wittering now if I wanted to be able to make tea.

'So, they must think it was just an accident, then?' said Sly insistently.

Joe had, in fact, phoned me in confidence to confirm that that was indeed what they thought. The pathologist's report had added very little to what we knew. The blows to Joyner's skull – and the damage to his panama hat – were consistent with his head having hit the brick wall of the well more than once on the way down. The alternative theory, that he had been hit with something before he fell, could not be ruled out, but had not been supported by the discovery of a bloodstained brick elsewhere in the garden, though that weapon could have just been lobbed in after him. The search of the well had revealed there were loose bricks in the detritus at the very bottom. Whatever the cause of the head wound, Joyner would, the pathologist thought, have been unconscious when he hit the water and would have drowned within a very short time. The discovery of his torch, also at the bottom of the well, suggested that he had been leaning over, peering downwards, just before he fell. Or perhaps he had dropped the torch and was craning his neck to see if it could somehow be recovered. Even if I had stayed with him, Joe had kindly added, there would have been nothing I could have done once Joyner had slipped. There would have been no way of getting an unconscious man out of the well in time to save him from drowning. He didn't say that I might have prevented his falling into the well at all. But so could we all have done that. And it was Joyner's choice that none of us had stayed with him. None of us should feel guilty.

And yet I did.

'There's no reason why the police should tell me

anything,' I said, not wishing to have Joe's confidence to me spread all over the village. 'I'm just a witness, the same as you. I'm sure they'll make a public announcement when they want to.'

'I'm sure they will,' said Sly. It sounded like a sneer, but that was how most things he said sounded, even condolences. 'Your mate in the police – he didn't suspect Henry Polgreen, I suppose?'

'He would scarcely tell me if he did.'

'No – especially since you are so close to Polgreen and might tip him off. But think about it: Joyner was a sharp cookie. He was keen we continued the programme of excavation on the site. That was the last thing Polgreen wanted.'

'If you say so,' I said.

Sly nodded. 'I do say so. I can keep a secret, Ethelred. I'm known for it. I don't tell tales out of school. Polgreen's a friend of yours, but you must realise that he thinks that if there are no further digs, nobody will find him out, and he'll avoid disgrace.'

'Disgrace?'

'Obviously my lips are sealed, under the circumstances, but the last dig – the last authorised dig – showed up some strange anomalies. I can't tell you any more than that. It wouldn't be right. Not since you're his friend.'

'I entirely respect your discretion,' I said.

'What I will say, though, is that it was quite clear somebody had been digging there who shouldn't have been. Now that could only be through Polgreen's negligence, couldn't it?'

'Not necessarily,' I said.

He looked at me with approval.

'Well, you've hit the nail on the head there,' he said. 'Like you, I can't see that Polgreen would fail to spot illicit digging on somebody else's part. So, it's more likely it would be Polgreen himself. The question is: what was he digging for?'

Sly's artless probing was beginning to annoy me. Anyway, I needed to go home, get the car, drive into East Wittering and buy some semi-skimmed milk.

'Really, I've no idea,' I said. 'It could be anything at all.'

'You think so?'

'Think what?' I asked.

'That Polgreen might be looking for anything at all. But, with a better knowledge of the site than you have, I can make a pretty good guess. Under cover of being chairman of the committee, your friend Henry Polgreen has been conducting illicit excavations to see if he can find the Madonna – and for his own gain, not ours.'

Sly was straying towards slander, and some friendly advice would not go amiss. 'Well, for your sake, I hope you can get proof of that,' I said grimly.

He nodded approvingly. 'So do I, Ethelred. So do I. But we won't if Polgreen stays as chair. And Iris Munnings as treasurer.' He spat this last name out as if it was a fat slug he'd eaten accidentally with a rather nice piece of iceberg lettuce. Whatever Iris had said to him in the garden had hurt him a great deal. 'I told her what Polgreen was up to, but would she listen? Just because she and Polgreen went to university and I didn't, she seems to think I know nothing. When I was eighteen, I'd already been working for two years. By the time Polgreen had graduated, I had five years of solid commercial experience under my belt, selling office stationery. You can't just ignore something like that – experience of that quality. But Polgreen thinks he can get away with anything, just because he has a history degree. And Iris Munnings is tied up in it somehow too. I don't have all the evidence yet, but it's pretty obvious, isn't it? Big house. Not much income, so they say. She needs the money. It's probably the two of them working together, don't you think?'

'I've no idea,' I said.

'Really? None at all? Then the one man who might expose them dies mysteriously. It must have crossed your mind that it could be murder?'

'Yes,' I said. 'I suppose it has.'

'Exactly. Then you'd have to conclude that the most likely killers are Henry Polgreen and Iris Munnings.'

'I wouldn't go so far as to say that.'

He nodded thoughtfully. 'Of course you wouldn't *say* it,' he said. 'Not publicly. Not yet. But thank you, Ethelred, for sharing your suspicions with me. I admire you for not letting your friendship with Henry Polgreen get in the way of discovering the truth. I won't breathe a word to anyone – and you know you can trust me when I say that. But an accusation of murder, such as you have just made, is a very serious thing. Especially when you're accusing Iris Munnings of being an accomplice. You can get into a lot of trouble that way, Ethelred. There's such a thing as slander, you know.'

'Thank you,' I said. 'That sounds like good advice.'

'So, Sly reckons Polgreen had been doing some illicit digging?' asked Elsie. 'With Iris's approval?'

'But is that possible?' I asked, readjusting the phone under my chin. 'The whole process of excavation is quite tightly controlled these days. I doubt you can just turn up with a shovel and dig, even if you are the chairman of the committee. Surely he'd never do that?'

'It's what I'd do,' said Elsie. 'If I had a key, I'd go down there at night with a metal detector and see what I could find. What's that rustling noise? Are you eating chocolate, Ethelred?'

'There are rustling noises other than opening a chocolate bar,' I said.

'Are there?'

'I was checking a book when you called. The Reverend Sabine Barclay-Wood. *Curious Tales of Old Sussex.*'

'That rings a bell.'

'It's the book we were all talking about. You've actually read it – or some of it. It had a bit of local history in it that helped clear up the Robin Pagham case a couple of years ago.'

'Oh yes, I remember that one. The story of "The Murderer and the Devil". That was a load of crap, that was.'

'But helpful. When you worked out which bits to believe. Well, the same book also contains *The Sidlesham Madonna*. Like I said, a little of Barclay-Wood goes a long way with me, and I hadn't yet read that story. So, I thought I'd see what he had to say on the subject. It does seem to be the basis for the whole Maltese Madonna legend, as we know it today.'

'So, is it crap too?'

'I don't know. I've only just started. Professor Cox was very rude about it, but there may be an element of truth in there somewhere. Barclay-Wood was petulant and indiscreet – hence his failure to become a canon of the cathedral and the action for libel taken against him by the Bishop of Chichester. And by the Dean of Chichester. But he did a great deal of meticulous research. When he got it wrong, he usually got it wrong deliberately in order to annoy somebody. What's that rustling noise at your end?'

'It might be a book,' said Elsie. 'Possibly one about Sussex.'

'You're eating a book?' I said.

'I'm hungry enough,' said Elsie.

'Is your assistant still keeping you to the diet, then?'

'Let me know how you get on with your story,' said Elsie. 'I might need to come down to West Wittering again and give you a hand with treasure seeking.'

'I might be too busy for visitors,' I said.

'Ethelred, I'm your agent. If you're ever too busy, I'll tell you.'

'Thank you,' I said.

'Don't mention it,' she said. 'All part of the service.'

AN EXTRACT FROM 'THE STRANGE TALE OF THE SIDLESHAM MADONNA' (PUBLISHED 1904)

by the Reverend Sabine Barclay-Wood

Once upon a time, there existed in the city of Constantinople, which was in those days Christian, two wonderful golden images of the Virgin Mary and our Blessed Lord, Jesus Christ. The man who had made these holy objects was more skilful than any who exist in our day, and nobody could set their eyes on the statues without wonder. The gold shimmered and gleamed in the Eastern sun, and the jewels that adorned the statues were beyond the powers of my poor pen to describe. Rubies and diamonds and sapphires and emeralds and garnets and pearls and opals and many other stones with strange and wonderful names studded the crowns that the statues wore and the edges of their robes. The Madonna's cloak, so I am told, was all of lapis lazuli, for her colour was and ever has been the deepest, richest blue. And Christ's emerald crown of thorns dripped with small blood-red drops of ruby. Their eyes were perfectly matched sapphires and their lips flawless rose quartz. It was said that, so long as the statues were in the city, it would never fall to an enemy.

But the Christians of Constantinople had many foes, including the fierce and implacable Turks, and the day came when these infidels had conquered all of the country right up to the mighty triple walls of the city. For weeks they laid siege to this last bastion of the true faith, but they could not break through or break the spirit of the Christians within, who prayed daily to God for deliverance.

There was, however, an evil man in their midst. Though he was called a Knight of St John, he was weak and unworthy of the title. His knees trembled at the mere mention of the enemy. I am pleased to say that he was not an Englishman but a Greek or an Italian, of whom there were far too many in the town. He refused to place his trust in Our Lord and told his neighbours that the Turks would most certainly slaughter them all. In spite of their laughing at his foolishness – or perhaps because they did so – he hatched a desperate plan. He would steal the two gold statues and use them to bribe the Turks to let him leave the city peacefully. This he did. Since he was a Knight of St John, nobody questioned him when he went into the church one evening after the day's service had finished. He quickly seized the two statues and concealed them under his cloak.

He waited until it was dark and then crept out through a small postern gate into the great emptiness of deserted olive trees and vines. He shivered as he looked up at the strong walls that had until then separated him from his enemies. Now they were behind him, immensely tall and pale lemon in the soft moonlight, he felt very small and alone. It was as if the cold eyes of the whole world were upon him. A Turkish sentry soon challenged the knight, for no Christians were permitted to cross the Turkish lines. He asked to be taken to the chief of the Turks, which they did in a most polite and civil manner, seeing the knight's fine armour and believing him to be an honourable soldier and a gentleman. Once in the presence of the infidel general, however, the knight cunningly produced the two images.

'Choose, O Mighty Pasha!' he exclaimed. 'If you allow me to pass safely through your army and into Greece, then you shall have one or other of these fine gold statues!'

At first, the chief did not know what to say, for he was a good and honest man, in spite of being a Turk. Then he said, 'But are these statues not of your Lord, Jesus Christ, and of his Holy Mother, the Virgin? How can you offer them up in this way? If they were of Mohammed, whom I worship, then I should never let them go, no matter how dreadful a death I suffered as a result.'

'They are just trinkets that I do not value,' said the knight. 'But you may only have one, for I wish to sell the other for my own gain and profit.'

'You deserve to keep neither, O false knight, but I will not compound this evil deed by robbing you. Go! Take the statue of the Virgin. I, for my part, will have the other, but I shall treat it with more respect than you have, for your Christ, whom we call Isā ibn Maryam, was a true prophet.'

And he was as good as his word. He not only let the knight go but gave him a bag of bread and some black olives and dates and a flask of wine to take on his journey, and also a letter of safe passage to show to any other Turk who might try to stop him. And the false knight went into

Greece and took ship for the island of Rhodes, where the Knights of St John then had their castle. So much for him.

Now there was, as you may imagine, much consternation in Constantinople the following day, when it was found that the statues had gone, and there was a great deal of weeping and wailing. Had it been an English city, I rather think that they would have pulled themselves together and jolly well got on with things, like the gallant defenders of Ladysmith and Mafeking, but they were merely foreigners and decided they might as well surrender to the Turks as not. Thus, Constantinople fell under the rule of the Mohammedans, and the Christians were all forced to flee or become Mohammedans themselves, which I am sad to relate some chose to do.

In the meantime, the false knight had arrived in Rhodes. It had been his intention to have the statue melted down and to sell the gold and become rich. But even as he gazed at the statue in his cabin on the ship, a sort of terror came over him. Surely after such a betrayal the statue must be cursed? And so, he did not sell the relic as he planned but presented it as a gift to the order. And he told his master a story of having saved the statue from the sack of Constantinople, after he had fought long and hard and killed the chief of the Turks in single combat. But he said nothing of the sale of the statue of Our Lord, and the commander of his order asked no questions, being very content with his prize. In the end, it did none of them any good, for the knight soon died of leprosy and the order was driven out of its castle by the Turks and had to wander Europe looking for a new home.

By and by, the Emperor took pity on them and gave them a new castle in Malta, which is now, of course, fortunate enough to be British but which at that time belonged to him, and the statue of the Madonna travelled there too, though this time not in a bag with the dates . . .

The phone had been ringing, I realised, for some time. I picked it up.

'Have you finished reading your little book?' asked Elsie.

'No, I'm about halfway through the story, I think.'

'Any good?'

'His style is, as usual, a sort of mock folk tale. A lot of it is rubbish but I think he knows it's rubbish.'

'Really?'

'There's stuff he can't possibly believe.'

'Such as?'

'He tells us that Muslims respect Jesus and that they call him Isā ibn Maryam, but at the same time he claims that they worshipped images of the Prophet Mohammed, something which would, in fact, have been repugnant to them. He must have known that they didn't. He claims that the Turks were fierce and implacable, and yet one of the few honourable and genuinely decent characters in the story is the chief of the Turks. It's as if he was laughing at his readers.'

'Writers!' said Elsie. 'What are they like? Let me know if he says where the treasure is now. Anyway, I've just remembered what I phoned you about the first time – before you started rambling on about diets. I've been doing some research on the Internet. You remember the gardener who died?'

112

'Yes, he accidentally fell into the well.'

'Maybe, or maybe not. Iris's grandfather was tried for his murder. His brief got him off. It was quite a famous case at the time.'

'I'll look it up. What was the name of the gardener?'

'*Sly*,' said Elsie with some emphasis. 'Walter Sly. Small world, eh?'

CHAPTER EIGHT

Ethelred

There are few things that cannot be verified on the Internet. You can check the weather in Tokyo, the exchange rate for the Vietnamese Dong, the shortest route from Chichester to Bristol, the day on which a full moon occurred in June 1657 and how to mix an Old-Fashioned cocktail. You can also find the outcome of long-forgotten murder cases.

The death of Walter Sly had caused a stir at the time and, almost sixty years later, a few ripples still lapped up against the vast edifice of the World Wide Web. On a site created for those who liked their crime real rather than fictional, I managed to discover the outline of the case.

Walter Sly had been the gardener at the Priory for many years before the Munnings family had bought the house. He had been kept on as part of a much larger labour force required to create the garden that the new owners required. Sly had, it was clear, resented both the desire to rip up the garden he had tended for so long and his demotion, as he had seen it, to a mere labourer amongst other labourers. For some weeks large quantities of earth had been shifted, walls built and the old priory carp pond re-excavated. Then, it would seem, Sly had got his way. Munnings apparently decided that fewer changes were needed than he had first envisaged. As if on an impulse, everyone except Sly had been dismissed, and for some weeks Munnings and Sly had worked on alone, side by side. When the last geranium was in place and the new lawn had been turfed, Sly was kept on in his old role, in a garden that was different, but less different than it might have been. Munnings was noted, even after a few months in the village, for his stubbornness and short temper. It did not go entirely unremarked that his gardener seemed to have an unusual influence over him.

Then Walter Sly had been discovered, drowned, in the well. He had failed to come home one evening. The following morning his family, having made enquiries at both village pubs and at the Priory, went to the police and reported him missing. Munnings told the police that, as far as he knew, Sly had left the Priory at about his usual time, though unaccountably not locking up the tool shed before he left. It was two or three days later that a proper search of the garden was conducted and the old wooden cover to the well was found to be broken. It was not easy recovering the body from the deep shaft. At first the case seemed straightforward. That Sly should have made a final tour of the garden before going home, that he should have stepped or leant on the rotten cover inadvertently, that he should have fallen, striking his head on the sides of the well – all of these things were quite possible. Then Sly's widow told the police that she was sure that her husband was in possession of some secret of his employer's. Sly had told her, a few days previously, they would shortly be very rich – something he had never envisaged before, neither drunk nor sober, not during the entire thirty-two years of their marriage. Even at the time it had worried her. The police returned to the Priory and conducted a more thorough search. From the depths of the well they extracted a large claw hammer. After almost a week's immersion, the hammer yielded only one verifiable fingerprint. That fingerprint belonged to Munnings.

At his trial, Munnings was represented by an eminent QC. The QC was able to argue that the wounds suffered by Sly were as consistent with a head striking a projecting flint – for some were mixed with the brickwork – as they were with a blow from a blunt weapon. It was true that the hammer had Mr Munnings' fingerprint on it, but then it was, legally, his hammer. There was no law, or none that he knew of, against owning one. Nor did Mr Munnings bear any blame for the tragic accident. As gardener, it was, arguably, Sly's responsibility to ensure that the well was safe – it was not to be expected that the master of the house would do this personally, if he employed relevant staff. Mr Munnings would in due course give evidence that he had asked Sly to do precisely this some weeks before. Only Sly's tardiness had left the cover in its precarious state. Surely what had happened was that, that afternoon, Sly had finally heeded his instructions, taken the hammer from the workshop in order to repair the cover, carelessly knelt on the rotten wood and fallen through. Mrs Sly had accused Mr Munnings of having some secret that her husband knew. Well, if she was going to accuse him, let her say now what Mr Munnings had been concealing.

Mrs Sly, to be fair, made a good witness. She stuck to her story that Munnings had a motive for killing her husband. Her husband had known something. She was unimpressed by the QC's suave manner or his silk gown. She was more than willing to answer back, a talent for which she was repeatedly reprimanded by the judge. In the end, however, she was no match for the eminent QC. He ridiculed all of her suggestions as to why Walter Sly might have been able to blackmail his employer. Finally, he asked her whether her husband was the sort of scoundrel who would stoop so low as to threaten the man who put bread into the mouths of his family. She paused, realising that both 'yes' and 'no' held dangers. The QC had smiled at the jury before she had a chance to reply and said, 'No further questions for the witness, M'lud.'

The jury retired and deliberated for two whole days. They would clearly have liked it to have been a case of blackmail and murder, and would have given a great deal – ten shillings each at the very least – to have been told what the secret was. In the end they were sufficiently impressed by the eminent QC to bring in a verdict of not guilty, but they left the courtroom with a vague sense of having missed out on something good.

'So,' said Elsie, 'it's obvious, isn't it? In the process of creating this new garden, they discovered the treasure. Munnings recognised what they'd found and knew that he'd have to hand the whole lot over to the Crown or the Knights of St John or somebody, probably with no compensation if it could be shown that Henry VIII had specifically reserved the stuff for himself. Munnings sacked the new workforce before they got wind of it, and started to excavate properly, with just himself and Sly, the trusted family retainer. They stored the loot somewhere – in that old ice house in the garden, probably – and started to look for a buyer who wouldn't ask too many questions. Meanwhile, they turfed over where they found it so nobody would know what they'd done. But then Sly got greedy and demanded a bigger cut of the profits. So, Munnings hit him over the head with the hammer and dumped him in the well. Because Sly hadn't trusted his wife with the full story – a warning to all men who keep secrets from their wives *or agents* – the jury didn't know about the Maltese Madonna and couldn't work out why Munnings would suddenly decide to kill a perfectly good gardener. If they'd been on to that, Munnings would have been hanged for sure.'

She took another scoop of her chocolate pudding and defied me to contradict her.

I was up in London for the day and was lunching with my agent. When I first joined Elsie's agency it was a small concern, and lunch consisted of a sandwich and a coffee, for which I often paid. More recently, the firm had grown and, when I phoned Elsie, it was usually one or other of her staff who took the call. I was, as Elsie pointed out at most of our meetings, now merely one of her much-loved but, frankly, less profitable clients. But that had been equally true when I joined her. It was just that she had moved on and I hadn't. Lunch now ran to three courses, with wine for me. Elsie rarely, if ever, touched alcohol, preferring not to waste calories that might otherwise be allocated to some form of chocolate.

'So, where's the treasure now?' I asked.

'Sold long ago.'

'It can't have been worth much. Iris seems fairly short of money to maintain the house.'

'Spent on riotous living.'

'Not Iris. Other than this new housekeeper – I suppose she could scarcely manage the place on her own – she has few extravagances.'

'Her parents spent it, then.'

'Maybe,' I said. 'I still know next to nothing about them.'

'They probably gambled it away in Monte Carlo,' said Elsie. 'Or Le Touquet.'

'And you base that assumption on what, exactly?'

'It's the most likely thing to have happened in the '50s. That's what people did then. Correctly dressed, in a double-breasted dinner jacket and black tie, they bankrupted entire families.'

'You can't just assume things,' I said.

A waitress approached us. 'A cappuccino for me,' she said, 'and he'll have a double espresso.'

'See?' I said.

'What?'

'You just assumed I'd have a double espresso.'

'Which is precisely what you *will* have. Because I've just ordered it. So, I was right, wasn't I? I never said you'd *like* a double espresso. I wouldn't presume to know that.'

'Thank you,' I said.

'My pleasure,' she said.

'So what happens after that?' I asked.

'I calculate the tip and pay the bill, then I go and do some work and you can play at being a writer.'

'No, what happens at the Priory apart from the treasure and gambling it all away? Iris said both her grandfather and her grandmother died quite soon after moving in, though she was strangely vague about exactly when the grandmother died.'

'The curse of the Maltese Madonna,' she said. 'Everyone who touches it meets a horrible end.'

'I doubt it.'

'Well, don't come hobbling to me when you get leprosy.'

'Why don't I try to find out some facts?' I said. 'Then why don't we have this conversation all over again, starting at the beginning?'

'Facts like in your book of Sussex folklore?'

'I still have to finish the story on the train back to Sussex. It may give us a clue to what happened.'

She shrugged. She was already calculating how small a tip she could get away with. 'It can't be of any importance now, can it? The police think Joyner slipped and fell. That will be what the inquest concludes too.'

'No,' I said. 'It can't be of any importance now. Hilary Joyner slipped and fell. A bit like Walter Sly.'

CHAPTER NINE

*Now it came to pass that a monk from Sussex had
undertaken a pilgrimage to Jerusalem and was returning on
a ship bound for the port of Chichester. It stopped at Malta
for fresh water and to give the sailors some recreation, of
the innocent sort that sailors commonly enjoy, for it had
been a long and stormy passage thither. The monk had a
kinsman who was one of the Knights of St John and so set
out from the port to visit him. And there, at the castle, he
was greeted with much joy and feasted in their hall so long
as the ship remained in Malta.*

*'Before you leave this island,' said the kinsman, 'you
must see our most precious relics – which include a statue of
the Virgin, which was saved by a brave knight of our order,*

many years ago, out of the destruction of Constantinople by the evil Turks.'

'We have a Madonna of our own at Sidlesham,' the monk said. 'It is English-made and very fine it is too.'

'But not as fine as ours,' said the cousin. 'Come and see the treasures that we hold here.'

So, by and by, he took the monk to their chapel and showed him, and the monk was amazed indeed. The gold shone, and the lapis lazuli dazzled. The ruby-red blood almost moved the monk to tears.

Now, the monk was a good Englishman and so he said to himself, 'Why should this treasure sit here in hot, dry, fly-ridden Malta, where nobody that matters can see it, when it might be in the lush green fields of Sussex, close to the great and populous city of Chichester?'

And so, the following day, just before the ship was due to depart, he visited the knights' chapel again on the pretext of wishing to see the Madonna one last time and to venerate it on his own in the quietness of the morning. And the chapel attendant, having seen him there the previous day, allowed him to pray undisturbed before the image. But as soon as the attendant had gone, the monk seized the treasure, stuffed it in his bag, and ran for the harbour, jumping on board the ship in a rather plucky way just as it was casting off.

Well, the Knights of St John soon saw what had happened and sent one of their own ships chasing after it. But the English ships then were better and faster than any foreign ship, just as they are today, and so the monk's ship easily outran its pursuer and got home safe to Chichester without any further adventures.

But, as the ship sailed through the cold northern seas, strange thoughts came into the monk's mind – he knew not whence.

'I was once content in my simple monastery,' he said to himself. 'But now I see that with the riches I possess I might be anything I choose. When we land in Sussex, I shall slip away to London and sell this treasure and become perhaps a great merchant. As for the monks of Sidlesham Abbey, they will think I perished on my pilgrimage, as so many do.'

When the ship docked at Chichester it happened that the Abbot was there by chance, visiting the town, and he enquired what the monk had in his bag that he clutched so tightly to his chest. And the monk was obliged to open it and give his treasure to the Abbot there and then. And it is said that the monk died of grief shortly after, not a morsel of food having passed his lips after setting foot in England.

But even as the Abbot rode back home on his mare, he pondered thus, 'Sidlesham is the least of the Abbeys of England and one of the poorest. Yet God has sent us this gift. He clearly has a purpose in doing so. He wishes to raise us high in the eyes of the Church and of the pope in Rome. We shall spread the word that we have such a marvel, and then folk shall flock here, and when they come they shall pay us well and we shall all wax fat indeed. I do not think that our brother obtained this by fair means, but, if anyone challenges us, we shall simply claim that it is the poor statue that we have always owned.'

And so it came to pass and the Abbey grew rich. But soon word of their fabulous wealth reached the King. The King *was, at that time, thinking of doing away with lazy monks and setting up the Church of England, to the immense advantage of the people. But he was also a greedy man and when he heard of the Madonna he wanted to possess it for himself alone. So he sent some of his men to Sidlesham.*

The Abbot had heard of the visits of these men to other Abbeys and knew that they would seize anything of value for their master. So, the Abbot invited the Prior of Wittering to dinner, and during the meal he dismissed all of his servants and spoke privately to the Prior.

'I have a great relic here, as you know, but the King means to possess it for himself. I would have you take it and hide it in your Priory. When the King's men come, we shall tell them whatever lies I think it good to tell them. Once they have left, then I shall call to collect the Madonna from you, and you shall return it to me, and all will be well.'

And the Prior agreed to this. But once he had the Madonna in his possession, strange imaginings ran through his mind too. 'Why,' he said, 'should I return this to Sidlesham, when it would grace our own Priory so much better? The Abbot said that God gave it to them by chance, and by chance it has now fallen to me. When the Abbot comes to collect it, I shall hide it and say to anyone who asks that it was never given to us. Then it will be ours for ever.'

Of course, the Abbot was wrath, but he could do nothing. He could not complain to the King without revealing his stratagem. Nor could he complain to the Bishop, who (like all Bishops) looked down on the monks and the hard-working parish priests, and who would most certainly have told the King if the Abbot had confessed where the statue was. The Abbot let it be known around Sussex that the Prior was a rogue and a thief, but he could do no more than that and he died shortly after of apoplexy.

Nor did the Prior enjoy his ill-gotten gains. A villager told the King's men that he was sure the Prior had taken the statue, and the King sent his commissioners to close down the Priory at once. But though they searched every building, they never found the Madonna. And the Prior was sent away, with his monks, and he, too, died soon after.

Some say that the new owner of the Priory found the statue buried in the monks' garden, others that it was never found and is still there today, in West Wittering, and yet others say that the Abbot spoke false when he said he had ever given it to the Prior, and that the statue lies slumbering somewhere under the soil of the Abbey cloisters. And which of those things is the truth, I dare not even attempt to say.

But what I can tell you is that the image never brought anyone any luck, and those who would place such nasty foreign things in our lovely and simple English churches would do well to heed the warning of this story.

'So,' I said, 'in the end, the story was just a protracted rant against the Oxford Movement. In Barclay-Wood's time they would have been putting statues of saints into a lot of the churches round here. It evoked strong feelings. He was opposed to the introduction of images, incense and candles. A story that showed that no good came of it would have appealed to him. He would have bent what few facts he had to fit the moral he wished to teach.'

'Then none of it is true?' asked Elsie.

'No, I think some of it is. But there are inconsistencies. For example, when the monk contemplates the statue of the Virgin, he is impressed by the gold and the lapis lazuli and the drops of ruby-red blood.'

'So?'

'The ruby-red drops were on the statue of Christ.'

'If you'd seen as many proofreading errors as I have . . .'

'Yes, but I think Barclay-Wood may have been offering a clue that the statue of Christ also made it to Sussex . . . Sorry, I didn't catch what you said just then?'

'Didn't understand . . . bit . . . what?'

'You're breaking up,' I said.

I tried walking over to the other side of the sitting room. Reception in West Wittering was usually bad and sometimes the phone works in one part of the house but not another. I put the handset to my ear again.

'. . . so you were dead wrong there,' Elsie was concluding.

'You'll need to start again,' I said.

'All of it?'

'You can leave out the bit about my being wrong, if you like.'

'I'll try, but it may not be possible. Anyway, what I was saying was that I sent our intern over to the newspaper archives to see if he could find anything more on the original death-in-the-well case.'

'And did he?'

'No. It involved handling paper, of course. That's not his strong point. Millennials don't really understand paper. They all had iPads in their baby buggies. Frankly, Ethelred, the problem with interns is that they make me feel old and out of touch with technology – though not as old or out of touch as you, obviously. It's always very reassuring talking to you, in that respect.'

'Thank you,' I said. 'I do my best.'

'And like all interns he can't write or think and can't speak without it sounding like a question. Young people these days always sound as if they're checking that what they've just said is really true. Anyway, he did find out something useful. Shortly after the trial, Mrs Munnings, Iris's grandmother, vanished.'

'Iris said that she died. She didn't say anything about her vanishing. That might explain why she didn't know exactly when she died.'

'I'm sending the intern – whatever he's called – back to check the rest of the story.'

'Good. But in what way does any of that make me wrong?'

'In what way does it make you right, Ethelred?'

'Not at all.'

'There you are, then.'

'But are you saying the deaths of Walter Sly and Iris's grandparents and Hilary Joyner were in some way connected?'

'Only by the curse of the Sidlesham Madonna.'

'If Barclay-Wood is to be believed, and I'm not sure he is, then possession of the Madonna incites insatiable greed, then death by leprosy or apoplexy. Did Old Man Munnings die of either?'

'Good point. I'll get the intern to check what he died of. If it was leprosy, then we're onto something.'

'I was joking.'

'Yes, but interns are dirt cheap. And it will keep him away from things he might mess up. It's win-win, when you think about it.'

It was a couple of days later that my phone rang and another small part of the story was revealed to me.

'I have to see you at once,' said Polgreen. 'The forces of evil are gathering.'

'What about tomorrow?' I asked.

'I'm quite close to you now,' he said.

'How close?' I asked.

'Very,' he said.

'Fine, just ring the bell when you arrive,' I said.

I put the phone in my pocket. The doorbell sounded.

'So, Sly went completely behind my back to the rest of the committee,' said Polgreen bitterly. 'He convened a meeting that I wasn't even to be informed of and told them that Iris Munnings and I were conspiring to deprive the Abbey of valuable items that we had dug up. He couldn't even claim what he was proposing was sanctioned by his bloody rule book. It was pure spite.'

He took a sip of coffee. We were now sitting on my patio, looking out over the new rose bed. The bush at the end was looking slightly the worse for wear. It was drooping. I'd need to water and feed it. But perhaps Polgreen's problems were worse than mine.

'That's outrageous,' I said.

'He also claimed that you told him that Iris and I had probably murdered Hilary Joyner.'

'He actually said that?'

'He implied it. You know what he's like.'

'Yes,' I said. 'I do. But nobody believed any of this, surely?'

'Some did. Sly pointed them to a rule saying that anyone on the committee accused of a serious crime, such as murder, had to stand down immediately.'

'Is there such a rule?'

'Sly had the only copy of the rule book. It was in there, apparently.'

'I suppose it's not unreasonable. But nobody has accused you of anything.'

'Sly's accused me. He got the committee to agree I have to explain myself to the next full meeting. If they're not satisfied, then I'll be suspended and they will investigate the site as Sly wishes, to see if my excavations are connected to Joyner's death.'

'That's ridiculous.'

'Not in Sly's imagination.'

'Would it even be possible for you to dig without people knowing?' I asked. 'I mean, a trench appearing overnight would be very visible.'

Polgreen looked slightly embarrassed. 'The site is closed between November and March,' he said. 'I look in once a week or so to check that all is well, but not many people go there then.'

'And did you see anything?'

Polgreen swallowed hard. 'Of course not.'

'You're not worried that they will find anything untoward, then?'

Polgreen sighed. 'It's not that they'll stumble across anything I've done that worries me. It's that they won't be able to tell the difference between an unrecorded dig thirty or fifty years ago and one that took place last month. It's all been dug over. Sly can claim that anything there might have been me.'

'But will the others believe him? If your conscience is clear, why not just let them dig? The less you protest, the less suspicious it will look.'

'Because it's just an excuse for Sly to reopen the excavations. He's had this thing for years that there's still something buried there somewhere – at the Abbey or the Priory. He thinks, if we found it, then we could get crowds of people in and fund a new museum on the site, of which he would be the curator.'

'Not unlike the Abbot's plan years ago,' I said. 'Get the Maltese Madonna to pull in the crowds.'

'At least the Abbot had the genuine goods,' said Polgreen.

'I'd still let them dig,' I said. 'From what you say, the damage has already been done, in archaeological terms. Anyway, why do you think I can help? I have no influence at all with the committee.'

'You could join the committee,' he said. 'There's a vacancy. We could co-opt you.'

'Do I have to?' I asked.

'You would be doing me an enormous favour if you did. A favour as a friend. And you do know some of the other members already.'

He handed me a list. I did know two vaguely. One was actually another writer, who lived in the village. I sighed. 'Why is Sly so convinced there's still something there to find?' I asked.

'There's always been a story in his family that half the

treasure was stored at the Priory and half at the Abbey. And I don't know if you know but his grandfather used to work as a gardener at the Priory.'

'Yes,' I said. 'Mr Munnings was accused of his murder.'

Polgreen nodded. 'There you are, then. What you may not know is that Sly's grandmother went over to the Priory after the trial and told Munnings she had finally worked out what his secret was.'

'Meaning what?'

'That's all Sly would tell me. It's probably all he knew. She went over there and accused him to his face.'

At this point a text message arrived. It was from Elsie. I opened it at once.

RE OLD MAN MUNNINGS, it read. HE DIED SUDDENLY OF A HEART ATTACK.

I texted back: HOW DO YOU KNOW?

CHAPTER TEN
Elsie

So, I'd found out like this.

A face had looked cautiously round the door. It was strangely familiar.

'Yes?' I enquired.

'I'm Aaron – your intern?' he said.

'Is it that you aren't sure whether you are my intern?' I asked. 'Or are you speaking Millennial?'

'I don't understand,' he said. 'I'm just speaking like I usually do?'

'So you are. Shouldn't you be at Colindale, sifting through newspapers? That *is* a question.'

'I've been there for two days. I hoped I could come back now. I'd like to learn about publishing?'

'No shit?'

'Yes. Really.'

Excellent. I could still impose on him then.

'First tell me what you've discovered so far about Walter Sly's death,' I said. 'Then I might let you have full and unrestricted access to the fabled slush pile.'

He opened the notebook that he had been clutching.

'I tried to go back to the very beginning,' he said. 'I've constructed a timeline.'

'Am I paying you to construct timelines?' I asked.

'You're not paying me at all.'

'You're an intern,' I said.

'My father said to point out to you that you were exploiting me,' he said.

'And so you *have*,' I said kindly. 'I'm sure he would be proud of you. At least be grateful you're not a writer. You will earn proper money one day.'

'Sometimes I think I'd like to be a writer.'

'You wouldn't.'

'Don't they enjoy writing?'

'Writers enjoy starting and finishing books. In between there is nothing but doubt, self-loathing and coffee. Their moments of happiness are brief and illusionary. So, just tell me what you've found out.'

'OK. As you know, work started on the Priory garden in the spring of 1959. Then in early May the workforce was dismissed and Mr Munnings and the gardener continued on their own.'

'Yes, I do know. Look, you may have another eighty years to live, but I don't. Can we fast-forward a bit? Like when you're streaming a video.'

'Do you know how to stream a video?'

'Yes.'

'A lot of older people don't.'

We stared at each other across a generational divide. 'I can do long division,' I said. 'And I've never paid more than two pounds fifty for a cappuccino.'

'Fair enough,' he said. 'So, in late May, the gardener vanished and was found in the well after three days. The trial took place in August. The verdict was not guilty. Then, in early September, Mr Munnings died suddenly of a heart attack.'

I nodded. 'So, when did his wife die? During the trial?'

'Some time after that.'

'How much after?'

'Nobody knows. Mr Munnings' son and daughter-in-law discovered his body, when he didn't answer the phone. They lived close by. They also discovered his wife was missing. At first the police thought she might have killed her husband and fled. There was a search for her – they checked whether she might have gone to her family or London or even left the country. But then the coroner reported that it was a heart attack that killed Munnings and the police decided that, since she had dementia, Mrs Munnings had just wandered off, once there was nobody watching her.'

'Dementia? That was what was wrong with her?'

'Yes. I didn't research dementia because I thought you'd already know more about it than I did. Older people often look that sort of thing up, just in case.'

'I'm younger than a lot of my writers.'

'You mean the dead ones? The ones whose estates you represent?'

'They're a lot less trouble than the living ones. What happened next, Aaron?'

'Well,' he said, 'they continued looking for the grandmother, but this time in the fields and woods round West Wittering.'

'And that's where they found her?'

'No. It wasn't until January 1960 that her body was found – up on the Downs, in a small area of woodland, just north of Chichester. It seems she had just wandered off on her own and that was as far as she could get. She'd died of exposure or hunger or something. By that stage it was difficult to tell. She must have just tramped across the fields, maybe for days. It's a bit sad, really. She stopped just short of a lane where somebody might have found her while she was still alive, but it took ages to locate her body. It was in the middle of a wood, under some bracken she'd managed to cover herself with. They identified the body mainly by her clothes and shoes, which matched what she had been wearing, and by the contents of her handbag.'

'Well done,' I said. 'Not leprosy then, in either case.'

'Sorry?'

'Just thinking out loud. It's what old people do.'

'Cool. Can I do some publishing work now?' he asked.

I looked at him. Could he be turned into an agent one day? Who could say? In the meantime, he was far better off being exploited by me than being released back into the community to write a novel. I was being cruel to be kind, though thinking about it, I was also being cruel to be cruel. That's how you get when your dementia stops you streaming videos.

'Of course,' I said. 'I'll forward you a couple of manuscripts from the slush pile. Don't worry – it's all electronic. I don't accept paper submissions any more. Even at my age.'

His face brightened up. 'Thank you,' he said.

'My pleasure,' I said. 'I'll do it now.'

I selected a couple at random from a folder marked 'The Usual Old Crap' and pinged them across. By tomorrow he'd be begging to go back to the archives in Colindale.

I picked up my phone and texted Ethelred with what seemed to me to be the one useful fact that we had uncovered.

RE OLD MAN MUNNINGS, I wrote. HE DIED SUDDENLY OF A HEART ATTACK.

CHAPTER ELEVEN

Ethelred

My landline rarely rings these days, other than for the usual quota of scam calls. When I answered it, I was ready to listen to an invitation to sue somebody for my recent accident or an explanation of how I could erase viruses from my computer by connecting to a website and allowing it to make unspecified but wholly trustworthy changes to my hard drive. For a moment I didn't recognise the voice at the other end of the line. Then I said, 'So how did you get this number? I hardly ever use it now.'

'Ah,' said Professor Cox. He laughed nervously. 'I'm afraid I got it from the development office. I said I needed to contact you urgently and that you would have no objection. They said it was the only number they had for you.'

'I probably gave it to them when I moved here,' I said. 'I didn't use my mobile so much then.'

There was quite a long pause, then he went on, 'Very unfortunate business – Hilary's accident. He will be much missed by us all. We must do something to commemorate his valuable contribution to the life and work of the College. He was Tutor for Admissions for a while – a very important post. And briefly deputy Principal, or at least acting deputy Principal, some years ago.'

I waited for a short but scathing critique of Joyner's abilities in one or other of these roles, but none came. Death pays all debts.

'I didn't know that,' I said. 'So, will there be a memorial service in the chapel? I'd like to come if there is.'

'A memorial service? I imagine there may be, in due course. I believe the home bursar is trying to establish the wishes of his family.'

'Well, let me know when you have a date,' I said, wondering if that was the sole purpose of the call.

There was another pause. 'I suppose that Hilary didn't leave a bag with you?' Cox added.

'Yes,' I said. 'I've already told the College that.'

'Of course. So you did. Excellent. Have you opened it by any chance?'

'No,' I said. 'I've had no reason to do so. It's none of my business.'

'Really? Quite right. Very proper of you. But . . . well, you see, he had some papers of mine, which I'd like to get back as soon as possible. They don't seem to be in his rooms – his new rooms – so I wondered if he'd taken them with him to Sussex. I could come over and pick the bag up. It would save your sending it on.'

'It's a long way for you to come.'

'I do need the papers urgently. They are critical to my research. I have a book to finish, and you know what

138

editors are like, Ethelred. Deadlines, eh?' He gave a little chuckle, one writer to another.

'I thought you were just starting a new book – Gladstone?'

'It's another book entirely. One I'm currently finishing.'

I waited to see if he'd tell me what it was about. He didn't.

'I can certainly see if they're there,' I said. 'What do they look like?'

'Ah, well there's the problem,' said Cox. 'I can't easily describe the papers, but I'd know them when I saw them, of course. I was planning to be down your way, so it would be no bother to collect the bag from you. Without your having to open it at all. I think your discretion in that respect does you great credit and I wouldn't want to make you do something that you thought was improper. My position is, of course, slightly different. I'd be acting on behalf of the College, in a way. It's the least I can do . . . for Hilary. To tidy up Hilary's affairs. Out of the great respect and affection we all had for him. Without troubling you or putting you to any unnecessary expense. After all you did for him, I owe you that much.'

Sometimes during a scam call there's a point where you know, if you didn't before, that all is not well. I'd just never received a scam call from a professor of modern history.

'Are the papers loose or bound, Professor Cox?' I asked.

'Both,' said Cox. 'I think. I lent him various things over the past few months and I'm not sure which he would have taken with him. That's why it's better I check them in person.'

'And what are they about?' I said. 'Or don't you recall that either?'

'Really, I don't think you need to take that tone with me,' said Cox.

'Professor Cox,' I said. 'I have undertaken to return the bag to Dr Joyner's family as it is. The College knows that. If it contains papers of yours, then I'm sure they will cooperate in returning them to you. I claim no credit for not examining the bag until now. It is light and, I felt, unlikely to contain anything of general interest. But I could check now and reassure you that the papers are safe. You just have to say what they are.'

'That seems a little inflexible, if you don't mind my saying.'

'That's how I am,' I said. 'I'm probably a bit old to change now.'

'Then I'm very sorry to have troubled you,' he said.

'No trouble,' I said. 'Happy to be of service. Have a nice day.'

After the call, I went up into the attic and retrieved the bag. It was a compact case on wheels – neat but solid. The contents were as unexceptional as I had assumed they would be. It contained Joyner's pyjamas, his toothbrush and a copy of Sabine Barclay-Wood's published memoirs, *Happy Recollections of a Sussex Clergyman*. There was also a large, but very empty, padded jiffy bag. There was no sign of any papers as such, bound or otherwise. I checked the side pockets, in case I had missed something, but Dr Joyner had travelled light. Not even, I was only slightly surprised to see, a spare pair of socks. It was a small piece of luggage by most standards, but a very large one for what it contained. Perhaps he had brought something in the envelope? Or perhaps he had hoped to take something back to Oxford with him? Still, there was nothing in the bag that was worth reporting back to Cox.

Feeling slightly guilty for having given way to curiosity, I returned the suitcase to the attic, descended the metal stairs, locked them back in place and closed the trapdoor. Then I dialled Elsie's number.

'It's strange how history has repeated itself,' I said. 'I mean two deaths in the well sixty years apart, both largely unexplained.'

'But the police think it's an accident,' said Elsie. 'Only Sly seems to be suggesting it's not.'

'He believes his grandfather was murdered in the same well,' I said. 'That must affect how you see things.'

'It's interesting the way Old Man Munnings died of a heart attack,' said Elsie. 'Just after Walter Sly's wife went to see him.'

'I'm sure that Walter Sly's death and the trial put a lot of strain on him,' I said. 'Even though he was found not guilty. Whatever Mrs Sly said to him, he might have had the heart attack anyway. Don't think I'm agreeing with Sly in any way, but it's Joyner's death that is starting to look a bit odd. I had Cox on the phone to me yesterday. Joyner had something that he needs badly, and he thought he might have brought it to West Wittering with him. Papers, he claimed.'

'And what did you say?'

'I said I hadn't looked in the bag.'

'And he actually believed that?'

'I really hadn't.'

'Yeah, right,' said Elsie.

'Anyway,' I said. 'I did look, after his call, because it was all so odd. But there's nothing in the case, except a book, his pyjamas and toothbrush. Oh, and an empty envelope that he planned to use to take something back or had used to bring something down.'

'But not papers?'

'If the envelope did once contain papers, there's no sign of them now.'

'Anthony Cox was mistaken, then,' said Elsie.

'So it would seem,' I said.

Then, remarkably, history did repeat itself. This time as farce, just like Marx said it does.

There was a ring on my doorbell and Iris Munnings stood there.

'I was just passing,' she said, 'so I thought it would be so nice to drop in and see you.'

It seemed impolite to point out that she had never done so before and, with one recent exception, I had never dropped in on her without having to buy a ticket in aid of the lifeboats.

'I was just making some coffee,' I lied politely.

'Perfect,' she said. 'Why don't we have it in the garden? I've always wanted to see your garden.'

I wondered how many untruths had been told since she rang my bell. I made that at least four between us.

I seated her on the patio and went and made real coffee. Fortunately, Elsie had not visited recently, so I still had biscuits. I carried them out, only to find that Iris was examining my flower beds. Compared with her own, mine would not have been of much interest.

'Your roses are doing well,' she said. 'Except that one, which looks almost dead.'

I looked where she had been pointing. One was certainly ailing. I'd noticed it when Polgreen was here, but it was showing no improvement. It was odd because it had had as much mulching and water as the others.

'I planted them this spring,' I said. 'The dry weather lately hasn't helped them much. That one was fine until recently. The soil around it looks a bit disturbed, now you point it out. Foxes, probably. They dig everywhere. But occasionally it just happens that one doesn't thrive, for no apparent reason. Maybe I should take it up, fork the ground over again and plant something else there.'

'Yes, probably,' she said, returning to her seat. 'They're cheap enough to replace.' She took a sip of coffee and made no further comment on any aspect of the garden. This would have surprised me only if I'd believed she genuinely had any interest in it. She put the cup down again. 'Ethelred, perhaps I should tell you the real reason for my coming here. Could I persuade you to join the Abbey preservation committee?'

'Yes, Henry has already mentioned it to me,' I said, sitting down beside her. I pressed the plunger down on the cafetière and poured the coffee. 'But wouldn't I need to be elected by the AGM or something?' I added.

'No, if there are vacancies, the committee can fill them pending the next AGM. Additionally, the chairman can personally co-opt up to three members with specialist skills.'

'I'm not sure I have any.'

'But you have an extensive knowledge of history. You write about it.'

'My historical novels are set between 1377 and 1399,' I said. 'Like most writers of historical fiction, I know just enough about a very brief period of time.'

'You are too modest,' she said.

'I've just joined the Crime Writers' Association committee,' I said. 'I'm not sure that I could manage to fit in another one.'

'There are only two or three meetings a year.'

'I thought Tertius Sly had increased them?'

'Well, we're decreasing them again. That man Sly needs putting firmly in his place. We just need one or two sensible people on the committee to try to reduce all of this unnecessary bickering. Sensible people from – how is one allowed to say it these days? – the right *background*. Please say you'll do it, Ethelred?'

'Two or three meetings?' I said.

'Think about it,' she said. 'That's all I'm asking. But I must go and powder my nose. I think I saw a cloakroom as I entered?'

'Yes,' I said. 'By the front door.'

'I can find it,' she said, getting to her feet. 'Don't get up. I remember exactly where you mean. I'll just be a moment.'

Iris vanished into the house. So, was the committee, rather than my garden, the real reason for her visit? If so, I wasn't sure why she hadn't got Henry Polgreen to just follow up his earlier suggestion – which, oddly, he'd never done. Anyway, I imagined that Iris's definition of 'the right background' was slightly more exacting than I could manage. She'd spot me pretty quickly for a mere crime writer. She'd already got me down as an incompetent grower of roses, which was bad enough.

I finished my coffee and was about to top up my cup and Iris's, when I noticed hers was still almost full. She had been away quite a long time. The lock on the cloakroom can be tricky and, fearing that she might be trapped inside, I went in search of her. But she was not there. The door was ajar and the room empty. I proceeded down the corridor past my study and the larger guest bedroom. Just before I reached the smaller one, I heard a noise of something being opened. I entered the room that Joyner had occupied, only to see Iris hurriedly shutting a drawer.

She looked up, startled.

'You seem to be lost,' I said. 'I thought you knew where you were going?'

'Yes. Very silly of me. I must have turned right when I should have turned left. Or something. Rather foolishly I have found myself here. But . . . was this by any chance Dr Joyner's room, when he stayed with you?'

'Yes,' I said.

She nodded thoughtfully, as if entering a bedroom in mistake for the cloakroom was quite normal, at least amongst those of the right background. 'I suppose he must have left his belongings with you – I mean, he wasn't in any position to take them with him. Not to where he is now. Sadly.'

'No,' I said.

'But his bag isn't here now?'

'No,' I said.

'I've just had a brilliant thought, Ethelred. I could take it to Oxford. By a strange coincidence, I'm driving up there very soon. If the bag is easy to find – obviously I wouldn't wish to put you to any trouble – then I could just take it with me now.'

'It's fine,' I said.

'Yes, of course. I'm sure that it is safe in your hands. But, if there's anything I can do to help tie up any loose ends for poor Dr Joyner, I'd be very pleased to help. Perhaps, if you've now looked inside, there might be something in his bag that puzzled you, but which I might be able to explain? As a committee member with a knowledge of the Abbey.'

'There's nothing in the bag that needs explaining,' I said.

'So, you *have* looked? But I thought . . .' She paused and bit her lip. I waited for her to say what she thought, but she did not.

'I've already had one enquiry about it,' I said, 'as you appear to know. So, yes, I did check after Professor Cox's call. There's nothing in the bag apart from some clothes and an empty envelope.'

'Empty?'

'Completely empty.'

'You're sure?'

'It's not something I need a second opinion on.'

'No, I suppose not. And the thing that was in the envelope – before it was empty – he couldn't have concealed it somewhere in the house?'

'Why would he do that?'

'I merely wondered.'

'If he did, I would have found it by now.'

Iris nodded. 'I just thought I'd ask. To ascertain the facts. In case I could help in any way.'

'Thank you,' I said. 'I've told the family that I'll return the bag to them, just as it is. I've told Professor Cox. And that's what I shall do, if anyone lets me.'

'I wasn't trying to interfere,' she said.

'I didn't say you were.'

'If you change your mind . . .' she said.

'You'll be the first to know,' I said. 'You, then Professor Cox. In that order.'

As she was leaving, she paused for a moment and frowned. She glanced back, through the sitting-room door, and out into the garden.

'That rose,' she said. 'You know, on second thoughts, I should be patient with it. Give it another chance. Plenty of water and compost. No digging. Just mulch the surface. Yes, that's what I'd do. Regard it as a challenge, Ethelred.'

'Of course,' I said. 'Thank you for the advice, Iris.'

After she'd gone, it occurred to me that she hadn't asked me whether I'd decided, on reflection, to join the committee. Perhaps, like Henry Polgreen, she'd decided it wasn't so very urgent after all.

The email arrived that evening. It was from Joyner's ex-wife – or perhaps I should now say ex-widow, if there is such a term.

Dear Mr Tressider,

My late husband's underpants and toothbrush have, for some years now, been of minimal interest to me. I have informed the College that I wish nothing to be forwarded – not clothes, not household chattels and certainly not history books relating to any period. Whatever it is you have in those bags, you may keep. I am sure Hilary would have wanted you to have it, so that's fine. Alternatively, if he'd have hated your having it, that's fine too. Either way, it's all yours, as a gift from me, and I wish you well of it. No need to

write and thank me. I'm happy just to imagine your
joy at the receipt of this email.
      Kind regards
      Lesley Joyner

This seemed eminently sensible. The cost of sending the bag to Spain would far outweigh its value. Then I noticed that she had mentioned bags in the plural, a natural mistake when I had not specified the number. There was just the one bag in the attic. Except, now I thought about it, hadn't there also been a rucksack that Joyner had been carrying at the Abbey? Where was that? I tried to remember us setting off for our walk. Joyner had been clutching his map in both hands. I was pretty sure that he hadn't had the bag with him then. And we would have noticed if he'd left it on the terrace at the Priory – if not when Iris and I arrived back there, then certainly later after his body was discovered. Unless Joyner's killer – if he had had such a thing – had stolen the bag while we were all still wandering round the garden?

That was possible. But there was a more likely solution to the mystery of the missing bag. I went outside and opened the door of my car. A small rucksack was stuffed underneath the front passenger seat. I pulled it out. I took it inside and unzipped it.

CHAPTER TWELVE

Elsie

'So that's it?' I said. 'That there?'

'Yes,' said Ethelred.

'You thought it was worth lugging that random paper collection up to London to show me, just in case I turned into an archivist since you last saw me?'

'This,' said Ethelred, 'is the original inventory of Sidlesham Abbey in 1530.'

He seemed to think I should be impressed and whip out some white cotton gloves before handling it.

'I thought Barclay-Wood nicked it?' I said.

'Well, Joyner seems to have found it again,' he said. 'It seems to be the genuine article. It was in the rucksack.'

I picked up the genuine original inventory. It looked like one of the dullest documents I'd ever come across, and I have drunken deep of many slush piles, electronic and paper. At least there was no covering letter telling me how much I was going to love it because it was just like an inventory that J. K. Rowling had written.

'What you're saying is that this is a list of stuff?' I asked.

'Yes,' said Ethelred.

'Dead monk stuff?'

'Exactly,' said Ethelred. He was pleased I finally understood and shared his boundless enthusiasm. 'Until the commissioners appropriated it, obviously. Then it was the King's stuff.'

'Lucky King.'

I tried to work out what the list said. It wasn't entirely clear.

'So, there was nobody around to teach handwriting until 1531 at least?' I asked.

'That's how they wrote in the sixteenth century,' said Ethelred, as if that ever excused anything.

It just looked like a load of squiggles to me. I explained this to Ethelred.

'The handwriting isn't that difficult to interpret, once you get your eye in,' he said. 'And thoughtfully they wrote it in English rather than Latin. Mainly, anyway.'

He talked me through: *Imprimis i golde and blew enamel chalis, shewing the Virgin enthroned* . . . then *vii sylver candelle stikkes* . . . then *iii sylver cuppes*.

'They certainly had crap spellcheckers in 1530,' I said.

'Spelling was rather looser in those days.'

'No shit? What does that line say?' I asked.

'It says: one gold and blue enamel pyx with St Peter and St Paul and the Lamb of God.'

'Which does what exactly?'

I waited for him to admit that he had no idea. But he was a man, so he didn't.

'A pyx? It's a sort of container ... or box ... or bowl ... for something or other,' he said with great authority.

'You don't know, do you?' I said.

'In very general terms.'

'Except you don't.'

'I'll google it,' he said.

He took his computer out of his bag and typed for a bit. 'There,' he said. 'It's a box for holding communion wafers.'

'Obviously,' I said. 'What else would you use it for? I was just checking whether you knew too. Everyone knows what a pax is.'

'Pyx,' he said. Whatever. He hadn't scored a point of any sort. He turned the screen round so I could see it. 'Like the one there.'

'So, that's St Peter and St Paul?' I asked.

'Yup,' said Ethelred.

'And that small and slightly deranged animal with a flag is a sheep?'

'Lamb.'

'You know it couldn't really hold a flag in his front hoof like that?'

'Yes, it can. It's a Lamb of God.'

'What other superpowers does it have?'

'It takes away the sins of the world.'

'Fair enough. They probably hadn't come up with X-ray vision then. And that's all blue enamel?'

'Absolutely.'

'So, what you're saying is that there's one on Google exactly like the one in the inventory?'

'Apparently.'

'They must be pretty common, then?'

'I doubt it. A lot of mediaeval English church plate was seized and melted down in the 1550s. Edward VI didn't like it from a doctrinal point of view, and he also wanted the cash. It's all quite rare now.'

Ethelred frowned and typed some more. 'That one is in the Stephenson Museum in Hadleyburg in the United States,' he said.

'Fine. Lucky they had one so we could see it online. And what would the chalice have looked like?' I asked.

'I doubt we'll be so fortunate this time, but let's try searching for a mediaeval gold chalice, also with blue enamel. There might be one a bit like it.' Ethelred fiddled around a bit more. 'Good. And now let's click on Images . . .'

He turned the computer screen to face me.

'Nice gold,' I said. 'Nice blue enamel. Nice Virgin enthroned.'

'I agree I hadn't expected quite so close a match,' said Ethelred. 'Let's see where that one is . . . that's odd. It's in the same museum – in Hadleyburg.'

He ran his finger down the badly spelt list. 'The Abbey had a gold reliquary pendant of St Catherine. There won't be too many of those out there . . .'

For a while he typed and frowned and frowned and typed. 'I don't understand,' he said. 'Almost everything in the inventory seems to be in the same museum.'

'Coincidence?' I asked.

He typed some more. 'Ah,' he said. 'For the pyx, it gives the origin as . . . Sussex County, United Kingdom. And the chalice is . . . Sussex County, United Kingdom. And the candlesticks are . . .'

'Sussex County, United Kingdom?'

'Yes,' said Ethelred slowly. 'All acquired about fifteen years ago – apparently.'

'So, does the Stephenson Museum also possess a gold statue of the Virgin Mary originating from Malta? It would be great if it did. We could wrap up the whole thing, go home and eat chocolate as a reward.'

Ethelred typed a bit more. 'I can't find a gold statue of the Virgin listed on their website,' he said. 'Obviously, they haven't put everything they possess on there. Just the more interesting stuff.'

'But if it was the finest gold statue ever made, worth several zillion pounds and capable of killing anyone who touched it, you'd think it might be worth a mention?'

'Quite. You'd think they'd refer to it in passing.'

'But it's in the monk inventory?' I asked.

'Yes, definitely. Right at the end. *An ancient image of the B. V. Marie.*'

I looked at the squiggles, which might have said almost anything. It was a good job I had Ethelred there. He definitely was, by a couple of centuries, the closest thing I was ever going to find to a sixteenth-century monk.

'So how did Joyner get his hands on this?' I said.

Ethelred shrugged. 'I've no idea. All of the papers should be in a museum too. Here in Sussex.'

'What else was in the rucksack?' I asked.

'Some other papers relating to the Abbey. And a notebook containing Sabine Barclay-Wood's journal in manuscript. It looks pretty much identical to his published *Happy Recollections of a Sussex Clergyman*, though I haven't yet compared it all line by line.'

'But the original notebook?'

'That's what it seems to be. If we're assuming that Barclay-Wood removed the inventory from the Abbey, then the combination of the journal and inventory here suggests that Joyner somehow acquired a whole stash of Barclay-Wood's papers. But it still leaves unanswered the question of how and where he got hold of it all.'

'And Cox was desperate to get his hands on it all?'

'Apparently. And Iris.'

'But is there anything remotely interesting there? A map with a big X on it, showing where the loot is buried?'

'Joyner had a map of some sort with him when he died.'

'The one that was reduced to mush in the well?'

'Yes. I caught a glance of it. It looked quite old. Joe said the ink had run so badly you couldn't make out anything now.'

'OK, maybe Anthony Cox and Iris wanted the map, then. What else is there?' I asked. 'Anything exciting?'

'Most definitely. A couple of documents confirming charters. What seems to be a list of manorial tenants. A letter from the King informing the Abbot of the coming visitation by the commissioners. Two or three letters concerning a lawsuit over grazing rights. Some general correspondence with the Bishop.'

'Sorry,' I said. 'I think I must have dozed off there.'

'Why did Joyner carry them all the way down to Sussex, though?'

'No idea,' I said. 'The map would have been helpful, but he could have left the rest behind.'

'Still, it could explain the padded envelope in the case,' said Ethelred.

'Great!' I said. 'There's a weight off my mind.'

'Iris seemed to find it significant,' he said huffily. 'She

asked what had been in the envelope before it was empty.'

'Not much happens round your way, does it?'

'I just meant, maybe the papers were in the envelope,' said Ethelred. 'That's why it was in the case.'

'Well, that disposes of the envelope problem, which might otherwise have kept me awake for several minutes tonight,' I said. 'Do you think Joyner knew that the Abbey's gold- and silverware was all in the US now? It didn't take us long to find out. Not once we knew what we were looking for. He had the list at the time he died.'

'Probably,' said Ethelred.

'Actually, wasn't the inventory published somewhere? Wouldn't a lot of people have seen it?'

'It's in a pretty obscure journal,' said Ethelred.

'But Polgreen might know? Or Sly?'

'Both, probably,' said Ethelred. 'But they've never mentioned to me the possibility that the Abbey's treasures might have been discovered and sold. I can't see Sly holding back on that if he knew. Or Henry, really.'

'Unless Henry found it at the Abbey and sold it. He'd keep quiet about it then. Very quiet.'

'Surely not?' said Ethelred.

'It's pretty much what Sly accused him of. Maybe there's more to the accusations than we suspected.'

Ethelred thought about it and shook his head. 'Or it was part of the hoard taken to the Priory. If so, then Iris's grandfather seems to have succeeded in finding a buyer before he died.'

'Except,' I said, 'if it was at the Priory and then acquired by the museum only fifteen years ago, that actually points to a sale by Iris.'

'Maybe I should contact the Stephenson Museum and ask them.'

'No,' I said. 'That's what interns are for. Let's go for a coffee.'

CHAPTER THIRTEEN

Ethelred

'So, how did he get on?' I asked.

It was the evening after my return from London and I was curious to know what Elsie's intern had found out. Curious enough to make a call to her mobile.

'I was very pleased with him,' said Elsie. 'He called Hadleyburg on the office phone and spoke to one of the junior staff there, intern to intern. He said he was an MA student writing a dissertation on mediaeval church silverware and wanted to know more about the museum's collection.'

'You have trained him well,' I said.

'Yes, he was entirely honest and law-abiding before I took him on. Anyway, he asked her if she knew how the various Sussex County items had been obtained and whether they had been obtained directly in the UK or from a third party in the US. The Hadleyburg intern said she would be delighted to help and would email the information to him.'

'And?'

'He got a reply from her within half an hour. The items were from an unnamed source – a donation.'

'Sounds as if she knows how to lie too.'

'I was deeply shocked when I heard. Young people always *look* so clean and trustworthy. So he asked if the unnamed donor was British or American and if she had found out when the silverware had moved to the United States. She said the museum had been gifted the items fifteen years ago, but they had no records that enabled them to find out when or how any of it had entered the country.'

'But they would have needed an export licence?'

'Aaron pointed that out. He's quite good. I almost wondered if I should pay him something . . . Anyway, he further enquired if the information he needed might be included on the licence, which they must still have. She said if such a thing had ever existed, it had been destroyed many, many years ago. In all likelihood before either of them had been born, though that obviously wasn't that long ago. She declined to answer further questions. She had, he said, become quite irritable.'

'How long ago was the museum set up, then?' I asked.

'It was back in the '50s. A wealthy local businessman, Howard L. Stephenson, left a whole sack of money to the town of Hadleyburg to establish a museum of art in his name. It made a number of notable acquisitions from various sources. Aaron also picked up a news item from some years ago, which suggested that the Stephenson Museum possessed a number of Italian marbles that may not have left Italy in an entirely orthodox manner.'

'Right, let's take another look at the goods,' I said.

I went to the museum's website and searched for the chalice. Then I searched for the pyx.

'They've gone,' I said. 'They've taken all of the Sussex items off the website.'

'Bad mistake,' said Elsie. 'As good as a confession of guilt. And pointless. Nothing that was on the Internet ever completely leaves it. Far better to have said that the items were exported to the US in the '20s or '30s when controls didn't exist, then donated later by their American owner.'

'Maybe deletion was the less risky option,' I said. 'At least nobody can now stumble across them accidentally. As for claiming publicly that the items were exported before the war, perhaps they're afraid somebody over here might simply know different.'

'Iris Munnings, for one,' said Elsie.

'I fear so,' I said. 'She said she managed to do some work on the house fifteen years ago. That suggests quite a large windfall then. It's too much of a coincidence.'

'Joyner had the inventory,' said Elsie. 'We've agreed he'd probably have tracked down the various items to the Stephenson Museum, just as we have.'

'So we should assume Joyner had got at least as far as we have before he died. Maybe further. He might have had more evidence than we have that Iris had made an illegal sale. Joyner said things had changed between my first meeting him and his visit here. Perhaps he had other reasons for wanting to see Iris – not just digging to find the Madonna. Perhaps he wanted to blackmail her, if he had good evidence she'd sold some items illegally. But maybe he wasn't after money – it's more likely he was just going to threaten her with exposure if she didn't allow him to dig there and get the publicity he was after. Perhaps Iris already knew most of this. That's why she was so quick to say he could come round and visit. Cox had already warned her that Joyner might know something. She wanted to talk and see just how bad it was. There's something that keeps worrying me. When I was in the garden, I saw somebody in a white jacket ahead of me and thought it was Joyner. Then I stumbled across Iris in her white jacket and decided I'd been mistaken. But what if I was right all along? What if I did see Joyner, heading in Iris's direction? He couldn't talk to her in front of everyone, so he waited until we'd all dispersed over the garden. Once she'd finished with Sly, he intercepted her. They went back to the well as a place where they could talk privately about blackmail, away from prying ears. I doubt if Iris took kindly to his proposals any more than she did to Sly's. They argued. She gave him a push. Maybe she'd even planned it that way all along. She was the one who removed the grill, after all. She even had the key with her to do it.'

'It's not surprising that she was searching Joyner's room,' said Elsie. 'She'd want to find and destroy any evidence he might have had. Maybe that's what had been in the empty envelope she'd been so interested in. The proof.'

'Which was?'

'How should I know? I hardly ever do blackmail. Not these days. We can rule out the papers you found in the rucksack, anyway. Nothing exciting or incriminating there, when you think about it.'

'I thought it was quite exciting,' I said.

'I know. But you find *Gardeners' World* exciting. What else was in the envelope? Cox wanted it. Iris wanted it.

But it's gone. Could Dr Joyner have hidden whatever it was at yours?'

'Yes, but where? If it was in the house anywhere, I'm sure I'd have come across it by now.'

'I'd wrap it up and bury it in the garden,' said Elsie. 'There are loads of places to hide things in a garden.'

I thought of Joyner's early morning walk round the garden. I thought of my inexplicably dying rose bush and the disturbed earth round it.

'I suppose that's just what he may have done,' I said. 'It's getting too dark now. I'll check once it's daylight and call you tomorrow.'

But the following morning, when I got up, I noticed that where the rose bush had been the previous day there was now a large hole. The shrub, already sickly, was lying on its side on the lawn, its roots bare and drying, its leaves visibly wilting – a horticultural lost cause. Joyner had found an ingenious hiding place. He just hadn't realised that disturbing the rose bush might ultimately reveal what he had done. Somebody else had spotted his handiwork. It didn't take me long to work out who that person might have been. Iris had noted that the rose was wilting and I had kindly alerted her to the fact that the soil round the rose had previously been disturbed. Then on mature reflection, having fruitlessly searched the house, Iris had advised me that I should on no account dig there myself.

I decided it was time to pay a return visit to the Priory. I looked at my watch. It was still seven-thirty. But if you sell works of art on the black market and murder the man who is about to expose you, then having the *Today* programme interrupted is probably the least of your problems.

Before I could fetch the car keys, however, there was a most insistent ring at my bell, followed by a loud banging on the door. Iris was not the only one facing early morning visitors, it seemed. And mine seemed determined to see me right away.

There were two men waiting for me when I opened the front door. Both were dressed in snappy suits, crisp white shirts and discreetly striped ties. But there was something about them – an ill-defined air of menace – that suggested they might not be Jehovah's Witnesses making a prompt start to the day. One was quite short, slim and carried a briefcase. The other more than made up for the first man's lack of height and breadth. He blocked out most of the daylight that would otherwise have reached West Sussex. There was very little about him that did not suggest he was a retired heavyweight boxer, down on his luck and ready to take on whatever crap job was on offer.

'Mr Tressider?' asked the small man. I'm no expert on American accents, but I'd have placed his as being somewhere halfway down West Seventy-Fifth Street, right by the hamburger joint.

'Yes,' I said cautiously.

'We are most sorry to trouble you, sir, and especially at this hour in the morning, but we wanted to ensure that we found you in. We think you may have an item that we are anxious to acquire.'

'That sounds unlikely,' I said.

The small man nodded thoughtfully, as if the improbability of his proposal had only just struck him. 'We recognise, sir, that our arrival here is unexpected, and that you might have cause to doubt our bona fides, but if you allow us in, I would be more than happy to explain our position. More than happy. We think that you will like the offer that we intend to make.'

'And if I don't want to let you in?'

'That is not an eventuality that we would wish to contemplate, sir. Not for our sake. Not for yours. My advice to you would be to talk to us, as I have just proposed. None of us wishes for any unpleasantness.'

The boxer cracked his knuckles. It was his only contribution to the conversation so far, but it was effective.

'I could call the police,' I said.

'Not if I'd broken your fingers,' said the boxer. He laughed, revealing fewer teeth than most people possess. He'd obviously taken more punches than he handed out, but my guess was that he was still a better boxer than I was. To be fair, Elsie was probably a better boxer than I was.

The smaller man turned slowly towards him and shook his head.

'Sorry,' said the boxer. He shrugged and started to pick his teeth with his thumbnail.

'My friend tends to jump to conclusions,' said the small man, turning back to me. 'He gets . . . ahead of himself. Sometimes as much as several minutes ahead of himself. I dislike unpleasantness, Mr Tressider. I dislike unpleasantness and I dislike blood almost as much as I'm sure you do. I'd rather we just talked, sir. You can put your cellphone over there on the hall table while we do so. It would ensure that there were no misunderstandings. You won't need any records of our conversation.'

'I'll make you both coffee,' I said.

'Black for me. White with four sugars for him,' said the small man. 'That must be your kitchen through there. Why don't we sit at the table, by the window? I always think you can negotiate better when you're relaxed and happy. We'd like you to be relaxed and happy.'

'So,' said the small man, primly sipping his coffee, his little finger extended. 'It's really just a question of agreeing a price.'

'A price for what?' I asked.

'I shall come straight to the point. Mr Tressider, you have an object that a client of mine wishes to acquire. He is willing to pay well for it. I can ensure that you are remunerated in cash, in whichever currency you wish to name. Pounds. Dollars. Roubles. Swiss Francs. Bitcoin. It depends very much how and where you intend to conceal the proceeds. Or I can arrange for the money to be paid directly into any account in any country in the world, if you would find it inconvenient to smuggle large quantities of banknotes yourself. Some people – those who trust us to transfer the money – do prefer it that way and we try to be accommodating.'

'You still haven't said what this object is that you are hoping to buy.'

'Mr Tressider, you are amongst friends. Your caution does you credit, but it is unnecessary. We both know that you know what I'm talking about. However, for the avoidance of doubt, the object in question is the Maltese Madonna. Now is my meaning clear, sir?'

'I don't have it.'

The boxer cracked his knuckles again and this time the

small man did not frown at him and tell him not to get ahead of himself. We were obviously already close enough to wherever it was we were going.

'We know that you do have it, sir. Don't think that by denying it you will get a better price. The offer is for a quick sale now. Today.'

'But why do you even think I have it?'

'Very well, Mr Tressider. If you doubt us, let me explain. We know, as you do, that the object was found here in Sussex County some years ago and has been in storage ever since at Wittering Priory. Some months ago, Mrs Munnings arranged for her agent to contact us and offer it to us, at a price that seemed excessive unless she was open to negotiation, as we believed her to be. We are used to sellers demanding a higher sum than they ultimately expect to receive. It is, you might say, standard practice in any sort of business, but especially in this one. Her agent very kindly sent photographs, which tended to confirm to our client that it might be what Mrs Munnings claimed it to be, but we were still sadly unable to agree a valuation, for reasons that, as the current owner, you will understand. Her agent invited us over to view the object for ourselves. Then, with minimal explanation, he emailed to put us off. We decided to come anyway, suspecting he had had a higher offer from elsewhere and wishing to persuade him that we were the better purchasers. But when we arrived, we were told that the statue was no longer in Mrs Munnings' possession. It had been stolen. A certain Dr Joyner, who I think was a friend of yours, broke into the rooms of Mrs Munnings' agent and removed the Madonna from his safe, where it had resided in a simple padded envelope. Dr Joyner brought the statue with him, here to Sussex County. Before he could do with it whatever he planned to do, however, he met with an unfortunate accident.'

'He fell down a well,' I said.

The boxer sniggered. 'Yeah,' he said. 'That's a very bad accident.'

'I have no reason,' said the small man, 'to believe that it was anything else. And it was certainly none of our doing, I can assure you, Mr Tressider. That is not how we do business. I have sent my most sincere and heartfelt condolences to his widow. Death is a terrible thing, especially when it is unexpected, as sometimes is the case. His widow replied, thanking me most kindly for my good wishes. In response to my enquiry about an object of great historical interest but purely nominal value that he wished to sell us, she said it would either be in his rooms at his college, or that it might possibly be in a bag that he had left with a Mr Tressider in West Wittering. We have established that it is not in his rooms at the College. The locks there are of an old pattern and not very secure. It did not take us long to track you down here. We're good at finding people. Wherever people hide, we find them sooner or later. I say that purely for information, in case you thought we couldn't.'

'We should'a been Mounties,' said the boxer. 'We always get our man.'

His companion gave him a very thin smile, then went on. 'Fortunately, we did not need to try very hard on this occasion. The Internet age opens many doors, Mr Tressider. And, as a writer, you are very visible.'

'Even if I have Dr Joyner's bags,' I said, 'the Maltese Madonna wouldn't be mine to sell.'

'On the contrary,' said the small man. 'Mrs Joyner made it quite clear that she had no claim on any of Dr Joyner's possessions. In any case, you are aware of the legal maxim that possession is nine-tenths of the law. There are many, many people who might try to claim ownership of the Madonna, including your British government and the Catholic Church. We are prepared to do business only with the person who actually has possession of it. That is, sadly, no longer Mrs Munnings or her agent. That is now yourself. Let me put my cards on the table, Mr Tressider. My client is willing to pay half a million for the Madonna. You would receive the cash as soon as we are able to verify that the object you hold is the real statue.'

'I can't do that,' I said.

'Very well. I was told to offer you half a million as my client's opening bid. I can see that there is no point in beating about the bush. Not with somebody as astute as you clearly are, Mr Tressider. We frankly don't have time. His final offer is a million. Pounds. I am not authorised to go higher than that. If you have any qualms about ownership, you may split the money with Mrs Munnings or the Catholic Church or anyone else that you choose. That would be your affair, not ours. But we will only deal with you. One million, Mr Tressider. Cash. And we need the goods today.'

'That won't be possible.'

'He won't go a penny higher, sir. When I say that *is* his final offer, that is his final offer.'

'I mean that I don't have it. Now I know the full story, I am pretty much certain that Dr Joyner buried the statue in the garden under one of my rose bushes.'

'Excellent. Then we only have to establish which one.

If you have a spade, then my friend here can do the hard work for us. He enjoys that sort of thing.'

'Come with me,' I said.

I took them both to the garden.

'Shit,' said the small man. 'Who did that?'

'I wish I knew,' I said.

'Who did you tell that Dr Joyner was visiting you?'

'Hardly anyone.'

'Did you tell anyone who wasn't at the Priory the day Dr Joyner died?'

'No,' I said.

The small man frowned as if counting off the guests that day one by one. 'Iris Munnings,' he said eventually. 'It can't be anyone else. So, the statue is back where it started. Except she has neglected to tell us. An oversight, I am sure. Thank you, Mr Tressider, sir. You've been most helpful.'

'I assume your offer no longer applies?' I said.

'We were never here, sir,' said the small man. 'You never even saw us.'

The large man cracked his knuckles eloquently for what I hoped was the final time.

They left.

When they had gone, I picked up my phone from the hall table and phoned Iris Munnings.

'I've just had a visit from some American friends of yours,' I said. 'A little one and a big one.'

'Bloody hell,' she said.

'They know about your gardening work last night,' I said.

'How do you know that was me?'

'Because it was.'

'It might not have been.'

'Your call,' I said. 'They don't have doubts, any more than I do, and they'll be with you in about five minutes. You'll know better than I do whether you wish to see them.'

'Five minutes? Oh God, what do I do?'

'Get in your car and drive to Apuldram Roses.'

'It won't be open yet.'

'Just park in the lane that leads up to it. I'll be waiting for you.'

'But—'

'Four minutes and counting,' I said.

'I'll see you there,' she said.

CHAPTER FOURTEEN

Ethelred

Iris was already waiting for me as I swung off the Chichester road, past the sign saying 'Now is the Perfect Time to Plant Roses' and into the rutted lane. I parked my car behind hers and got out.

The morning still felt fresh and full of promise for somebody. The sky was blue. The sun had started to warm the dry soil of the fields around us. A gentle breeze eased its way through the elms. A blackbird sang. We were a long way from the hamburger joint on West Seventy-Fifth.

'Thank you for the tip-off,' she said. 'You're a gent. That might have been awkward.'

'My pleasure,' I said.

Iris was again wearing black jeans, but this time with a white blouse and a grey cotton jersey. The jeans still had traces of earth on the knees. My earth, enriched with my own garden compost, as I would shortly point out to her.

170

'I'm not sure why you did it,' she said. 'You don't exactly owe me anything.'

'I'd just like to know what's going on,' I said. 'My guess is that you can tell me. I've saved you an awkward meeting, so, in exchange, why don't you do just that?'

'Didn't Sammartini explain?'

'Is that the big guy or the little one?'

'The little one. I don't think the big guy has a name. He just cracks his knuckles and smiles.'

'Sammartini explained a bit,' I said. 'How long have you had the Maltese Madonna?'

'You know that my grandfather found it? That and some assorted church plate?'

'When they were doing the garden?'

'Yes.'

'And old Walter Sly knew about it?'

'I suppose so. My grandfather kept him on after he'd dismissed everyone else.'

'And that's why Walter Sly was killed?'

'No, I think that really was an accident. My grandfather was quite old by then. I doubt he'd have had the strength to attack Walter Sly and kill him. Anyway, he was found not guilty. I'm entitled to believe that he didn't do it.'

'So, what did they do with the treasure after it was found?'

'They hid it all in the ice house. But my grandfather died and my grandmother died and Walter Sly died and there was nobody left who knew what had become of it. My parents told me that my grandfather had excavated something, but it was only when, years later, I decided to try to clear the ice house of rubbish that I found it all. It was obvious what it was as soon as I saw it.'

'So, about fifteen years ago, you sold the chalice and the reliquary and the pyx and the candle sticks to the museum in Hadleyburg?'

'I had a boyfriend then – Piers – he said he had contacts in America. He could sell the less identifiable objects at least. So that's what he did. But I don't think we got a great deal. The museum questioned our title to the goods and consequently drove a hard bargain. The items were encased in plaster, which completely changed their shape, and shipped over as modern copies of Greek artefacts. I had a certain talent for sculpture. Piers and I fell out over it in the end, which was rather sad. I have never had many boyfriends. He was the last. I decided that the Madonna – the only piece left – might as well stay where it was. I thought that it was a bit too identifiable, if you see what I mean. Then, a year or two back, I realised that either I raised some serious dosh for repairs or I was going to have to sell the Priory. I mean, I was only the third generation to own it, and I've nobody to pass it on to except my nephew, but still, you don't want to be the person who sold up the family home . . . So I looked for help elsewhere.'

The sun was slightly higher in the sky and the day was already getting warmer. The noise of traffic from the main road, at first intermittent, was becoming a constant hum, as the day trippers headed down to the beach.

'Sammartini mentioned an agent,' I said. 'I assume that was Professor Cox?'

'He'd contacted me about the lost treasure of Sidlesham Abbey. I get two or three letters a year from people who'd like to dig here and split the proceeds with me – very

172

generous. His interest was slightly different. More to put one over on Hilary Joyner than anything. I was cautious with him at first, but we got on well. He seemed quite an expert on mediaeval gold and silver. And he is charming when he wants to be – he reminded me a bit of Piers, to be honest. Eventually I told him what had become of everything. He said he had contacts at some US museums, from his work on church plate – including the Stephenson Museum – and would see what he could do. Failing that, he thought we could try one or two Russian billionaires who liked upmarket bling but weren't too worried about provenance. I think he rather enjoyed it being all undercover. I mean, when you spend most of your time in libraries poring over the archives of dead politicians . . . And he rather liked the idea of Joyner hunting in Sussex for a statue that was actually in America or Novgorod or somewhere.'

'So he got in touch with Sammartini?'

'Sammartini represents the Stephenson in purchases . . . like this one. He's worked mainly in Iraq and Syria lately, where things are a bit easier, but thought we could do a deal. Anthony took the statue to Oxford so that he could get somebody's opinion on it and then ask Sammartini over and do the deal.'

'Why did you need any sort of opinion?'

'Because, to be perfectly honest, we realised the Madonna isn't quite what one might expect it to be. The only descriptions of it are in the inventory, and that is very sketchy, and in Barclay-Wood's account, which is very fanciful. The statue must have been under the ground for the whole of Barclay-Wood's lifetime. He could never have seen it in real life. Everything he says about lapis lazuli and sapphires and rose quartz was pure guesswork. So, we needed to be sure that what we had was genuinely eighth-century Byzantine or whatever it was supposed to be. I wasn't planning to be ripped off again.'

'Didn't Cox know what it was?'

'Frankly, Ethelred, Anthony Cox is a bit of a bullshitter. He's written a couple of papers on English mediaeval church silverware, in the context of its use in the sixteenth century and its wholesale destruction under Edward VI, but that's not quite the same as knowing Byzantine gold- and silverware inside out. In fact, it's not remotely the same. He could tell it was sort of old, but so could I. It looked a bit Byzantine, but it looked a bit English too. If the museum tried to get the price down by casting doubts as to its origins, we needed to be sure what we had.'

'So what was it?'

'We never found out. Before Anthony could show it to one of his mates at the Ashmolean Museum, it was stolen by Hilary Joyner. You see, Anthony had taken over Hilary's old rooms in College when he became the senior history tutor – very nice, seventeenth century, south-facing and overlooking the main quadrangle. Hilary had been fobbed off, under protest, with a larger Victorian set of rooms in a gloomier and more obscure part of the College. What Anthony did not know was that Hilary had kept a bunch of keys to the front door and, more important, to the safe, which was too big to move – at least, that was what we worked out afterwards. There was no sign of a break-in. Our guess is that when Hilary got wind of what Anthony was doing, it was easy enough for him to sneak in there with his keys and remove the Madonna from the safe. We didn't realise what he'd done until after he came down here. Then it was much too late.'

'So, you killed Hilary Joyner by drowning him in the well.'

'Why would I do that? I've told you: at that point we didn't even know that Hilary had stolen the statue. He was a nuisance, but he wasn't going to stop us – or so we thought. And if you're planning to sell something like that quietly, the last thing you want is the police swarming all over the house, checking every inch of the garden for clues.'

'Joyner could have reported you for not declaring the find.'

'He could have reported my grandfather and Walter Sly for not declaring it. As for the sale of the pyx and the reliquary, he'd have needed to get the museum to admit to purchasing the goods from me, and they and their lawyers and their Swiss bankers weren't going to do that. I could safely have admitted finding the Madonna in the ice house – that in itself was no crime. Old houses are full of all sorts of stuff that the owners have only the vaguest idea they ever had. Until we'd done the deal with a museum, and shipped the goods, there was nothing he could have accused me of. Anyway, Walter Sly's death in the well gave me horrors enough. Why would I want a second death in my garden and the old well as a constant reminder? No, I certainly did not drown him.'

'Who did?'

'Nobody. He just fell in. Like Walter Sly. They were both idiots.'

'What I don't get,' I said, 'is why Joyner came here at all, if he had the Madonna already.'

'Search me,' she said.

We looked at each other.

'Well, at least you now have it back,' I said.

'Me? No, you have it . . .'

'I saw the rose bush, Iris. You dug it up and took the statue. You have it.'

'I dug up the rose bush, but there was nothing under it. I heard a noise in the house and ran off, leaving everything as you found it. I assumed you'd realised where the statue was buried, after I so stupidly drew your attention to it, and had already found it and moved it elsewhere. The joke was very much on me.'

'No,' I said. 'I just mulched and watered. It's what the RHS website says to do.'

'So, Joyner could have hidden it there, then somebody else dug it up and replaced the rose before I could . . .'

'Badly and without watering it in or applying bonemeal . . .'

'It never stood a chance,' she said. 'Absolutely criminal.'

We listened for a while to the wind in the trees and a blackbird singing, not so far away. It was good to be reminded that this was England. Maybe not Barclay-Wood's England, secure in its traditions and low church certainties, but England for all that.

'So who has the statue now?' I asked.

'Not Sammartini, clearly,' said Iris. 'And not me. Sammartini no doubt thinks we've pulled a fast one on him. I'm going to lie low in Waitrose until the coast is clear.'

'You don't think Sammartini shops at Waitrose?'

'God, no.'

I nodded.

'What will you do?' she asked.

176

'I'll wait until Apuldram Roses opens,' I said. 'I need to buy a new bush.'

It was not an ideal time to plant roses. The weather had been hot and dry for weeks, and this day promised no respite. The lawn was parched. The rainwater butts had long since run dry; I scarcely noticed they were there any more. But I reckoned, with plenty of irrigation with the hose every evening and a regular mulch, I could get the new bush properly bedded in. I stood back and admired it, now in the rose bed, a little shorter than the ones I'd planted earlier, but strong and healthy and with several large buds about to produce blooms.

It was only on the second or third ring that I heard the doorbell inside the house. I had nothing to fear from Sammartini, or his friend. This was, after all, Sussex, not New York. We had a police force that didn't beat people up in alleyways and, more to the point, signs at the entrance to the estate saying 'Residents Only'. It was, however, with a certain amount of caution that I opened the door.

'Dr Tomlinson . . .' I said.

'I'm sorry to drop in out of the blue, Ethelred, but I was passing.'

She smiled as if there might be much more to it than that. Elsie's voice in my ear told me that it was unlikely she was lusting after my middle-aged body, whatever I might hope.

'On your way to where?' I asked.

'Oh, I just thought I'd take a run out into the country. I was heading for . . . Brighton.'

I noticed Professor Cox's Mercedes parked in the drive.

Their relationship extended to his insuring her to drive his car.

'You'd have been better on the M25 and then the M23,' I said.

'Who wants to drive on motorways on a day like this?'

'Somebody who wants to get to Brighton,' I said.

'Anyway, I thought, wouldn't it be fun to go and see my friend Ethelred? I'm a great fan of your books.'

'Are you?'

'Isn't everyone?'

Elsie's voice in my ear conceded it was marginally more likely that Fay was lusting after my middle-aged body than that she actually thought I was a good writer.

I offered her a coffee. I'd offered coffee to almost everyone else, so why not her? She at least claimed to be a genuine fan of traditional crime fiction.

'That would be lovely,' she said. 'Why don't we go into the garden? I'm so looking forward to seeing it.'

'The garden,' I said. 'Yes, of course. Let's go there.'

Fay toyed with her cup for a moment and then put it back on the table. 'Perhaps I should come clean with you, Ethelred,' she said.

'I've lost track of the number of people who have used those words over the past few days,' I said. 'They're usually followed by a string of lies and half-truths, but do by all means let me hear yours.'

Fay's smile flickered into a thin line of disapproval, then picked up again as if the power failure had been only momentary. 'You are very cynical, Ethelred. But I rather admire that. It's attractive.'

She stretched out her legs in case I hadn't noticed them

before. She was right. They were nice legs. They were both equally good.

'So, tell me why you're really here,' I said.

'You know that Anthony has been working for Iris – trying to sell this statue thing?'

'Yes,' I said. 'I had a visit from Sammartini.'

'Oh, him,' she said. 'He represents the Stephenson Museum. It's hardly a big player.'

'Isn't it?'

'Not in the top twenty in the States.'

'Strangely, he didn't tell me that.'

'Of course not. Anyway, Iris already knew the Stephenson Museum. She'd done business with them before. Anthony was scarcely doing her any favours simply suggesting they went back to the same place that had ripped her off last time. But I had contacts at one of the very top museums. One with an international reputation. You'd be quite impressed if I told you.'

'And will you tell me?'

'Not yet. You'll find out when the time is right.'

'So who represents this other museum?'

'Nice try, Ethelred, but the contact is mine. The museum was willing to deal with Anthony and me so long as he was the one with the goods. But he isn't any more. He's out of it.'

'Have you told him?'

'He doesn't need to know. We wouldn't want him causing trouble for us. Not until money has changed hands and we're both out of the way.'

'Will this museum worry at all about a lack of export certificates?'

179

'Not if we can provide them with evidence that it has been in the US for some years.'

'And we can do that?' I asked. 'Bearing in mind that it hasn't.'

'For the right price, Ethelred, we can do anything. We're partners. I, and only I, can do the deal. You, and only you, have the statue. What do you say?'

'What I say is that I don't have the statue. I'm not just playing hard to get. I really don't know where it is. You're right that Joyner left it here. He buried it in the rose bed. From where somebody removed it – I'm not sure when. But it's gone.'

'Shit . . . But are you sure he buried it? It couldn't be elsewhere – maybe in the house?'

'I'd have found it. It's certainly not in either of his bags. Iris has already tried the rest of his bedroom. I just have an empty envelope.'

Fay thought about this for a bit.

'So the partnership offer is dead in the water?' I asked.

'Whoever stole it must have known that Joyner was staying with you and could have hidden the statue here.'

'True.'

'So, how many people is that?'

'Apart from you, maybe four or five. Not many more.'

'And they are . . . ?'

I smiled at her.

'Iris?'

'No, not Iris,' I said. 'That was Sammartini's guess, but he's wrong. She dug, but the bird had already flown. Her disappointment when I explained things was very genuine. I don't think she was bluffing.'

'So, somebody else? And you might be able to work out who that is? And get the statue back?'

'Possibly. But why should I wish to do any of that?' I asked.

'Because then our deal's back on, Ethelred. We sell it, split the proceeds down the middle and we head off together to the Caribbean.'

'Together?'

'Why not?'

I considered all of the reasons.

'I might not want to,' I said.

'You'll never get a better offer.'

'That may be true. But, looking at it from your point of view, you'd be throwing away your Fellowship at the college.'

'The History Fellowship? I thought that was what I wanted. But then I realised what I could do with the money we'll make on this. Whatever Sammartini offered you will only be a fraction of its real value. If I'm right, this thing may be worth three or four million. Do you know what academics get paid, Ethelred?'

'More than writers,' I said. 'And it's regular indoor work with long holidays and membership of the Universities Superannuation Scheme. Are you really willing to ditch Anthony Cox, though? Your relationship with him must run to more than borrowing his car. Doesn't he want to lie on the beach? I'm sure he'd like the West Indies too.'

'He can go back to his wife. He probably would have done anyway. They always do. The deal was that, if I helped him, he'd make sure I got the Fellowship when Joyner retired. That was all. He took a modest fee from the sale.

The rest went to Iris. Or that was what he said. He was probably lying.' She reached out and touched my arm. 'But you wouldn't lie to me, Ethelred. You're the only man I've ever met that I would trust entirely. You wouldn't let me down. You're the sort of guy who is wholly dependable.'

If that's what she thought, it seemed unlikely she'd discussed my general character with Elsie. Or they hadn't covered book sales, anyway.

'So, your plan is that we do this together?' I said.

'Yes.'

'And we spend the rest of our lives sunning ourselves on a beach in Antigua?'

'Or St Lucia. Your call.'

'There's one good reason for running away with you,' I said, 'and that would be to see my agent's face. She considers you well out of my league.'

'That's all she knows. You can play Arthur Miller to my Marilyn Monroe.'

'That didn't work out well last time round.'

'History doesn't really repeat itself. Old man Marx was wrong. Trust me. I'm a historian.'

'Fay, you are beautiful, without moral scruples of any kind, and might be the next Regius Professor of History but three. Let's face it, it's an irresistible combination for any red-blooded male. You are so far out of my league that you are playing in the premiership and I am playing Subbuteo on the mat in the nursery. Sometimes you have to concede that your agent may be right.'

'Who does Elsie consider is in your league?'

'She'd probably rule out anyone who still had all their own teeth,' I said. 'Otherwise the field's pretty much open.'

'So, what are you going to do?'

'Nothing,' I said. 'I never wanted the Madonna and, when I had the Madonna, I never knew I had her, so not having her now is more than OK. Sammartini and his friend may not be major league, but they're good enough to frighten me.'

'Well, they don't frighten *me*,' she said. She stood up. She didn't bother to ask if I was a man or a mouse. People rarely ask mice searching questions.

'Take the road back to Chichester,' I said, 'then turn right onto the A27.'

'Sorry?'

'That's the best way to Brighton,' I said. 'That's where you were heading.'

'Yes, Brighton,' she said slowly.

'I'd get going,' I said. 'It can be busy this time of year. Especially the Arundel bypass.'

She bit her lip. A very small tear was forming in her eye – perhaps one of regret, though more likely one of extreme disappointment. She'd hoped to be leaving with four million pounds worth of Madonna tucked under her arm.

'Ethelred, I meant it,' she said. 'You. Me. The West Indies. Wads of cash in our pockets and a lifetime in which to spend it. That is what I want. That is what you could have. If you wanted it too. As much as I do.'

'Thanks for the offer,' I said. 'I appreciate it.'

I watched her turn and then go back into the house, her skirt swishing, her heels clicking on my floor, her perfume still hanging enticingly in the air. I didn't follow her. After a while I heard the car engine start up. The estate was treated to the sound of a Mercedes being driven as fast as the speed bumps would allow, then there was silence.

Of course, Elsie was right. Way out of my league. Still a week or two in St Lucia would have been nice. It wasn't as if I had any other plans.

'You can't hide in London for ever,' said Elsie.

'I'm not hiding,' I said. 'I just needed to do some research at the British Library.'

'Right,' said Elsie. 'Except it's six o'clock and I want to lock up the office and go home. When are you going back to Sussex?'

'I'm not sure,' I said. 'I thought maybe I could stay with you.'

'Are you frightened of Sammartini or Fay Tomlinson?'

'Neither. But I'm not going to sit there in West Wittering waiting for somebody else to turn up and ask me where the Madonna is.'

'And where is it?'

'It used to be under a rose bush. Then somebody took it. Ask them.'

'But Fay said it must be somebody who knows your garden well. They didn't dig up all the roses, did they? Just that one. They didn't dig up the Miscanthus. They didn't dig up the peony, though God knows they should have done. It's too big for that bed.'

'True,' I said. 'It would have been much better if he'd hidden it under the peony.'

'So, who'd even been in your garden since Joyner was there?'

I thought about it. 'Apart from you?' I said. 'Iris.

Polgreen. He was there when I first noticed that one of the roses was dying. I've already thought of him. But he simply wouldn't do that.'

'Ethelred, if Barclay-Wood was right, the Madonna has corrupted everyone who has come into contact with it. Why not Polgreen as well?'

'The Madonna is just an inanimate object. It has no mystical powers.'

'How much is it worth?'

'I don't know. Millions, apparently.'

'And that won't corrupt anyone?'

'No more than any other valuable object.'

For a while neither of us said anything.

'You like Henry Polgreen, don't you?' said Elsie.

'He seems essentially decent,' I said.

'And "essentially decent" is basically your highest form of praise?'

'There's nothing wrong with being decent.'

'But you don't much like Sly?'

'He never grew out of being the school sneak. Actually, he's probably eased nicely into the role over the years. He's good. He's taken sneakery to new levels.'

'So, if anyone killed Joyner, you'd like it to be Sly?'

'If anyone would hit somebody on the back of the head with a brick and push them down a well, it would be Sly.'

'And yet, Sly had no possible motive for killing the one person who was on his side. He had nothing at all to gain by it. Polgreen, on the other hand, might have genuinely had something to fear from Joyner. For whatever reason, Polgreen did not want the excavations to recommence. Sly said he could be ruined if they did. Joyner was keen to dig everywhere, and quite possibly had something on Iris that would have got her to vote with Sly and agree to new excavations. And you've just said that Polgreen was one of the few people who knew where the Madonna might have been buried?'

'Yes.'

'And you saw somebody in a white jacket close to the well. A white jacket not unlike Polgreen's?'

'Yes.'

'But you'd still like the killer to be Sly anyway?'

'You don't have to labour the point. I do understand.'

'Are you sure? I could run through it all again.'

'Yes, I'm sure.'

'So, you need to go back to West Wittering and talk to your friend Polgreen. Polgreen the prime suspect.'

'If there's been a murder, then it's the police who need to talk to Henry Polgreen.'

'But they won't. They think it was an accident. They're not interviewing anyone. Anyway, they're not going to recover the statue of the Virgin and hand it over to you.'

'I don't want it, it's not mine.'

'I'll have it.'

'I wouldn't want to corrupt you.'

'I'm a literary agent. We can handle stuff like that. You'd be surprised.'

'Well, it isn't going to happen, anyway,' I said. 'Unless Henry Polgreen decides to hand it over. And I've no idea why he'd do that.'

'Just remind him of the curse,' said Elsie. 'Anyone who goes near it dies horribly. He'll die horribly too, unless he gives it back to somebody who won't be corrupted by it.'

'He doesn't need reminding. He's the world expert on it. That's the best reason of all why he wouldn't touch it.'

'Everyone in the story knew there were consequences if they stole the statue. They still did it.'

I sighed. 'I used to think that my life was an Agatha Christie novel,' I said. 'A little convoluted, but essentially well-ordered and civilised. I'm beginning to think it may be more Raymond Chandler.'

'How many scheming dames with mouths like a scarlet gash have tried to seduce you for their own crooked purposes?'

'Just the one,' I said. 'I turned her down.'

'How many times have you been beaten up by a corrupt cop in a grimy alleyway?'

'Not at all,' I said. 'Just scammed by academics.'

'Doesn't sound like Chandler,' said Elsie. 'Maybe Edmund Crispin on a quiet day.'

'Fine,' I said.

'Just don't end up in a James M. Cain novel. Nobody gets out of one of those alive.'

'I'll bear it in mind,' I said.

CHAPTER FIFTEEN

Ethelred

I should have followed my instincts and begged Elsie to let me stay in London for a while. It would have been a small reciprocation of her frequent visits to Sussex. But I reluctantly took the train back to Chichester and, having missed the last bus, paid twenty pounds for a taxi to take me from Chichester Station into West Wittering.

Sure enough, the following morning I had a visitor.

'You'll forgive the intrusion,' said Sly with unjustified confidence.

But it was not as if there were any other options on offer. He'd already intruded. 'What can I do for you, Mr Sly?' I asked.

'Tertius, please,' he said, though it was clear that he felt his membership of his parish council entitled him to be addressed more formally if he so chose. 'As to what you can do for me . . . I understand you wish to join the Abbey preservation committee?'

'Yes,' I said cautiously. I had no wish to be churlish.

'Well, I'd be happy to support your application,' said Sly, with what he clearly imagined was great generosity. 'We need men of your calibre, Ethelred, to carry forward our important work. I'm assuming, of course, that we are of much the same mind?'

'I'm sure we must be on some things,' I said.

Sly looked dubious. He had not expected qualification of any sort. 'If I'm to give you my support, Ethelred – my full and unreserved support – I'd need to be certain that our views were wholly aligned. I realise that Henry Polgreen is a friend of yours, but you have already conceded that his activities are illegal. We now need to work together to have him unseated. Once I am chairman, I would be happy to relinquish the secretaryship to you, Ethelred. You could act as my deputy, working to support me as best you could. Of course, at your age, you couldn't expect to succeed me as chairman, but I can assure you that secretary of the Abbey preservation committee is a position of considerable power and influence and not just in West Wittering. As you are aware, it gives me a certain kudos throughout the entire Manhood Peninsula: East Wittering, Bracklesham, Sidlesham – even Selsey. It would do the same for you. You would gain respect that you couldn't possibly have under normal circumstances. For somebody like you, it is an amazing opportunity. So, Ethelred, do we have an understanding?'

I sighed. Perhaps churlishness was the better option after all.

'I haven't yet decided what to do,' I said, 'but thank you for your offer of support, should I choose to join.'

Sly looked disappointed in me. 'You need to make up your mind,' he said. 'You'll never get anywhere in life if you dither like this. Look at me. When there was a vacancy on our parish council, I threw my hat straight into the ring. *Carpe diem*, as the Bard so rightly said. *Carpe diem*, Ethelred.'

'I'm sure you're right,' I said, as I so often said to Elsie, and with equal conviction.

He sat back in his seat. As with most of my visitors, it was taking him some time to come to the point. The real point.

'Is there anything else I can help you with?' I asked.

'Well – I'm just curious – have you had any further discussions with your policeman friend?'

'Joe? No, not lately.'

'You don't have the low-down on what they are thinking? About Dr Joyner?'

'Only that it was an accident. I told you that.'

'You did, Ethelred, you did. I thought our discussion was very interesting, and I hope you found my advice helpful. But they've had no second thoughts?'

'None that they have told me about.'

'You didn't put your idea to them that it might have been Henry Polgreen who killed him, with Iris Munnings' help?'

'No,' I said. 'No, I decided not to.'

'But you must agree that was what happened? Dr Joyner's book, when he'd finished it, would have exposed Polgreen for what he is. A man of Joyner's integrity would not have been bribable. Polgreen had to stop him any way he could. So, he had to kill him.'

'I think that's very unlikely,' I said. I had no intention this time of making myself unclear in any way.

Sly frowned. 'But consider, Ethelred. Surely what happened was this? The rest of us were touring the garden. Dr Joyner had remained by the well. Polgreen returned, crept up behind him and smashed a brick into the back of his skull as he knelt there. He gave Dr Joyner a gentle push and then watched as his body tipped forwards and plummeted helplessly to the bottom of the shaft. There was a muffled splash. Polgreen gave a guilty start and looked behind him, but nobody had seen or heard a thing. So, he breathed a sigh of relief. He crept away, shaking, and rejoined the group as if nothing had happened. Doesn't that fit the facts as we know them?'

'If the police say anything at all along those lines, I'll certainly let you know,' I said.

'Thank you, Ethelred,' he said. 'That's kind of you. Any little snippet that you hear – even if you do not entirely understand its significance yourself. Just tell me, all right? Well, I'd best be on my way. Lots to do when you're on two committees, and secretary to one of them, as you will discover yourself, if you play your cards right.'

'Of course, Councillor Sly,' I said.

'*Tertius*,' he said. 'There's no need for formality between us. Do you know, Ethelred, I think we're going to be great friends.'

I decided that it was my turn to drink coffee and lie about my intentions. Accordingly, I took a stroll to the edge of the village and walked up the front path of a small, modern bungalow, built of anonymous beige brick, with a nice display of roses in the garden. I didn't need to ring the bell. Polgreen suddenly emerged from behind a large buddleia, glasses balanced on the end of his nose, a pair of secateurs in his hand.

'Ethelred!' he said. 'This is a pleasant surprise!'

'I was just passing,' I said.

'Really? On your way to where?'

'Brighton,' I said.

He looked at me oddly. 'That will take a day or two on foot.'

'Unless I'm stretching the truth slightly, Henry. As you seem to be.'

He quickly glanced round. 'Let's go to my study,' he said. 'We can talk privately there. My wife's pruning the wisteria over the back. A technically more difficult task, so she tells me. She'll only want to make you coffee if she knows you're here.'

He led me along his hallway and into what had probably been intended as a nominal third bedroom. Inside the cramped space was a desk, some bookshelves stuffed with local history books and several heaps of lever arch files on the floor. He peered out of the small window, then closed the blinds as a precautionary measure. He sat down in the typist's chair in front of the desk and motioned me towards the only other seat in the room – a vinyl kitchen chair that had already acquired a few dents before The Beatles released their first EP.

'So, why do you think I've been lying to you?' he asked.

'Everyone else has,' I said. 'But more to the point, much though I dislike Tertius Sly, there is usually some small grain of truth in what he says. He's convinced that you are conducting illicit excavations. If I'm to join your committee, I'd like to know the truth. Tertius, as I must apparently now call him, will support my application only if he and I are of one mind. In that singular mind that we must now share, you're guilty as charged.'

Polgreen looked at me for a long time. I wondered if he was going to speak at all. Then he said, 'Yes, he's right. For what it's worth, I've done a bit of digging on my own account. But he's wrong that that's the reason why I don't want further excavations carried out.'

'So what exactly have you done, Henry?'

Polgreen got up and went to his bookcase. He extracted a battered copy of *Happy Recollections of a Sussex Clergyman*.

'You've read this strange little volume, I take it?' he said.

'As with *Curious Tales of Old Sussex*, I've dipped into it,' I said. 'I can't claim to have read it all, or even most of it. I suspect, with both books, that Barclay-Wood made a great deal of it up.'

'But you know that it is put together in the form of a diary, each entry dated?'

'Yes,' I said.

'And you know that, during some of the period covered, Barclay-Wood was busy excavating the Abbey site?'

'Yes.'

'Now, a lot of the references to the Abbey might not have meant much to you, if you read those sections, but they did to me. I could follow his fieldwork almost yard by yard. And, to the trained archaeologist, it made little sense. Recent digs have been to establish where the monks' dormitory was, where the kitchen was, what the monks ate, how the Abbey expanded over the years, and so on.'

'Yes, of course,' I said.

'Barclay-Wood's excavations on the other hand showed

a complete lack of curiosity for facts such as these. The earliest – this would be the early 1890s – was right in the middle of what he would have already known was the monks' herb garden.'

'Not a lot to find there, I would imagine.'

'That took three summers of painstaking labour. He then switched his attentions to the cloisters – not the buildings around the quadrangle, but the centre, where we believe there was a rose garden. Do you see any pattern emerging?'

'So, it was the vegetable garden next?'

'I'm not sure there was one within the Abbey – though there would have been fields beyond it, of course, for that sort of thing. No, he started to dig right in the middle of the Abbey church, where we know some of the Abbots were buried. That took several years, and did result in the discovery of bones, a couple of rings and a crozier. Then in 1902 he suddenly stopped. For the next forty years there was no excavation of the site at all. What does that suggest to you?'

'He'd found whatever it was he was after,' I said.

'Precisely. So, let's consider where he'd looked: herb garden, rose garden, tombs.'

'Places where the Madonna might have been buried to hide it from the King's commissioners,' I said. 'And in 1902, he found it.'

'That's what I think too.'

'What does Tertius Sly think?'

'I haven't discussed it with him. Not worth the risk. Think about it, Ethelred. Archaeology has advanced enormously since I studied history. Ground-penetrating radar. Shallow geophysics. X-ray fluorescence spectroscopy measurers. Light detection and ranging technology. Google Earth. You can do so much these days without even lifting a trowel. Quite a bit without even leaving your own study. You don't need to destroy the soil in order to find out what's underneath the surface. Best we leave things, as much as we can, for future generations with even better techniques. The last thing I wanted was for Sly to decide that, where one valuable object was found, there must be a lot of other loot to dig up.'

'So why did you decide to dig yourself?'

'I just wanted to confirm that that was what had happened. That there was no point in further digging to locate the Madonna, because Barclay-Wood had taken it. When it was quiet, I went over the old chapel with what technology I had – a cheap metal detector. My theory was that Barclay-Wood wouldn't just dig up the Virgin – he'd leave something behind too.'

'And did he?'

Polgreen opened a drawer in his desk and took out a clear plastic bag. He spilled the contents onto his desk.

'Pennies,' I said. 'Edward VII.'

I picked one up. They'd been common enough when I was a child. The familiar profile on one side, Britannia, and the date on the other.

'Not just Edward VII,' said Polgreen. 'They were all minted in 1902. The leather purse they were in had rotted, but the coins are in a good condition, bearing in mind they've been buried for over a hundred years. I don't think they were ever in circulation. Their sole function was to date, to the year, when the ground had last been disturbed.'

'Barclay-Wood telling you that you were on the right track,' I said.

'Don't tell me it's just a weird coincidence. Over the years, I've got to know Barclay-Wood and what he found amusing. The moment I checked the date on the first coin I knew what I had discovered. The question is: are there further clues somewhere else or is that it?'

'But you know where the Madonna is . . . or was,' I said.

'Do I?'

'You dug it up,' I said.

Polgreen shook his head and looked at me as if I had not been paying attention. 'I've told you. It was just the pennies. There was nothing else there. That's the whole point of my story.'

'I mean in my garden.'

Polgreen's gaze was now completely blank. 'Why on earth would it be in your garden?' he asked. 'That would have been just fields in the sixteenth century.'

'So, it wasn't you?'

'It wasn't me doing what?'

I took a deep breath. 'The Madonna was actually buried at the Priory, just like the story says. Iris's grandfather dug it up. He hid it in the ice house, where Iris later found it. She gave it to Professor Cox to value, and possibly sell. Joyner stole it from Cox and buried it under my roses. Somebody – I had assumed you – then removed it.'

He shook his head. 'Not me . . . Bloody hell. Iris knew all that and never told me? *You* knew that and never told me?'

'Sorry,' I said.

We looked at each other for a while.

'I'm sure Barclay-Wood found it at the Abbey,' he said.

'So that must mean he then reburied it at the Priory . . . Yes, of course. He could have done that. It's no distance to the Priory from the Abbey. But *why* would he do that? Even by his standards, it makes no sense at all.'

'Well, there's no doubt it was at the Priory by 1959, waiting to be found. But I think you may be wrong about Barclay-Wood moving it there. Iris thinks Barclay-Wood never saw the Madonna at all. She conversely has seen it and says the description in his book – all the rubies and lapis lazuli stuff – is just plain wrong. If that's true, then your supposition that he ever found it at the Abbey must be wrong too. Maybe he buried the pennies for some other reason that he found equally amusing.'

'Then why does he stop digging when he does?'

'He just lost interest,' I said. 'Or perhaps he was looking for something else entirely and did find that.'

Polgreen shook his head. 'What else could it have been? He was obsessed by the Madonna. He wrote about it. He spent almost ten years digging for it. I'm telling you, he found it. He saw it. It doesn't surprise me that he sexed the statue up a bit. That's what he did all the time. For an evangelical clergyman, he was a liar of quite exceptional ability.'

'All right, then why – and how – did he then bury it at the Priory? I suppose the how is the easy bit. He had about forty years, between 1902 and his death, to walk or ride or drive over to the Priory and hide it there. But it still leaves the why.'

'He just found it amusing,' said Polgreen grimly. 'He'd clearly worked out where it was and decided it was too easy to find. So he moved it somewhere less likely, where it could do no harm.'

'But the Priory? That was the other place everyone thought it was.'

'I suspect that generations of owners have declined to have their garden dug up – especially since the treasure might prove to belong to the Crown and not them. So, the Priory may have actually been safer than most places.'

I shook my head. It still didn't feel right. But Barclay-Wood was always the joker in the pack. As long as he was involved almost anything was possible.

'Do you think Joyner knew all this too?' I asked. 'He had all the evidence. I think it was the Priory where he really wanted to dig.'

'He seems to have done,' said Polgreen. 'But you say he actually had the Madonna at that point. So, why dig at all? What was he doing looking in the well for something he knew was buried in your garden?'

'Iris said the same thing, more or less. Why did he come to West Wittering when he had the object he was supposedly searching for? Perhaps he knew something that we still don't know. He had put together quite a collection of papers, including what seems to be the original inventory of the Abbey – or a very early copy.'

'Well, I wouldn't mind seeing *that*. It's been missing since Barclay-Wood's time. How did Joyner get it?'

'I've wondered about that,' I said. 'He told me that he used to take his aunt to boot fairs round here, years ago. Maybe her interests extended to auctions and antiquarian bookshops. He seems to have ended up with a collection of books owned by Barclay-Wood and papers belonging to the Abbey.'

'So, in one place or another, he stumbled across Barclay-Wood's library being sold off?'

'Something very much like that. The collection doesn't look very exciting unless you know how to read sixteenth-century handwriting. He did.'

'But that would be an odd coincidence – he's interested in the Abbey and he just happens to find a collection of papers on it.'

'More likely the other way round, don't you think?' I said. 'A chance find at a boot fair years ago led to his researching the background to the dissolution of the monastery.'

'Those papers really belong here,' said Polgreen. 'By rights.'

'Probably,' I said.

'And the Madonna, if it's out there.'

'If you really want it,' I said. 'I can't see why you would. Barclay-Wood made up a great deal, but he was right about it being cursed. It certainly brought Joyner no luck and he probably had it only for a few days.'

'True,' said Polgreen. 'Though falling down the well seems to have been entirely his own fault.'

'Where were you when he fell?' I asked.

'On the far side of the garden, probably,' he said. 'I certainly never went near the well after we all left together. Actually, I scarcely saw anyone from the moment we left the well to the moment we all got back to the terrace. I ran into Elsie and Anthony Cox, but that was all.'

'Are you sure?'

'Of course.'

'It's just that I saw somebody in a white jacket. I thought it was Joyner, then I lost sight of the person, then I came across Iris and assumed it was her that I'd seen. But you were wearing a white jacket too.'

'I'm a bit taller than Iris or Joyner.'

'It was only a brief glimpse. A flash of white. Thinking about it, it could have been any one of the three of you.'

'And where was that?'

'Near the ice house. Not far from the well.'

'What are you saying, Ethelred? That you think I came back and pushed Joyner down the well?'

'That's Sly's theory.'

'I bet it is. And what is my motive supposed to be?'

'To save your reputation. He gave quite a detailed description of you by the well, including the moment you gave a guilty start, but I think, like Barclay-Wood, he has a rather gothic imagination.'

'I'd better get back to the garden,' said Polgreen. 'I'm supposed to be deadheading, not dealing with Abbey business.'

I nodded. I was divorced myself, but I knew that most marriages operated on delicately negotiated, often unspoken, compromises. It was, in my experience, unlikely that Mrs Polgreen shared Henry's enthusiasm for archaeology or considered it more important than timely garden maintenance. He needed to be seen deadheading something and quickly.

'I'll email you my application to join the committee,' I said. 'Will just a quick statement of my wish to join plus a brief CV and contact details do?'

He nodded. He was no longer quite so sure he wanted me. That was progress of a sort.

'I'll pass it on to Iris and Tertius Sly,' he said. 'Sly's bound to want some kind of formal vote amongst the three of us. He always does.'

I walked back down the path to the main road and turned right, in the opposite direction from Brighton. I needed to check something in Barclay-Wood's journal. Not the printed book but the manuscript version that Joyner had felt so worthwhile bringing with him.

CHAPTER SIXTEEN

Ethelred

To my right was a large mug of coffee. To my left was my copy of *Happy Recollections*. In the centre of my desk was Barclay-Wood's original journal.

I had always suspected that *Happy Recollections* was largely fiction. In the event, about half of it was true – or at least half of it was as true as the journal.

The published book began on a jolly note, with Barclay-Wood moving into the vicarage in Selsey on a sunny April morning and his giving thanks to God for being able to serve a parish in such a beautiful part of the country. He recounted an amusing conversation with his churchwarden, Mr Cornwallis, and a bracing walk along the beach with seabirds flying overhead. The journal, from which the book was supposedly derived, told a very different story. Barclay-Wood was despondent at having to live, as he put it, amongst congenital idiots and miles from any sort of civilised society. He deeply regretted having turned down the opportunity to run a mission amidst the bright lights of Omdurman. He hated the vicarage, which was damp, too large and inconveniently situated. He hated the church, which was not quaintly mediaeval, and which possessed not only a job lot of alabaster images of saints but also an incense burner recently manufactured in Wolverhampton. He intended to take a hammer to the lot at the first opportunity. He despised his churchwarden, who clearly approved of everything his Romish predecessor had done. He loathed the sound of the sea and the constant rush of pebbles up the beach, which, alternating with the rush of pebbles down the beach, would continue until Judgement Day. He set out, in some detail, his plans for buying a gun to send the seagulls back to Satan, whose minions they undoubtedly were.

Reading the two texts in parallel provided many insights into the true meaning of the published work, which had previously escaped me. It was, for example, now much clearer what he meant when he had said that the previous vicar and the churchwarden had fully deserved each other. And when he said that the choirmaster had taught the boys to sing almost as well as he did himself. And when he said that the vicarage was every bit as beautiful as it was comfortable. And possibly when he said that the church authorities in Chichester (with whom he would later have the protracted legal dispute) were as wise as they were devout. After a while you looked for a double meaning in almost every sentence, and usually found it.

His account of the excavations at Sidlesham was, as might be expected, fuller in the manuscript journal. Though Polgreen had implied that Barclay-Wood dug at random, the journal showed him working his way systematically through the herb garden and the cloisters, stopping when checked by the foundations of some building, then renewing his carefully planned progress across open ground. Each find was meticulously recorded, but it was clear from his notes at the end of each season that he had not located what he was after. In 1899 he had started on the nave of the chapel. Again, this was no amateur at work. He identified each tomb with some accuracy, often from a few fragmented Latin phrases on a coffin. His treatment of the bones, however, reflected his increasingly bitter correspondence with the Dean of Chichester. His reburial of the remains of past Abbots (as recorded in the journal, anyway) was haphazard and perfunctory. He had no time for senior clerics of any sort.

The 1902 excavations ended in *Happy Recollections* with the words: *And so another season comes to its conclusion, I having discovered more than I could have hoped for. I resolved to allow the bones of the pious monks to sleep undisturbed next year. May God bless and watch over them all!* But the entry in the journal for the same day was slightly different.

And so my work here comes to an end, having discovered more than I could have hoped for, after so much wasted effort and idiotic advice from the rest of the committee. The question is now what to do with what I have discovered. I shall conceal them in the place that people will least suspect – a place where they deserve to be and can do no further harm.

Conceal *them*. So, whatever he had found, he had more than one item to hide? If Iris was right and he had never seen the Madonna, then he might conceivably have meant the pyx and, say, the chalice. But how could they do any harm? More likely, especially in view of his reference to the ruby drops of blood, he had unearthed not only the Madonna but the statue of Christ as well. Then, for the Madonna to have been found in West Wittering in 1959, he must have buried that and quite possibly the second statue at the Priory. Joyner, having doubtless conducted a comparison similar to the one I was engaged in, would have known this. But nothing in the remaining pages of the journal mentioned such a burial or gave details of which location at the Priory he had chosen – it annoyingly stopped soon after the discovery of the treasure. Either it had been discontinued or the later volumes had been lost.

The printed version of *Happy Recollections* did record two later visits to Wittering Priory, either of which might have allowed him the necessary leisure to bury the loot. The first entry that mentioned the Priory was brief and gave no clue as to what he might have done there. The second, however, was slightly more expansive. And, checking Joyner's copy, I saw there was a slip of paper already marking the page.

The food and conversation were every bit as good as on my last visit to this interesting house. But, fortunately, West Wittering is too far from Selsey for me to come here often. After dinner, my host again pleading his infirmities, I had a chance for a stroll alone in the gardens, where the monks of Wittering once took their exercise. I spent some time on the flower beds and paused for a while by the quaint old well, which must have been in use in King Henry's day. Thus, I unburdened myself of some of my troubles.

The first time I had read that, I had assumed 'fortunately' was a printing error. Now I was no longer so sure. But it was the final phrase that really caught my eye. I had previously skipped over it, assuming it meant no more than that the visit to the garden had allowed him to forget temporarily some of his problems with the Bishop and with his churchwarden. But, with the other information I had, I placed a very different interpretation on Barclay-Wood's reference to unburdening himself of his troubles at the well.

I could see why Joyner, with exactly the same information, had felt that it was worthwhile searching where he did. You could never be quite sure, of course, when Barclay-Wood was telling the truth. But I felt I had just read the passage that had lured Joyner, already in possession of one statue, to his death in pursuit of the other.

'So, in summary,' said Elsie, 'your mate Henry denies killing Dr Joyner and you believe him?'

'Yes, I do believe him,' I said. 'Your unconcealed scepticism is noted, however.'

'And you believe that in spite of his having admitted a motive – that is to say that he had been conducting illicit excavations, which would have been detected as soon as Sly, backed by Joyner, began work again. He would have had to resign from the committee. The Abbey is pretty much his whole life.'

'He also gets to deadhead roses,' I said. 'At least in the summer.'

'He'd have had to watch Sly take over as chair.'

'They wouldn't have elected Sly, not so long as Iris was on the committee.'

'I'm surprised Iris thinks she can stay on the committee,' said Elsie, 'once the others know she's sold off silverware that originally belonged in Sidlesham. They could scarcely approve of that.'

'They don't know.'

'I bet it would all have come out the moment they announced the discovery of the second statue. That would have raised all sorts of awkward questions. Maybe Iris had more to worry about than we thought.'

'Yes, but I still believe her. She didn't kill him.'

'Like Polgreen?'

'Exactly.'

'So, neither of the people with really good motives killed Joyner. That's nice to know, isn't it? It was actually Sly who decided to randomly bump off his only friend.'

'Yes. If anyone killed Joyner, it was Sly.'

'With deductive skills like that, Ethelred, it's no surprise that you're constantly at the top of the bestseller lists,' said Elsie.

'I'm not at the top of the bestseller lists,' I said.

'No, you're not, are you?'

'I'm going to take a trip to Selsey,' I said.

'Not enough sea air where you are?'

'I'm seeking divine inspiration,' I said.

* * *

'It was kind of you to see me,' I said. 'Especially at such short notice.'

'I've always enjoyed your books,' said the vicar – 'Father Thomas' as the noticeboard outside the church invited us to address him.

'The J. R. Elliot ones or the Peter Fielding series?' I asked.

'Amanda Collins,' he said. 'Just the thing when you can't get to sleep.'

'A lot of people tell me that,' I said.

'Two or three pages does it for me,' he said. 'Never fails. So, how can I help you? You said you were researching one of my predecessors?'

'Sabine Barclay-Wood,' I said.

'Ah, yes, composer of "God of Sunshine, God of Love".' Father Thomas hummed a few bars experimentally. 'I can't really remember all the words, of course – nobody sings that hymn much now. But I do recall it from primary school. It fell out of favour for some reason – I think it wasn't terribly politically correct – some feminists objected very strongly indeed. And the Commission for Racial Equality. And the Royal National Institute for Blind People. And the verse about the all-consuming fires of hell was quite disturbing for small children. Traumatic, actually. Even when I was young, they'd stopped singing that bit. Still, that's the hymn he's mainly remembered for. Nice tune, of course.'

'He also wrote a couple of books,' I said. '*Curious Tales of Old Sussex* and the *Happy Recollections of a Sussex Clergyman*.'

'The one that led to that protracted libel action?'

'That's it.'

'Oh, that was him, too, was it? Yes, of course, so it was. There's a copy of the book in the study. My predecessor left it behind. As his predecessor did. It's not a book you'd necessarily want to take with you. It may have been Barclay-Wood's own copy. Old Mrs Hardcastle once told me that he left quite a collection of papers when he finally died.'

'Do you still have any of them?'

'Not that I know of. There was a big clear-out some years ago – probably when the old vicarage was sold off. I'm surprised that those two books survived it, to be quite honest. Now I'm responsible for three churches, we've had to cut down on old files. They don't have much relevance to the Church today. Dusty old ledgers and minute books. The important stuff is now safely in the National Archives, where neither moth nor rust doth corrupt, and where thieves do not break through or steal. You can also view it online, so I'm told. Moths can't get at it there either.'

'Barclay-Wood did a lot of archaeological work over at Sidlesham,' I said.

'Really? I didn't know that.'

'He wouldn't have left anything from the Abbey here . . . ?'

'If he had, it would have gone with everything else,' he said, smiling. 'Thirty years ago, at least. But I'm sure they wouldn't have thrown out anything that was at all valuable. There's a museum at Sidlesham. It would almost certainly have been sent there. You could enquire with the chair of the committee that runs it – a Mr Poldark, I think.'

'Polgreen,' I said.

'You already seem to know him, then. We're a church, not a museum, as I was saying to Old Mrs Hardcastle only the other day.'

'That's the same Old Mrs Hardcastle who told you about the Barclay-Wood papers?'

'Yes, indeed. Constantly.'

'How old is Old Mrs Hardcastle?' I asked.

'Oh, gosh – we celebrated her ninetieth birthday just after I arrived here. So that would make her ninety-two . . . maybe ninety-three. She's very good for her age. Dear, dear Mrs Hardcastle. What would we do without her?'

'She'd remember Sabine Barclay-Wood personally?'

'Only too well. And most of my other predecessors. She has a bottomless fund of stories about them. And their wives. And their children. And their dogs. And their cats. So very many fascinating stories.'

'So where could I find her?'

'She's in the church now arranging flowers. She said she might drop by for a chat when she's done. I'm expecting her any moment.'

'Could I perhaps go and talk to her in the church for half an hour or so?'

A look of relief flooded Father Thomas's face. 'Would you really?' he said. 'That would be immensely kind of you. I can't say how grateful I am.'

The church was vast and late Victorian. On a warm summer's day, it felt like a mislaid piece of January. The harsh red-brick arches, which soared up to the roof, showed many patches of powdery white, where the damp had penetrated the ageing, but not yet ancient, structure. The window over the altar showed St Augustine preaching to what appeared to be a group of Victorians in fancy dress, perhaps about to take part in a re-enactment of the Battle of Hastings. A scroll with the words '*Non Angli sed Angeli*' hovered over them ominously, though they had not yet noticed it. One's eyes needed to drop some way before they encountered the twenty-first century, in the form of pictures of Palestine, executed in crayon by children of the local primary school and pinned haphazardly to a board. Most were set in biblical times, and were replete with yellow flat-roofed houses, green palm trees, brown camels and grey asses. But, in one, an Israeli soldier was pictured mowing down a crowd of Arab protesters with a machine gun that fired red tracer bullets in a strangely curved trajectory. The artwork had been graded by the class teacher. Most pupils had received full marks, regardless of any questions of artistic merit, but the massacre was for some reason accorded only eight out of ten.

Mrs Hardcastle was fighting with some tall and rather top-heavy blooms on the altar itself. They seemed a little too large for the vases and much too large for her. Gardening parishioners had probably donated surplus flowers to the church without dwelling too much on their suitability. For somebody of her age and size she wasn't doing a bad job. She rammed a final lupin into place amongst some hollyhocks and ferns, swore at the flowers with remarkable fluency and turned to face me.

'*What?*' she demanded.

'Sorry, are you Mrs Hardcastle?' I asked, being careful

not to condescendingly address her as 'Old'.

'I'm called Old Mrs Hardcastle, ducky,' she said. 'I usually do the flowers on Saturdays. My daughter-in-law, who does the flowers for special occasions, is called Young Mrs Hardcastle. Her daughter-in-law is called Amanda, but she doesn't do flowers on account of having joined a satanic cult in Eastbourne. Which of us did you want, dear?'

'Sorry,' I said. 'I should have made myself clearer. Father Thomas said to look for Old Mrs Hardcastle.'

'Did he? Condescending little prick. He's not that young himself. Well, you've found me, ducky. What do you want? I haven't got all day and I'm ready to go home. The last thing I want is to find, when my time comes, that I've dropped dead in this bloody place, just because some idiot kept me talking.'

'I'm sorry,' I said. 'Father Thomas told me that you might be able to assist. He said that you knew the Reverend Sabine Barclay-Wood.'

'You from the police?'

'No,' I said.

'It's just that they're digging up all sorts of cold cases these days.'

'That's not why I'm here,' I said.

'Good, because I'd have told you to piss off if you were.'

'I just wondered if you knew anything about his archaeological work.'

'Not really. Was that Sidlesham Abbey?'

'Yes.'

She shook her head. 'He'd stopped that some time before I first met him. He had one or two bits and pieces

212

in his study, though – a ring from an old Abbot and some bones. He reckoned they were some dead bishop's fingers, but they could have been sweet-and-sour spare ribs for all I knew. He used them to clean out his pipe.'

'What happened to his stuff?'

'Thrown away, about thirty or forty years ago. For a long time, you see, the priests here were all bachelors. The house was enormous – it's half a dozen flats now – but it wasn't very nice. You could call it a gothic monstrosity. Always chilly and never-ending cleaning and dusting. They tried to get married men to take it, but the wives looked at it and told their husbands to find a job elsewhere or find another woman willing to run the village fete and have their children. But some years ago, we did get a married couple. The first thing they did was to clear all of the accumulated junk out of the unused bedrooms and repaint from top to bottom. Mrs Roberts – yes, that was their name, Roberts – declined to dust all of the old books either, so they went, too.'

'So, where did this so-called junk go?'

'I don't know, dear – there was probably a man come and took most of it. I couldn't tell you who. Not now. And they had a bonfire of the rest. I do remember that. It was a very nice blaze and the kiddies all got to throw stuff on, though one did get hospitalised. Still, the others had a good time, which was the main thing. And I have to say the house looked much better for it.'

'You knew him well?'

'Well, everyone knows "God of Sunshine, God of Love", don't they? Or they used to. It's banned in thirty-one countries now, according to the *Guinness Book of Records*.

He was the vicar here when I was a little girl. I've always lived here in Selsey, except when I was away during the war – I was a Wren. Had a ball. You baby-boomers think you invented sex, but you don't know the half of it. There's nothing you did in the '60s and '70s that I hadn't done twice by 1943. As for the Reverend, he died about the time I came back. He was, you might have said, a broken man by then. Bloody bishops. But he was fun before the war. He'd put bits of the *Daily Herald* editorials in his sermons and claim it came from St Paul's Epistles. Sometimes he'd wink at me during prayers, because I was the only one who'd got it. "Blessed is the union of those who labour," he'd say. And he'd watch as the *Daily Mail* readers muttered, "Amen". He was a card, that one. I'm so glad the police never caught up with him.'

'So, were you always involved in the church?'

'No choice. My father was churchwarden for years and years. He and the vicar had a real ding-dong about saints' images. The church was full of them when Barclay-Wood arrived, and my father wanted to keep them. The vicar wanted them gone.'

'And they all went?'

'My father was eventually allowed to keep two. Horrible things. John the Baptist and St Mary Magdalene, according to the vicar, but they all looked the same to me in the gloomy corner they were stuck in. Could have been Fred Astaire and Ginger Rogers.'

'Gold and encrusted with gems?' I asked, optimistically.

She laughed. 'No, they were cheap things – white stone – what do you call it?'

'Alabaster,' I said.

'That's it. My memory isn't what it was. A sort of dirty white – like bad emulsion. I suggested once that a lick of paint might actually improve them. Now I think about it, that's what he did. By the time I joined the Wrens they were matt black. It made them worse, if anything – the black showed up every fault. You could see just how cheap they were. Not life-like at all. Sort of stretched out and very stiff. He really hated those statues, did the Reverend. But then he hated all statues of saints, bless him. Said they were the spawn of Satan and could drag you down to hell by the tits. Nobody ever forgot that sermon.'

'Are they still around?'

'Haven't seen them for years, my love. He probably smashed them up, around the time my father died – Dad went to London, you see, to be a firefighter during the Blitz and he never came back. The Reverend might have thought that was his best chance – before they appointed a successor. If it wasn't then, they probably went at the same time as all of the Reverend's papers. I used to clean the church, so I'd remember if they'd been around lately. Haven't seen them for years and years. Haven't missed them, but they were rubbish, like I say.'

'Thank you,' I said. 'You've been very helpful. Sorry – I didn't really introduce myself – I'm Ethelred Tressider.' I handed her one of my cards.

'Betty Hardcastle,' she said, stuffing the card in an apron pocket. 'Betty Cornwallis in the days I knew the Reverend. He'd have married me and Stan if he'd lived another year, but he died just before the war ended. I always thought him and Stan would have got on well.

Stan was an awkward bastard too. I miss them both.'

We belatedly shook hands.

'I'd better go and see the vicar now,' she said, 'and tell him a few anecdotes. He's heard them all, of course, but I like to pretend I don't remember I've done them before, then I can watch him trying to be interested. It's the closest you can get to fun at my age. That and trolling on Twitter. I've been suspended twice, but you can always set up under a new name. Or sometimes even under the old one. It's surprising what you can get away with.'

It was a couple of days later that a small package arrived for me. The covering letter was in spidery handwriting, that sloped across the page. It was from Old Mrs Hardcastle.

After you'd gone, she wrote, *I remembered I'd got some old papers of Dad's. He left them behind when he went to London. I found this lot. I'd always wondered where the statues went. Looks like the Reverend sold them. Can't trust anyone these days, can you? No idea how Dad got the enclosed, but I can see why he might have wanted to keep it if he fancied a bit of blackmail. And who doesn't, eh? Love and kisses, 'Old Mrs Hardcastle'*

'The enclosed' was a yellowed envelope, addressed to the Reverend S. Barclay-Wood at the vicarage. It was postmarked 3rd July 1940, but the letters it contained were of various dates from 1938 onwards. They were all from an auction house in Bond Street.

Dear Reverend Barclay-Wood,

Thank you for your letter of the third inst. Let me say at once what a pleasure it was to receive a communication from the author of 'God of Sunshine, God of Love', one of my favourite hymns at school, though for some reason less sung now than of old.

I should warn you that the market for jewellery of all sorts is not as it once was. The photograph that you sent me of the ring is, however, most interesting. It is, I would have said, thirteenth-century English and a very fine specimen – the sort of ring that a Bishop or Abbot might have worn. You are most fortunate to have been left it by your aunt. If you were willing to let us sell it for you, I would place a reserve of £250 on it, and would hope that it might fetch as much as £500, even in the present depressed market.

I do understand that wills can cause unpleasantness within families, if certain members who had hoped for a bequest do not receive one. We would, of course, be happy to avoid adding to your embarrassment and will just say that the current owner is a gentleman living in Northumberland, if that is still how you wish us to describe you.

Please let me know in due course what you would like me to do and, if you wish to commission us to sell it, then please send the ring by registered post in a small cardboard tube.

I beg to remain, sir, your most humble servant.

J. Partington (Partner)

Dear Reverend Barclay-Wood,

Thank you for the picture of the second ring. It is, if anything, finer than the first, though a little later in date. I think that it might fetch rather more than the £600 that we obtained for your aunt's other ring. Your aunt must have been a most knowledgeable collector. I wish any of my own aunts had her good taste! I do wonder, however, if we would be wise putting it on the market quite so soon after the first, which excited a certain amount of interest and speculation, bearing as it did the arms of Sidlesham Abbey. I would suggest that you send it to us, and we will put it in one of our sales early next year and perhaps under a different name to avoid any mistaken impression of impropriety.

I beg to remain etc. etc.

J. Partington (Partner)

Dear Reverend Barclay-Wood,

We are in receipt of your letter of the 29th ult. and the very curious photograph of the statue that you say is St James the Less. I would hate to contradict a clergyman, but are you sure that it is not intended as a figure of Christ? There is a distinct circlet round his head, which seems to be a crown of thorns. Whatever the subject, however, it is most certainly in a Byzantine style – and, if original, then of the eighth or ninth century. You say that it is painted black, making me think that it is more likely to be a modern copy, though a very good one. Your final question puzzles me a little: you ask, hypothetically, what its value would be if, under the paint, it was in fact solid gold, studded with gems. It is not clear why you think this might be the case. I have consulted my partners who agree that, if you could bring it to London for our inspection, we would be very interested to see it and perhaps, if you permit it, remove a little of the paint. My partners have asked me to point out, however, that, should it prove to be as you suggest, then we could not sell it without carrying out some enquiries into its provenance, beginning perhaps with the Dean in Chichester. I said that I was sure that you would raise no objection to this, but I shall take no further action until I hear from you.

This final letter was signed Acting Lance Corporal Partington (Partner), the war having broken out the year before and many men too old to join the army having volunteered for what would later become the Home Guard. There were no letters after that one, though that didn't mean he hadn't concocted a convincing story for the acting lance corporal or indeed tried another, less suspicious auction house.

So, in 1940, he had at least tried to sell the statue of Christ, which tended to confirm, if further proof were needed, that he had indeed found both statues in 1902. The place of safety for them, referred to in the journal, appeared, however, to have been inside his own church, disguised with black paint. So how, then, had the Madonna got to the Priory in time for Iris's grandfather to find it there in 1959? Barclay-Wood could, of course, have visited it during the war, long after the visit noted with a bookmark by Joyner. But it did not clear up the mystery of why he should want to do that. Even by Barclay-Wood's standards, this tale was . . . well, becoming Byzantine in its twists and turns. There had to be a simpler explanation that would fit all of the facts.

I packed the letters away and went to bed.

CHAPTER SEVENTEEN

Ethelred

I saw the police car draw up on the drive as I was making toast, and then heard the doorbell ring.

'I hope you don't mind my dropping by,' said Joe. 'Or the police car parked prominently in front of your residence.'

'Most people round here know that a house guest of mine died in an accident. It was reported in the *Chichester Echo*. They won't be that surprised to see you following things up. Anyway, as a crime writer, I'm expected to live beyond the normal limits of good taste. Can I get you a coffee or anything?'

'I won't, thanks. It's a short visit. But don't let me stop you having your breakfast.'

I buttered the toast and got a jar of home-made marmalade from the fridge. I joined Joe at the kitchen table.

'OK,' I said. 'I'm all ears. What can I do for you?'

Joe produced a photograph and showed it to me. 'Do you know this guy?'

'He calls himself Sammartini,' I said. 'I don't know if that's his real name. He takes a gorilla with him on house calls, but I've never been properly introduced.'

'It seems to be his real name. His friend is called Einstein – Chuck Einstein. How did you make their acquaintance?'

'They came to see me early one morning.'

'What were they after?'

'The Maltese Madonna.'

'Why did Sammartini think you'd be able to help him?'

'Dr Joyner apparently had it. Then he hid it somewhere. Sammartini thought it might be here.'

Joe frowned. 'But Joyner was supposed to be searching the well for it,' he said. 'Are you saying that he actually had the Madonna all the time?'

'Some of the time,' I said. 'If I'm right, then by the afternoon that he died, he'd found it and already concealed it again.'

'Here?'

'In the garden. At least, the evidence points that way. But, if it was ever here, it's gone now.'

'So, what was Joyner searching the well for, in that case?'

'The second statue, I think – the one of Christ. Have you read Barclay-Wood's memoirs?'

'I know of them. Are they any good?'

'No. But there's more than a hint in there that two statues may have made it to England. It would appear that Barclay-Wood knew this was the case because he'd actually excavated them both at the Abbey, then hidden them again. Possibly at the Priory. Joyner knew that.'

'So, Joyner had found one and was looking for the one that was still missing?' Joe asked. 'Then he'd have a matching pair or something?'

'Or something. What he didn't know was that there was a second possibility: the second one may have been sold via a London auction house back in 1940.'

'Really? You've proof of that?'

'I've proof Barclay-Wood tried.'

Joe whistled through his teeth and then sat there thoughtfully.

'You didn't mention any of this earlier,' said Joe, with more than a hint of official disapproval.

'I didn't know when we last spoke. Anyway, if Joyner's death was an accident, then it doesn't make much difference to your enquiry, does it?'

'It would still have been helpful to know.'

'It doesn't change the fact that Joyner was looking for something in the well.'

'I suppose not. There's nothing else like that you'd like to tell me?'

'Not exactly like that,' I said. I was, of course, aware that Iris and Cox had been planning an illegal sale, but that also didn't seem to affect anything. Or not as far as I could see. 'Can I get you a coffee after all?' I asked.

'Might as well,' he said. 'Just in case you remember any more statues over the next couple of minutes.'

I got up and boiled the kettle. When I'd made the drink, I set it in front of Joe, but he didn't touch it straight away.

'So, let's get this right,' he said. 'Joyner's got the Madonna, or had it?'

'Yes,' I said.

'So, where did *he* get it from?'

'It was a fairly tortuous route.'

Joe looked at me. 'How tortuous, exactly?'

'Tortuous enough to be tricky to explain – on the record, anyway. I'm assuming this is off the record?'

'Yes, if it was an accident. If a crime has been committed, then you know as well as I do that I may have to ask you officially. But, if it helps you in any way, I won't make you tell me now – not just to satisfy my own curiosity. So, Joyner had it, however he got it, and he knew Sammartini was after it. He therefore hid it in your garden?'

'And from here somebody, but not Sammartini, stole it. But I've no proof of any of this. All I actually have is a hole in the garden and an empty padded envelope. Joyner had the opportunity to hide the statue here, but equally he might have lost it in the pub in Chichester.'

Joe sat there, his coffee slowly getting cold in front of him. 'Or he could have taken it to the Priory? Like Barclay-Wood?'

'I'd thought the same thing,' I said. 'He had a rucksack with him that day – I remember him carrying it at the Abbey. But at the Priory, he left the bag in the car.'

'Did he have time to get back to the car, after he made sure you all left him alone?'

'Yes,' I said. 'But it was locked . . . no, actually, now I think about it, I was going to lock the car, then Joyner distracted me by complaining about Cox's Mercedes being parked there. I probably didn't lock it. I just put the car keys in my pocket and rang the bell.'

'So, he gets rid of you all, then he goes back to the car, removes the statue, returns to the garden and conceals it somewhere – God knows why – after which he goes back to the well, as if he'd been there the whole time.'

'It's possible,' I said.

'That also explains how he might have fallen in. Coming

in from the strong sunlight, it was quite difficult to see very much under the trees. Until your eyes adjusted, you could easily trip over a tree root or something. I did it myself. But, once you'd had a chance to get used to the light, you'd be fine. Joyner had been there a while when you all left. He'd have seen well enough. But if he went out and came back in again from the bright sunshine outside – maybe in a hurry, to cover up what he'd really been doing . . .'

'Still making his death a complete accident, of course. Well, the neatness of your theory appeals to me. It's how Agatha Christie would have done it. She'd have gone on about how gloomy it was in there, making you think that she was telling you somebody could have crept up on the victim. But later you'd realise the point was that you could easily slip if your eyes weren't accustomed to the dark. But she'd have made you suspect one or more of the guests at the Priory very strongly first. She'd have given them all very sound motives. Having talked to most of the people since, I'm still not sure we have a sound motive between them.'

Even as I said it, though, I knew that I had doubts about Iris at least. And maybe about Henry. But without new evidence that was all it was.

'Well, there's something I haven't told you,' said Joe. 'We have a new witness statement.'

'Really? I thought everyone had already given you statements.'

'So they did. But one witness had second thoughts. Mr Tertius Sly. He came to see me. Said he now recollected something that he'd forgotten before.'

'When one of my characters says that in a book, they're lying,' I said. 'Either about the thing or about the forgetting.'

'I'm not ruling out either possibility. Sly says that he now recalls seeing somebody in a white jacket close to the well, as he was returning to the terrace. He thought nothing of it at the time, but now he feels that it was almost certainly Henry Polgreen. He's willing to testify under oath. He reminded me that Joyner was about to expose Polgreen for misconduct in high office.'

'High office? You mean as chairman of the Abbey preservation committee?'

'That was how he categorised it.'

'That's nonsense,' I said.

'He's a friend of yours?'

I recalled Elsie having said much the same thing to me more than once. 'That wouldn't influence my judgement,' I said. 'Not in any way.'

'And you don't like Sly?'

'Not much. But again, that has nothing to do with it.'

'I don't like Sly either, to tell you the truth,' said Joe. 'And, after he'd been in, I checked our records. He's got previous – of a kind.'

'Perjury?'

'Oh no, nothing like that. A couple of years ago we got two 999 calls in quick succession. Two motorists claiming to be the victims of road rage. When we sent a car out, Sly and another driver had taken a dislike to each other and got into a fight over who had been endangering life by their driving on a quiet country road. They'd both called the police to claim assault by the other. No damage seemed to have been done to either car or driver, so the constable involved just told them not to be so stupid and to control their tempers in future. He said he'd keep a record of the incident and they'd better watch out next time.'

'So, Sly's told lies before?'

'Who knows? Maybe the other guy really was a maniac. There wasn't any CCTV out that way. But the point is that he's been accused of being violent before now. I think he'd be capable of killing somebody. Anyway, the fact that Sly could have seen Polgreen also places Sly right by the well at the right time. He can't have that both ways.'

'No,' I said.

'But you didn't see either of them?'

I took a deep breath.

'You remember that I thought I saw Joyner in his white jacket, then decided it must have been Iris in hers?'

'Yes – about the same build and height.'

'I've wondered since if it was Henry Polgreen. Sly may be right – about that, anyway.'

'Henry Polgreen's much taller.'

'I only saw the flash of white.'

Joe shook his head. 'A flash of white won't convince a jury. Nor will a hunch on my part. But Sly had the opportunity and he was capable of it. We're just back to the lack of a motive of any kind. If I could think of one, I'd arrest him this afternoon.'

'Do you want me to heat that coffee up for you?' I asked.

Joe took an experimental swig. 'No, it's fine. You get used to cold coffee when you're interviewing somebody.' He picked up the picture of Sammartini and looked at it again. 'Sorry – I got distracted,' he said. 'I was going to tell you about Sammartini. Interpol contacted us. They want him in connection with a theft of some antiquities in Italy. They've traced them to a museum in the States.'

'Hadleyburg,' I said.

For the first time Joe looked impressed. 'How did you know that?'

'Lucky guess,' I said.

'There are a number of items in the museum that seem to have been obtained in a less-than-honest manner. It has a lot of cash at its disposal, and few scruples, it would seem.'

'Gold corrupts,' I said.

Joe nodded. 'I'm not in a position to speak from personal experience, though we do get a good pension scheme. Anyway, Interpol said the museum had some items from Sussex. They'd heard that he was negotiating to get something else from over here. Wondered if it was the same source. They thought I should know. It sounds as if you were a step ahead of me on that.'

'Half a step,' I said. 'And I wish I wasn't.'

'Well, if he contacts you again, just be careful. The Italian police also want him for murder.'

'I'll bear it in mind,' I said.

CHAPTER EIGHTEEN

Elsie

Tuesday passed me the note as I came out of the meeting.

'When authors phone,' I said, 'just say the cheque is in the post and no, they can't have any more time to finish the book. That covers ninety-eight per cent of queries.'

'We pay everyone by bank transfer now,' said Tuesday.

I looked at the note. 'Even Ethelred?' I asked.

'Even Ethelred,' said Tuesday. 'I think you should call him. I think he needs help.' She looked at me sternly, like the head prefect she once was.

'It will be the Maltese Madonna, then,' I said. 'Send the intern out for some chocolate. This sounds like a three-Twix problem.'

'Aaron was reading some manuscripts. Are you sure this is more important?'

'It's *chocolate*,' I said.

* * *

'So,' said Ethelred, finally coming to the point, 'it's a bit of a mess. I found myself withholding all sorts of information from the police – for example that Iris had sold the church plate illegally to the museum and Anthony Cox was helping her. I felt guilty about that. On the other hand, I told Joe that Henry may have been quite close to the well at one point. I felt guilty about that too.'

'Ethelred,' I said, 'your loyalties are to me, as your agent, and to whichever publishers haven't dropped you yet. That's not many people, is it? Beyond this small charmed circle, you have no need to feel guilt of any sort. Screw them, I say.'

He muttered a bit about standing by friends, but he could see I was right, because I'd trained him to do that.

'Don't I have your interests at heart?' I asked.

'Sometimes,' he said.

'For example, have I ever been wrong about any of the women you've got entangled with?'

'Yes,' he said.

'But not very wrong,' I said. 'Because, in the end, they all let you down, didn't they? They have all gone. Whereas I am still here, returning your calls, sorting out your little problems.'

'I can manage my own life,' he said.

'But not as well as I can manage it,' I said. 'If it hadn't been for me, you might have been remarried ages ago to some floozy with a chest size twice her age.'

'Yes,' he said, but he sounded strangely ungrateful.

'There you are, then,' I said. 'And all for fifteen per cent.'

'Plus VAT.'

'Cheap at the price. Is there anything else I can do for you today at all?'

'Possibly,' he said.

He gave me an account of his studies of the collected works of Sabine Barclay-Wood and of his visit to Selsey.

'So both statues were in the church until the last war?' I said.

'Mrs Hardcastle – Old Mrs Hardcastle – said there were two sacred images, possibly Fred Astaire and Ginger Rogers, but more likely, in my opinion, Christ and the Virgin Mary. Mrs Hardcastle thought they looked a bit cheap, but they'd been painted black and dumped in a bit of the church that the sun never reached. Barclay-Wood tried to sell a black statue in 1940, but the auctioneers got a bit suspicious when he speculated that it might be solid gold underneath the paint. They couldn't work out why he thought that. They threatened to ask the Dean if it was all OK. He seems to have quietly dropped the matter – for a while, anyway.'

'I bet. So, the Madonna somehow made her way to the Priory, to be discovered about twenty years later. And the other . . . ?'

'. . . has vanished,' said Ethelred. 'Unlike Joyner, I don't think it was hidden in the well. The police would have found it when they searched there for a murder weapon – both this time and when the gardener drowned.'

'So, where's the Madonna now?' I asked.

'Joe thought maybe Joyner actually *hid* the Madonna at the Priory, while pretending to search, but I'm not convinced. Too difficult to recover later. Fay thinks he did bury it under the rose bush and that it could have been taken by somebody I know well, who spotted the rose bush had been disturbed.'

So, Fay Tomlinson was now the world authority on where

the hell things were? This was certainly breaking news.

'Hold on,' I said. 'Can we just rewind that? I'd like to hear the reverential way you said Fay's name, just one more time.'

'I didn't say her name reverentially,' he said. 'I can mention her without being infatuated by her.'

'Except you are, aren't you? I can tell from your voice. It's the voice you use to defend completely unsuitable women against my very reasonable objections. Has she by any chance suggested that you sell the Madonna and run away together on the proceeds?'

'Yes,' he said. 'To Antigua or St Lucia. My choice. I told her I wouldn't.'

He clearly expected praise of some sort.

'And you are still wondering what would have happened if you had said yes?' I enquired.

'A bit. She compared me to Arthur Miller.'

'Ethelred, a woman who would compare you to Arthur Miller has no shame at all. Don't trust her.'

He said nothing.

'Can you really see yourself on a palm-fringed beach with her – she in a skimpy bikini, which scarcely covers the legal minimum amount of flesh, you in your knee-length swimming trunks, high factor sun cream and panama hat?'

'Obviously, I can imagine that very well. But you don't have to worry. I know I'd be stupid to listen to her blandishments.'

'When has knowing you were stupid ever stopped you listening to blandishments?'

'Sorry, Elsie, but I think there's a danger we're both being unfair to Fay. When she came to visit me, I, like you, was very suspicious of her. But the more I think about it, the more I worry about Henry and Iris and Anthony Cox and what their motives are. Fay is at least absolutely open. Maybe she is genuinely the only person I can trust in all this—'

'Ethelred, this is an order: step away from that woman! Pull down the blinds and take cover on the floor with your hands over your head. I'll come and fetch you and take you to a place of safety.'

Then there was a strange beep.

'It's a text,' he said. 'I think it may be from Fay.'

He said it softly. And it was almost like praying.

'What is she graciously commanding you to do?' I asked respectfully.

'I'm not sure. I can probably check my texts without cutting you off on the—'

The call terminated abruptly. I waited. I wrote a few emails. I waited. I ate a Twix. Somewhere out there life went on, saplings grew into giant trees, mighty empires rose and fell. Then my phone rang.

'Sorry, I think I cut you off,' said Ethelred.

'Not a problem at all if it was a genuine text from Fay,' I said. 'I completely understand. You are so wise to check the moment Fay wants you to. It's what she'd want, so it must be right. No need to worry about me, your agent, sitting here, waiting patiently for you to call back.'

'Good . . .' he said, then he realised that I might not actually mean any of that. 'It's quite serious,' he added.

'Tell me what she said. I'll tell you exactly how much of a shit to give.'

'OK,' he said very cautiously. 'The text said to come to

Oxford at once. She couldn't risk explaining herself, but she was in danger.'

'Couldn't risk explaining in what sense? Who does she think is likely to be arsed to read your texts?'

'I suppose she may not have thought that through.'

'No shit? And so you said you'd drop everything for her?'

'No. I tried phoning but just got a recorded message. It said Fay couldn't come to the phone right now but—'

'Yes, Ethelred,' I said. 'I have heard a recorded message before, though I'm sure Fay's is the very best of its kind. You must play it to me sometime.'

There was a pause. He knew, deep down, I probably didn't mean that either.

'I'm going to drive to Oxford now,' he said with a sudden determination.

'You don't know where she lives.'

'She gave me the address in her text. Banbury Road.'

'Then forward the text to Anthony Cox, who is a hundred miles or so closer to her than you are, and tell him to go round in his nice white Mercedes.'

'What if she's in danger from him? From what she told me, I'm not sure they're still on the same side.'

'In that case Chief Inspector Morse will already be examining the body, and you'll only need one ticket to St Lucia. Or you could take me. I've got a bikini.'

Ethelred, for some reason, ignored my offer. 'She was OK a minute or two ago,' he said, 'when she sent the text. Now she's not replying.'

'Women!' I said. 'They just can't make up their tiny little minds, can they?'

234

There was another long silence as Ethelred tried to work out whether it was better to agree with me or not.

'I'm going,' he said. 'I've decided.'

'You're not.'

'I am.'

'You're not.'

'You can't delay me indefinitely by repeating the same words over and over again. I'm going.'

'You're not.'

'I mean it.'

'Then I'm coming with you. You protect her from Sammartini, or whoever it is. I'll protect you from her. And don't think you've got the short straw.'

'I'm going straight there. I'll text her to let her know. There's no time for you to travel down to Sussex.'

'I'm going straight there too. There's a thing called a train. You can pick me up at Oxford railway station in . . . hold on . . .' I checked the timetable. 'One hour and forty minutes.'

'I'm not sure I can drive there that fast.'

'Then I'll wait for you,' I said. 'And don't you dare go to her house without me. Whatever you think she may be prepared to offer by way of sexual or other favours, I can totally screw it up for you.'

'I know,' he said meekly. 'I know.'

I'd been waiting for twenty minutes when Ethelred's Volvo finally pulled into the station forecourt and came hesitantly to a standstill on a double yellow line. I strolled over to meet him.

'Get in quickly,' he said. 'I'm not supposed to stop here.'

'For a person who writes about murder, you are very worried about parking infringements,' I said. 'Anyway, there are no traffic wardens around. I think you may have just committed the perfect crime.'

'And do your seat belt up,' he said.

'For a person who writes about murder . . .' I said.

'This is real life,' he said. 'Anyway, we need to get to Banbury Road. Fast.'

'She'll be fine,' I said. 'Even if Fay has been tied up and gagged – which I am led to believe is standard procedure in these cases – the villains always like two or three chapters to taunt her in a cruel and merciless manner. She'll probably only be at the stage of weeping pitifully and wondering why you have abandoned her. And you can slow down, Ethelred. The penalties for exceeding the speed limit are considerably higher than those for parking on a double yellow line. I've seen your latest royalty statements and you can't afford the fine, unless I can sell some more foreign rights.'

But I shouldn't have mentioned the probability of Fay being mercilessly taunted. Our tyres screeched alarmingly as Ethelred put his foot down and the Ashmolean Museum flashed past the passenger window in a blur of Cotswold stone. The option of crashing straight into Balliol College, currently forty yards or so ahead of us on the far side of the traffic lights, was briefly considered and rejected. We hung a left into the broad, open and relatively safe spaces of St Giles, its colleges and pubs prudently set well back on either side. 'Any other advice?' he asked.

'Are we talking Raymond Chandler or Agatha Christie?'

'Either.'

'If this is Raymond Chandler, then as you enter the house, you'll be slugged from behind by your policeman friend, Joe, who is actually working for Sammartini. You'll wake up, drugged, in a private sanatorium in Headington, from which you'll escape by climbing out of the window. You'll go back to your office and drink whisky out of a dirty glass. Your faithful secretary will put a sticking plaster on your cuts. You'll be fine. If it's Agatha Christie, Fay will have vanished, leaving behind a cryptic note that makes sense only when you view it upside down in a mirror towards the end of the book.'

Ethelred nodded and swung the car suddenly across the road, taking the right-hand fork. A number of cars hooted us but, surprisingly, nobody died.

'Banbury Road!' I said. 'Can we stop so I can take a selfie outside Colin Dexter's house?'

'No,' said Ethelred.

We slowed suddenly so that he could check the numbers on the houses, then we accelerated again. Somebody we had failed to kill back at St Giles overtook us doing sixty miles an hour. They knew that, if they stayed anywhere near Ethelred, they would become just another road deaths statistic.

We hadn't even got close to Colin Dexter's place when Ethelred swerved neatly across the bus lane and into a driveway. There was a brief crunch of gravel and we were stationary. I gave thanks to God for watching over me in my hour of peril and looked up at the tall red-brick mansion, a merciful hair's breadth beyond the car's bonnet.

'Flat C,' Ethelred said, jumping out of the car.

'Don't smash the front door open,' I advised. 'That

Victorian woodwork is stronger than it looks. At least try ringing the bell first.'

He looked at me and nodded thoughtfully. Four strides took him up the steps. He pressed the button for flat C very firmly indeed.

Fay's voice answered at once, crackly music to Ethelred's ears: 'Hello?' she said. 'Who's that?'

'Ethelred,' said Ethelred.

'And me,' I said.

'I'll let you both in,' she said.

Well, that was a bit of an anticlimax. Not a Chandler or Christie plot, then. Who was good at anticlimax?

'L. C. Tyler,' I said to Ethelred, with a sudden flash of insight.

'Who?' he said.

'Don't worry, he's not that well known. Let's just go up and see Fay.'

We heard the intercom buzz and the front door latch click open. Ethelred pushed the door very gently and we walked in. Nobody at all hit Ethelred over the head with anything. Nobody pushed past us, heavily disguised in a false beard, sunglasses and thick winter overcoat.

We started up the stairs, towards flat C.

CHAPTER NINETEEN

Elsie

'I don't understand,' said Ethelred, his default position with any attractive woman who wanted to use him for her own evil purposes.

'I didn't send you any texts,' said Fay. 'It's not even my number.' She took out her iPhone and showed him, allowing her body to get as close to his as was permissible in the presence of his literary agent. 'See?' she breathed huskily.

'The text was signed by you,' he said. 'The answerphone message said it was you.'

He had, poor lamb, been so looking forward to rescuing Fay, possibly partially clothed, from the menaces of a band of vicious but easily overcome crooks. We could have almost been in Sydney Horler territory there. The tea and Battenberg cake, before us on the table, was only partial compensation from his point of view. He took a manly bite out of his cake and chewed.

'Somebody's gone to a lot of trouble to get you to Oxford,' said Fay.

He nodded. 'Yes, that's true.'

'Not that much trouble,' I said. 'They've bought a cheap pay-as-you-go phone, sent a text signed "Fay" and then quickly arranged for the answerphone message to claim you can't take the call, which was perfectly true. Compared with getting Ethelred a decent advance, that's a walk in the park, that is.'

'You haven't got me a decent advance,' he said.

'There you are, then,' I said.

'Well, at least you're in no danger,' said Ethelred to Fay.

Fay reached across the table and touched his arm with the tips of her fingers. 'It was brave of you to come,' she said, with what one person in the room at least recognised as sick-making hypocrisy. 'And you, too, of course, Elsie. Very brave of both of you.'

'It was our pleasure, Fay,' I said. 'Though a phone call from Ethelred to your friend, Anthony Cox, might have saved a couple of hours of my very valuable time.'

'Yes . . .' said Fay. 'Maybe it's as well you don't say more to him than necessary – about anything.'

'Not say more than necessary? Why is that?' asked Ethelred, entering devotedly into his new role of Fay's straight man.

'I have a confession to make,' she said. I wondered whether to point out that fluttering her eyelashes like that was causing a nasty draught, but I let her continue. 'You see, I didn't tell the police the whole truth . . .'

'Really, Fay?' I said, beating Ethelred to it by a microsecond. He looked hurt. He'd wanted to say that.

She nodded and continued, 'I said that Anthony and I were together the whole time in the garden. In fact, we weren't. We had a slight disagreement on something. I stayed where I was, on a bench on the far side of the woods, quite calmly and unconcerned. He stomped off towards the house – and towards the well, of course, because, as I later realised, they were *both* in that direction. I waited for ten minutes or so, then went to find him. He was on his way back to me. He looked . . . agitated. That puzzled me.'

Ethelred nodded sympathetically. Things often puzzled him too.

'Then, after poor Dr Joyner's body was found, Anthony said to me, "It would be best to say we were together the whole time. That way neither of us will get accused of bumping the old fool off, *much though he deserved it.*" Stupidly, I agreed to go along with his plan. Later I saw how terribly wrong I had been, but it was too late . . . too late . . .'

She blinked back the tears with her false lashes, and I again felt a chill wind – west, veering north-west, 5 to 7, occasionally 4 later. She was good. They could have named a cyclone after her. Or anything that was twisty and wrecked everything in its path.

'You shouldn't blame yourself,' said Ethelred. 'Loyalty is important.'

Well, as Fay's new personal lapdog, he would have known.

'Dr Joyner had worked out that Anthony was negotiating with Sammartini,' she said. 'I came into the Senior Common Room one morning, and they were in the middle of a very heated discussion. They stopped as soon as they saw me, but I'm sure that's what I overheard. If Dr Joyner had chosen to report Anthony to the police, Anthony's career would have been finished – no book deal, no TV deal, no College Fellowship, no chair of modern history. He knew he had little choice. Dr Joyner was not a large man. Anthony would have been able to overcome him quite easily and . . . and . . .'

Ethelred put his arm round Fay's shoulder. 'It was very brave of you to tell us of your suspicions,' he said. 'I'm proud of you.'

'Except,' I said, 'there's no evidence that Anthony Cox did any of that. Ethelred says that Sly has already accused Henry Polgreen, having had a revelation similar to your own, except for one minor detail. If you want to accuse Professor Cox, however, then please do go and join the grasses' queue at Chichester Police Station.'

'Fay has a point, though,' said Ethelred. 'Anthony Cox had the best motive of anyone. There was a strong mutual dislike and Joyner could have ruined him. That's now clear. And whereas, before, we thought he had no opportunity, now we know he did: he had time to creep up behind Joyner, in the gloom, and hit him with a brick.'

'Exactly,' said Fay. 'Except you put it so much better than I could.' She gave his hand a squeeze and then completely forgot to release it. Of course, most people's memories deteriorate as they get older.

'Right,' I said. 'I think we've done all this stuff as thoroughly as we need to. The fun is over. If you don't mind letting go of him, Ethelred needs to drive me back to the station. I'm delighted you are still in one piece, Fay, rather than in any other number of pieces. But we wouldn't wish to take up any more of your afternoon . . . would we, Ethelred?'

He looked at me as if he'd temporarily forgotten I was there.

'I guess not,' he said reluctantly. 'I'm sure Fay has important work to do. Though I could stay here tonight if she felt at all threatened.'

'I—' said Fay.

'She doesn't,' I said. 'And it's not her safety that I'm worried about.'

'I'll run you to the station,' he said to me.

I watched them exchange a chaste, hesitant kiss on each cheek and Ethelred head off downstairs. As I left, I whispered in Fay's little ear, 'Don't think I'm not on to your game, Dr Tomlinson. I shall be watching your every move from now on.'

'Do,' she said. 'You might learn something.'

'You've already admitted you and Cox weren't together the whole time. That puts you in the frame every bit as much as the professor. I think you've just blown your own alibi, Fay.'

If she said anything in reply, she was too slow for it to catch me as I descended the stairs. I closed the front door and joined Ethelred in his Volvo. He reversed carefully onto Banbury Road, narrowly missing only one bus, and we were soon travelling south again.

'You look pleased with yourself,' he said, as he crunched the gears.

'Just thinking back over this afternoon,' I said.

He looked at me suspiciously. 'You sometimes have a very selective memory,' he said.

'In what way?'

'I wouldn't want you recounting the story the way you sometimes do – I mean, making it sound as if I was infatuated with Fay Tomlinson. Or making Fay appear scheming and manipulative. Or making yourself sound as if you were the only one with any common sense. That's not how it was this afternoon.'

'I'd never do that,' I said. 'I'd tell the plain, unvarnished truth. You can trust me one hundred per cent.'

'Really?'

'Cross my heart.'

Again, he looked at me suspiciously. I wondered whether, when telling the story, I should finish it by having Fay hissing and turning into a long green snake? It was pretty much what had happened, after all. Then a text arrived on his phone. I grabbed the phone before he could, knowing that there were two lanes on each side of the road and we could end up in any of them once he started to try to access a message.

'It's from Pippa,' I said.

'One of my neighbours,' he said.

'The one with the garden that's much better than yours?'

'Yes,' he said.

'And who is also—'

'Yes,' he said.

'OK. Just wanted to clear that up. She's asking if your cleaning firm was any good. She wondered whether to recommend them to a friend who needs a cleaner.'

'Which cleaning firm?'

'I don't know. I'll check.'

I sent a reply and waited for a moment.

'She says the one that was at your house all afternoon – F. T. Cleaners and Gardeners. Hang on . . . there's another text from her. Yes, she went round to see you and their van was there. She rang the bell but nobody came, though she was sure somebody was inside. She tried again ten minutes later but the van had gone. There was no phone number on the side of the van, which she thought was odd, and wondered if you had it.'

So, a fake text sends Ethelred to Oxford, while a dodgy van, with inadequate advertising for the company that purportedly owns it, turns up in his driveway in West Wittering and somebody somehow gains admittance to the house. When the doorbell rings, they make themselves scarce. Hmm.

'Change of plan,' I said. 'Don't drop me at the station. I think you're going to need me back in Sussex. Head for the M40 and, once you get there, don't worry about speeding fines. That isn't your biggest problem any more. In the meantime, I'm going to text Pippa and say I wouldn't get those cleaners in, not if I were her friend.'

CHAPTER TWENTY

Ethelred

The side door was unlocked, though I was certain I had locked it when I left the house.

'Or you stupidly forgot,' said Elsie supportively.

'No, I'm sure.'

'Like you were sure Fay was in danger? That sort of sure?'

'They must have used a key,' I said. 'I noticed that a spare key for this door was missing a few days ago. I keep it for guests – it's usually with the other keys in the box in the hall. I meant to ask you if you had it.'

'A bit late asking me now.'

'Yes,' I said.

'You think somebody decided that the treasure could be hidden in the house rather than the garden and lifted the key when he or she visited?'

'It looks like it, doesn't it? I was sure I'd have spotted it if Joyner had hidden anything inside. But it should still have occurred to us that somebody else might think differently.'

'Should have occurred to *you*,' said Elsie. 'I wasn't there when this occurring was going on.'

'Well, let's hope they haven't made too much of a mess. I'll check the annex and the sitting room. You check the bedrooms. Then we'll know the worst.'

Actually, it was not as bad as it might have been. The intruder had been systematically through every room in the house, opening drawers, pulling out jerseys and socks and shirts, checking behind books. But it was just a matter of folding and replacing and restoring in alphabetical order of author. A small stash of euros in my bedside table was untouched. So, unfortunately, was my aunt's Victorian silver teapot and milk jug, for which I've never found a use or the resolve to sell. It is well insured and is always left in a position in which an intruder could not possibly miss it.

'Well, I at least have the consolation that I was right,' I said. 'It wasn't in the house. If they'd found what they were searching for they'd have stopped searching and gone off with the loot. They've clearly tried every room in the house, which suggests they almost certainly didn't discover it.'

'Do you reckon it was Sammartini?'

'That's my guess. He or his much larger friend pocketed the key when they visited. It's true that other people might have taken it, but I can't see anyone else setting the whole thing up as they did – the fake text to get me away from the house for a few hours, the recorded message. The text genuinely seemed to come from Fay. My other recent visitors – Sly or Henry Polgreen or Iris – wouldn't have had Fay's address. But Sammartini was in touch with both her and Cox.'

'So, Sammartini had maybe three hours to throw your socks around and found nothing – what would he do next?'

'Back to the garden,' I said.

Sure enough, they had also toured the garden, digging in the flower beds, even removing a new section of turf that I had put in in the spring. They were, after all, a cleaning and gardening company.

'They didn't have as much time in the garden,' said Elsie. 'But we know they were interrupted. Maybe your intruder was onto something. Could it still be here somewhere?'

For a while we searched amongst the bushes but without success.

'Let's just stand back from it all for a moment,' I said. 'If he was going to hide it, it had to be somewhere that nobody would look for a while and from which he could easily retrieve it. He'd worked out that people might search his room or elsewhere in the house, so he looks for the most obscure place in the garden.'

'A shed?'

'Both locked on the morning he was here.'

'The compost heap?'

Not willing to risk damaging an antique statue with a track record of putting curses on people it didn't like, I donned gloves and emptied the bin by hand. There was nothing other than vegetation in varying stages of stench and decay.

'What are we missing?' I asked. 'What is it that we can see but that we haven't thought of searching?'

As I spoke a car drew into my drive. Iris got out.

'I'm glad I've caught you,' she said. 'Sammartini's around in the village. You tipped me off last time. I thought I'd return the compliment.'

'I already know,' I said. 'He's just turned the house over. But I don't think he found what he was looking for.'

'Excellent,' said Iris. 'Though it doesn't look as if you have either.'

'I'll make you a coffee,' I said.

'Sounds good to me,' she said.

We were seated in the garden again, overlooking Sammartini's excavations. Even the longest summer day comes to an end, and the sky was growing red over the coastguard cottages, beyond the garden hedge.

'Joe thought that Joyner might have hidden the statue at the Priory,' I said.

'That's your policeman friend? Yes, the same thought had occurred to me. Once the police tape was down, I conducted as thorough a search of the grounds as I could. Joyner can't have gone far from the well – one of us would have seen him – so I focused on that part of the garden, and the ice house. I found a pair of secateurs that I lost the year before last and a pound coin – the old sort, not a new one – but no Madonna. With her reputation for being able to mess things up, I wasn't too sorry she was elsewhere. I always kept her in the ice house when I had her. I would check it occasionally by torchlight to make sure nobody had taken the statue away. I had mixed feelings every time I found she was still there. The family has been cursed since my grandfather found it. I don't regard it as any coincidence that, having taken it from its resting place, I find my life is now in the mess that it's in, with another dead body in the well and a pair of American gangsters prowling the village. That's what it does best. Barclay-Wood was spot on there. You say he found it in 1902. Up to that point, his career as a clergyman was quite successful – not exactly what he wanted, but perfectly OK. It was after that that it went so badly wrong. He died bitter and forgotten, over forty years later, having gratuitously thrown away his only chance of promotion by quite needlessly libelling the Bishop and Dean.'

'It seems that the churchwarden at Selsey insisted that the Madonna – and another statue – should stay in the church, when Barclay-Wood wanted to get rid of them,' I said. 'He died in the war – volunteered as a firefighter, went off to London and never came back. There was no need for him to do it. He could have lived out the war quite happily in Sussex. Even the Madonna's friends were not immune to the curse, it would seem.'

'There you are, then,' she said. 'Everyone who gets too close to that pretty little object ends up unnecessarily dead. I'm pleased you don't appear to have it either. You've avoided a lot of bad luck.'

'I'm not sure that having your house broken into is especially good luck,' I said.

'What was the churchwarden's name?' asked Elsie. 'The one who died?'

'Cornwallis,' I said. 'Mrs Hardcastle said that was her maiden name – and I think it's what Barclay-Wood calls him in the book. Does that have any relevance?'

'Maybe,' said Elsie. 'I have a hunch.'

She took out her phone and made a note.

'Making the definitive list of everyone the statue's killed or ruined?' asked Iris.

'Just the one,' said Elsie.

'If we ever find it, you could always give the statue to Sly,' I said to Iris. 'He'd have no hesitation in taking it.'

'And pass the bad luck back to his family? That has its attractions.'

'You really don't like him, do you?' I asked.

'He thinks – quite wrongly – that my grandfather killed his grandfather. But, and this is indisputable, his grandmother killed my grandmother. She went round to see my grandfather and gave him a heart attack. She probably left him dying on the floor, in the full knowledge that my grandmother was upstairs with nobody else to look after her or stop her wandering off on her own. It was months before they found my grandmother, and God knows what she went through in the days and possibly weeks after that, drifting, lost and confused on the Downs. I hope it was quick for her, but she did get an awful long way before she finally lay down to die of exposure.'

'That's not his fault.'

'No, nor is his general character his fault, most likely. Partly hereditary. Partly watching reality television. He has a genuine interest in the Abbey. And he'd work as hard for it as Henry has – harder, probably. Sometimes I think, why not let him be chair of the committee after Henry steps down? Nobody else really wants the job. He deserves it, just for the hours he's put in. Then I think, no – he'd just turn it into Disney World with students and out-of-work actors dressed as monks in polyester robes and fake tonsures. Well, he can stay as secretary, if he wants to, typing up the minutes and sending out circulars. That's what he's good for.'

'Does he know all that?'

'Oh yes, I made myself very clear when he and Henry came over the other day. The discussion got quite heated. He told me that I was a perfect example of middle-class entitlement and privilege. He told me his grandfather was worth ten of mine – not that I ever had any plans to have more than two. Well, I gave as good as I got, I can promise you. I doubt he'll be paying to visit the garden in aid of the hospice next year.'

'Well,' I said, 'that may be clear, but I've still no idea how the statue got from Selsey to the Priory between 1940, when Barclay-Wood was trying to sell it, and 1959, when it was found. And what happened to the second statue?'

'I don't think the second statue was ever at the Priory. I'm pretty sure my grandfather would have found it with the other treasure.'

'Where did it go, then?'

'That's exactly what I need to check,' said Elsie. 'I think I have an idea.' She put her phone away and smiled at us.

CHAPTER TWENTY-ONE

Ethelred

I didn't recognise the mobile phone number. I answered the call with a certain resignation, wondering what wild goose chase I'd be sent on this time.

'Hello,' I said. 'Ethelred Tressider here.'

'It's Anthony Cox. Don't hang up, Ethelred. Whatever Fay Tomlinson may have told you, we're on the same side, you and I.'

'She's told me very little,' I said.

'Really? Fine. Just hear me out.'

'OK,' I said. 'You've got five minutes to convince me of whatever it is you wish to convince me of.'

'Sorry, Ethelred, it will take a bit longer than that. We need to meet.'

'Professor Cox, it's not that I no longer trust you. It's more that I no longer trust anyone. But if you wish to come to my house, then I'd be happy to make coffee for you.'

'That won't be possible. My colleagues and I are worried that your house is being watched.'

'By Sammartini?'

'No, Sammartini is one of my colleagues.'

'Sammartini has just turned my house over.'

'When?'

'Sometime yesterday afternoon.'

'Not possible. He wasn't in West Wittering yesterday afternoon.'

'You expect me to believe that?'

'I agree we've done nothing to earn your trust. But, as I say, we'd still very much like to meet you. To explain. To discuss things. To agree certain things. But not at your house. It's not safe.'

'Where, then?'

'Where would you suggest?'

'The beach,' I said.

'Is it secluded enough?'

'The far end of it is. Even in summer not many people go there.'

There was a whispered conversation.

'Right, we can be there in twenty-five minutes.'

'I'll give you instructions.'

'No need. One of my colleagues knows it well. He says we'll spot each other easily enough.'

He hung up. I looked at my watch. I could just about walk there in twenty-five minutes if I left straight away. I thought I'd rather be there first if I possibly could. I wasn't expecting an ambush, but from now on I was ruling nothing out at all.

* * *

I saw their shapes in the distance. The tall figure of Professor Cox. The very much smaller one of Sammartini. His assistant, Einstein, shambling ape-like behind them. And then, off to one side, as if he'd coincidentally just decided to take a stroll out that way, Henry Polgreen.

It was one of those high summer mornings when the sky seems limitless and the thirty-foot dunes the narrowest of lines between the sky and the sea. It was low tide, and the hard, dark, rippling sands shone unevenly in the sun, neither land nor sea. A breeze gusted off the Channel. Small sandstorms skipped across the drying surface, rising eagerly then dissipating into nothing. As I had predicted, the beach by the car park had been crowded, but out here at the far end of East Head the family groups were sparsely scattered, sheltering anonymously behind colourful windbreaks. Their voices were vague and distant. The strolling dog walkers were further out still, where the retreating salt water lapped gently against the damp sand.

Slowly the little group approached, and I was able to admire Sammartini's immaculate pinstriped suit, perhaps the only one that the beach had seen that summer. He wore a white shirt and paisley-patterned tie, with a gold tiepin large enough to be seen even at the distance. From time to time he took a handkerchief from his breast pocket and mopped his brow. Cox was wearing red cotton drill trousers, a dark-blue polo shirt and a very white panama hat with a black band. Polgreen looked as if he had come straight from gardening, which he probably had.

It was Sammartini who held out his well-manicured hand in greeting.

'I am very pleased to see you, Mr Tressider,' he said. 'You have a fine beach here. A very fine beach, sir. I congratulate you on your fine beach.'

I nodded, taking full credit for the work of the local wind and waves, and shook hands with the man who had disarranged my library.

'I assume you didn't find what you were looking for yesterday?' I said.

'As Professor Cox explained to you, Mr Tressider, that wasn't us. I'm pleased, however, that whoever did search your house failed to find anything. It means that they probably don't have it and are still looking. As indeed we are.'

'Maybe you'd like to tell us what happened, Ethelred,' said Cox. 'Then we can decide what we all do.'

I gave them a brief and slightly selective account of the text, purportedly from Fay, and my journey to Oxford.

Cox nodded. 'You see, Ethelred,' he said, 'the sides have shifted a little. On the side of truth and light, as it were, we have myself and Mr Sammartini and your friend Henry Polgreen. On the side of darkness, we have Fay Tomlinson and Tertius Sly. Fay has been negotiating with another possible purchaser, letting me have as little information as she could without arousing my suspicions. She has now made her move. But she needed an ally here – somebody who could help her track down the missing Madonna. Fay had said to me at one point, when we were still supposedly colleagues, that she was working on the most gullible and easily seduced of those involved in this case, in the hope of getting his cooperation. I must apologise for having thought that might be yourself. But

256

Mr Sly's vanity, credulity and desire to be accepted would have been far more susceptible to her unsubtle charms. She probably persuaded him that, once they'd sold the Madonna, the two of them would go off to the West Indies or somewhere together.' He laughed, inviting me to share the joke.

I nodded. I probably wouldn't tell Elsie any part of that.

'Having heard your account,' he continued, 'I think I can see what happened. You say the text message sounded exactly like Fay. That's because it came from Fay, who would also, of course, know her own address, unlike Mr Sammartini here. She could have got your mobile number from Sly.'

'I've never given it to him,' I said.

'It's on your application to join the committee,' said Polgreen.

'There you are, then,' said Cox. 'But neither Mr Sammartini nor I have it. As you are aware, I have only your landline number. If you just consider these simple facts, you can see that few combinations of people, other than Fay and Tertius Sly, could have tricked you as they did. Once you'd texted to say you were on your way, she alerted Mr Sly, who had already hired a white van and purchased some cheap magnetic signs to stick onto the side – easily done. He drove round and entered using a key that he or Fay had taken from you on a previous visit. Had either been here recently?'

'Yes, both,' I said.

'But Fay hasn't just been complicit in turning over your house,' said Cox. 'I am afraid that I lied to the police on the day that Hilary Joyner died. I told them Fay and I were together the whole time. We weren't. She engineered an argument with me and then stormed off. I didn't see her again until just before we all met up on the terrace. I think she may have killed Hilary.'

'Why?'

'I doubt that her deal with Sly was her first attempt to cut me out of the sale of the Madonna. I think that she was already plotting with Hilary. You see, that theft of the Madonna from my safe – it's true Hilary had a key, but I doubt that he sneaked in regularly to check the contents, just in case. So, how did he know it was there to be stolen? Because Fay had told him. I think that Fay went back to talk to Hilary by the well and discovered that Hilary's plans were rather different from her own.'

'He wanted publicity, she wanted cash?'

'What Hilary wanted desperately was one successful book. A secret deal with a museum would not have appealed to him. He may have omitted to explain that to her.'

'So, she killed him?'

'I imagine there was an argument, in the course of which Hilary stumbled against the wellhead and fell in. Or something like that. It was, as people have constantly reminded us, rather dark in there.'

'It is indeed a point that's been made quite often,' I said. 'So Fay was left without the Madonna and without her partner in crime?'

'Yes. She needed help to recover the statue. I thought she might try to recruit you but, as I say, she found an easier victim.'

'Sly may be her victim, but he's no worse off than we are.'

258

'On the contrary,' said Polgreen. 'We've had a thought. Sly's watching the entrance to your road at the moment but he can't stay there for ever. He has a job to go to during the day, albeit in the village. We think the Madonna must be in the garden somewhere. Joyner brought it down. There's honestly nowhere else he could have hidden it. It's just that none of us has looked in the right place yet. We'll bring my metal detector round tomorrow and have a go with that.'

'I don't care whether it's found or not,' I said. 'But why have you teamed up with these two? Sammartini represents the museum that spirited away your church plate. You said it belongs back at the Abbey.'

'Well . . .' said Polgreen.

'It's like this,' said Sammartini. 'We've reached an agreement. Provided we find the Madonna, the museum will agree to regard all of the Abbey silver as legally belonging to the Abbey trustees, on loan to the museum for a period to be decided. It would . . . ah . . . regularise the current state of affairs, should anyone choose to question them. In return for the loan, the museum will generously fund the construction and staffing of a new visitor centre in Sidlesham, together with a substantial contribution to annual running costs for as long as the loan continues.'

'What if somebody else claims ownership when you announce all this?' I asked.

'We plan to announce the museum's generous donation to the Abbey site. There may be no need to trouble people with the rest of it.'

'It's a good deal,' said Polgreen. 'We could hardly house

thousands of pounds worth of silver in the hut we have. And if it's not on-site, then it might as well be in Hadleyburg as in the V&A or somewhere. Everything becomes legally ours. And we shall finally have enough money to maintain the site properly.'

'Precisely,' said Sammartini.

I looked at Henry Polgreen. He was now staring out to sea. Did the generous funding include a regular payment to the committee chair? The Madonna's power to corrupt seemed capable of endless variations.

'Good for you,' I said.

'So,' said Cox, 'we seem to have cleared everything up very nicely. We just need to find the Madonna.'

'Do you have any objection if I tell Iris Munnings what the plan is?' I asked.

Cox flashed a glance at Sammartini, then smiled. 'The Madonna was clearly the property of Sidlesham Abbey, as Iris would have to acknowledge. The Prior merely hid it for the Abbot. And nobody is asking her to repay the money that she obtained from the earlier sale. Under the circumstances we have nothing to hide from anyone,' he said. 'And certainly not from Iris.'

It was a pleasant walk back from the beach, across the broad, empty sands and then along the sea wall, with the glistening green marshes on either side of me and the seabirds constantly whirling overhead. I had been back at my house for only a short time when my phone rang.

'I'm coming down tomorrow,' said Elsie. 'I've got some news for you.'

'Do you want to tell me now?' I asked.

'Aaron discovered it. He may as well take the credit for what he's done.'

'Really? You'd actually let him do that?'

There was a long pause. 'I see your point. Well, he can this time, anyway.'

CHAPTER TWENTY-TWO

Ethelred

The following day dawned bright and clear. Cox was the first to arrive, with Sammartini, Einstein and Henry Polgreen in tow. Henry set to work with his metal detector, walking systematically up and down the lawn, sweeping from side to side, then making a return run that overlapped the first. Polgreen politely declined Cox's suggestion that he should take over. This was a job for the expert.

Like Iris, I soon found myself the owner of a collection of small metallic items – several coins, a small coil of barbed wire, an old tablespoon. Polgreen's attentions were switched to the vegetable patch, then to the flower beds. As before, we were left scratching our heads. I served coffee to Cox and Polgreen, a beer to Sammartini and lemonade with ice to his friend.

'Hilary hid it here, I'm sure of it,' said Cox. 'I just don't see why we can't find it.'

'Maybe it's at the Priory, after all,' said Polgreen. 'That

could be awkward – I mean, if Iris does object to being cut out of the deal with the Stephenson Museum. She might acknowledge she has no claim on it, but she doesn't have to let us search there.'

Sammartini simply nodded. I suspected that his position remained completely flexible on the question of ownership, but he was growing impatient.

'I don't think it's at the Priory,' said Cox. 'Iris has checked the obvious places. And Hilary scarcely had time to bury it deeply.'

'When we were first invited over to England,' said Sammartini, 'we were assured most categorically that the Madonna was available. My clients won't wait for ever. They were more than a little suspicious of the authenticity of the goods in question. I would not stop you searching anywhere you wish, but I think, gentlemen, that the deal may very shortly be off.'

'Hold on,' said Cox. 'We've all spent a lot of time on this. Let's not be hasty.'

Then Elsie and Aaron arrived.

Aaron had travelled down with Elsie in her ancient Mini. Every time I saw the car, I was amazed that it had not succumbed to rust and was still on the road. Aaron clearly wanted to be there this morning, even at considerable risk to his life.

Elsie introduced Aaron, neatly cut off an attempt on his part to praise my writing, and gave me instructions for coffee and biscuits.

'So,' she said to the assembled group, 'I sent Aaron off to research Barclay-Wood's churchwarden. He seemed to have been a victim of the curse of the Maltese Madonna, having died quite unnecessarily in the Blitz, but, unlike almost everyone else, he didn't seem to have been corrupted by her.'

'Not at first sight,' said Aaron. 'But it was worth checking that he might have been. I first went through the electoral rolls for Selsey for 1939 to establish his full name. It was Hector Alexander Cornwallis. This was fortunate in the sense that it was unlikely that I'd find two people of that name. I then tried to establish when he had died. I looked first at newspapers from September 1940 onwards. I found no reference to a firefighter called Cornwallis until December, at the very height of the bombing raids – the night that is referred to as the Second Great Fire of London. Amongst the reports was one of a missing firefighter – Alex Cornwallis. I kept checking to see if there was anything more about him, but that was that. Of course, that night the Luftwaffe was dropping three hundred bombs a minute. There would have been a lot of people who died and who were just never found. Temperatures reached up to a thousand degrees centigrade – that's about a hundred degrees hotter than a crematorium furnace. I checked for death certificates issued in London.'

'Did he have one?'

'Yes, I found it online. It was issued about two years later, but giving his date of death as 29th December 1940. It seems that it took that long before they gave up hope that he might still be out there somewhere.'

'So, much as expected,' I said.

'Not quite,' said Aaron. 'He apparently had a second death certificate. That was issued in Penzance in 1972. A second Hector Alexander Cornwallis. Same year of birth as the first one. It seems that he used the Blitz as an opportunity to vanish and start a new life elsewhere.'

'Could you do that then?' I asked. 'If he'd been declared dead in London, wouldn't that have caused problems for him in Penzance?'

'Well, there were no computer systems then to help correlate information. People had a much lower public profile. If you arrived in Penzance with a valid ID card saying who you were, and a ration book, then you had a good chance of getting away with it. Nobody was looking for him in Penzance, after all. With most of the men away at war, it wouldn't have been difficult for him to find work in his new hometown.'

'So, in 1940, he just started again from scratch?' I asked. 'That must have been tricky.'

'In which case, he didn't make a bad job of it. Here's a shot of the house he lived in in Selsey in 1939.'

Aaron showed me his iPad. There was a view on Google of a modest terraced house. 'Here, conversely, is his house in 1972.'

Aaron switched to a view of a large detached house, with extensive gardens.

'Nice,' said Sammartini. 'Classy. All that wrought iron wouldn't have been cheap.'

'You can't tell from this, but it has uninterrupted views of the sea,' Aaron said. 'According to Rightmove, it sold last year for just over two million pounds.'

'Very nice,' I agreed.

'I checked the local Penzance papers for the early '70s. According to his obituary he owned a chain of grocery stores in the south-west. He was quite well off.'

'So much for the curse of the Madonna,' Elsie said. 'He would have been how old in 1940?'

I quickly counted off the years on my fingers. 'If he was there, as an established figure, when Barclay-Wood arrived in 1891, he'd have probably been born before 1860, so in 1940, he'd have been at least eighty and he'd have been over a hundred and twelve when he died . . . no, that can't be right.'

Aaron shook his head. 'That confused me at first, but there were two Cornwallises, father and son, both churchwardens. Hector Alexander took over from his father around 1930. He was about forty-five when the war broke out.'

'But still,' I said, 'to start again with nothing at forty-five and die rich thirty years later . . .'

'Unless,' said Elsie, 'he had acquired some capital.'

'You mean the statues?' I said.

'Exactly.'

'They were in the church,' I said. 'They were tucked away in some gloomy corner. Nobody cared for them very much or would have missed them, except possibly Barclay-Wood. Cornwallis was churchwarden and would have had access to everything.'

'But, in that case, how did he know they were worth taking?' asked Elsie. 'Tucked away in a gloomy corner, one statue would look very much like another. You'd have scarcely known which was the boy and which was the girl, let alone their price tags.'

'Because Barclay-Wood had been trying to sell one of them. Cornwallis came across the correspondence and worked out what was going on. Years later, his daughter found the same letters amongst his papers and sent them to me. So, Cornwallis knew the statues were valuable, even if he wasn't sure exactly how much they were worth. And we know *both* statues vanished around then. What I still don't get is how the Madonna makes it back to the Priory by the late '50s. Cornwallis never came back. His daughter never saw him again and, anyway, he surely wouldn't have risked it?'

'Well,' said Sammartini, 'the mechanism for returning the Madonna is, I agree, not without interest. But it was undoubtedly at the Priory for Mrs Munnings' grandfather to find, and that is all we need to know. Can we please focus on where the Madonna is now?'

Aaron quickly scanned the garden. 'Joyner needed to hide it, because he didn't want to risk taking it back to Oxford,' he said. 'He hid it out here because he reckoned somebody might well search the house for it.'

'That's right,' I said.

'Except, it occurred to you all pretty quickly to search your garden. It wouldn't have taken Joyner long to work that out too. So, that's not what he did.'

'So, what did he do?' I asked.

Aaron looked around again.

'That's a nice garden next door,' he said. 'Well-established flower beds. Nobody is going to dig in those until the autumn at the earliest. All you'd need to do is a bit of weeding and deadheading. A statue would be safe there for months.'

Elsie nodded. 'Joyner had taste,' she said. 'Why would he bury something in Ethelred's garden when he could bury it there? It's obvious when you think about it.'

'I'll get working with the metal detector,' said Henry.

'I'll go and ask Pippa,' I said. 'I'm not sure she's any keener than Iris is at having archaeologists in her garden, but she may be curious to find out what's under her roses.'

In the end, the archaeological work was mercifully brief. Joyner had chosen a spot close to the boundary hedge. Once the metal detector had located our prize, it took me less than a minute, with one of Pippa's trowels, to uncover the bundle of bubblewrap that protected the statue. I lifted it carefully, brushing away the warm soil as I silently unwrapped it.

Pippa looked at it. 'It's definitely not one of mine,' she said. 'And I don't think Bugsy buried it there with one of his bones. You may have found what you were after.'

We took it back to my garden and set it on the table. I looked at it, finally standing there for all to see, gleaming softly in the sunlight.

'It's not quite what I expected,' I said.

'No,' said Elsie. 'I thought it would be gold, with diamonds and rubies. But it's black – sort of like Mrs Hardcastle's description.'

'But not painted black,' I said. 'That's just the way silver tarnishes. There are one or two gems – I think those are small garnets in her crown.'

'Well, that's it, anyway,' said Cox. 'Or it's the only one that I've seen.'

'It's beautiful,' said Polgreen. 'Far better than anything I'd hoped for.'

The body was sinuous and draped in flowing robes. The face was calm and serene. Her head was inclined towards a small child, whom she carried in her arms. It was skilfully done, but there was nothing Byzantine about it. There was no dazzling blue cloak, no coral lips, no eyes of sapphire.

'But this can't be the one that Barclay-Wood found,' I said. 'If it were, he would have known what it was like. In its way it's very fetching – much nicer than a mass of gaudy stones he lists in such detail. He'd have had fun describing her enigmatic smile. And there's something very tender about the inclination of her head. But he chose instead to come up with this fantastic account of an invented image. This is nothing like the statue in the book.'

'Maybe this statue was too English to be evil?' asked Elsie.

'Whereas what he described in his story was clearly a showy foreign import – something that by definition lacked good taste? I suppose so. But from his point of view, a Romish image was a Romish image. He didn't like the incense burner made in Wolverhampton, either.'

'So this was on display in his church?' asked Elsie.

I examined it more closely. 'Both Mrs Hardcastle and Barclay-Wood talk of it being *painted* black. There's no trace of any sort of paint. Not even in the crevices – and there are plenty of crevices. And Mrs Hardcastle described the statues at Selsey as ugly. Even painted black, this would still be elegant and well proportioned. And last, but not least, he told the auctioneers that the statue might well be gold and encrusted with jewels. This can't be the same one. I'm going to phone Iris and get her to come over straight away.'

'Well, that's Iris's statue,' said Cox. 'It's the one she gave me.'

'I'll phone her now,' I said. 'She can be here in ten minutes.'

* * *

Iris carefully picked up the little figure. 'Yes,' she said slowly. 'That's it all right. The Curse of the Munnings. And many others before us. Honestly, this is only the fourth or fifth time I've handled it. It never looked right – I mean, compared with Barclay-Wood's description. That's why I got Anthony Cox in. I'm no expert, but it just didn't look Byzantine – more English mediaeval. And it's clearly silver, not gold.'

'It's fairly clear to me,' said Polgreen, 'that both of the statues that were in Barclay-Wood's possession went to Penzance with Cornwallis and never came back. This is something else entirely.'

'I agree,' said Aaron. 'It's all pretty obvious when you read Barclay-Wood's account. The Abbey claimed that the Madonna on display was an old one they'd always owned. They probably wouldn't have done that if they hadn't possessed one. That's what this is. The Abbot sent this to the Priory along with the other gold and silver, hoping the King would find it and not look further. The real treasure, as he saw it – the statues that were worth more than all the rest put together – were safely buried in the nave of his own church, where Barclay-Wood later discovered them.'

'So, there's no curse on this one?' asked Iris.

'Not according to Barclay-Wood's version,' said Polgreen. 'This one is as clean as a whistle. The curse applied only to the Byzantine images.'

'Well, it may not be cursed,' said Sammartini, 'but these are not the goods as described to us. I'm very sorry, gentlemen and ladies, but the museum was promised the genuine Maltese Madonna. As I said before, my employers were a bit surprised when they saw the photographs, but they figured that if that's what the Madonna looked like, then they'd have it anyway. I mean – with a backstory like that it was still pretty interesting. But we now know the real Madonna is clearly elsewhere. Which is good in a way. The museum wanted gold and gems and I can still give them gold and gems, if I can just find the proper one. The trail is far from cold, ladies and gentlemen. I can be in Penzance in a few hours. In the meantime, I can hardly take back this cheap piece of shit, with no provenance at all worth talking about, and hope my employers will settle for the red herring in the story.'

A text came through on my phone. It was from Fay.

WE NEED TO TALK. I'M COMING RIGHT OVER.

The news was greeted with no great enthusiasm. I just had time to make a quick phone call before Fay arrived. Tertius Sly followed just behind her. They stopped when they saw the now large gathering in the garden, then looked open-mouthed at the statue on the table.

'So that's the famous Madonna?' asked Sly contemptuously.

'Yes,' said Fay. 'That's it.'

'And, as I have explained to these good people, I want no part of it,' said Sammartini. 'The deal is very much off, Dr Tomlinson. And, if you'll excuse me, I am very much off to Penzance.'

'What if we did a discount?' asked Sly.

'Not at any price,' said Sammartini. 'It's the real Maltese Madonna or nothing. And you don't have one.'

'That's the end of that, then,' said Polgreen.

'Hold on,' said Fay. 'Mr Sammartini may not want the statue, but it's valuable nevertheless and I still have my own contacts. That is a unique piece of English church

271

silver. Ownership is still a bit iffy, but certain museums would fight for it. If we all agree to keep quiet and split the proceeds between us, it must be worth fifty or a hundred thousand each. That's still worth having.'

'I agree,' I said. 'We could split the proceeds between us all.'

Polgreen looked at me as if I had just passed wind, but Fay nodded approvingly. 'Now you're talking, Ethelred,' she said.

'All of us except one,' I said.

Fay frowned. 'OK. But who are you saying gets nothing?'

'One of us here killed Hilary Joyner,' I said. 'I think we should agree, however we divide up the money, that person gets nothing. And this is perhaps as convenient a moment as any to tell you all who that was.'

'Because all of the suspects are rather improbably gathered in your garden?' asked Aaron.

'Yes,' I said.

'Really?'

'No, not really. It was just something Elsie said earlier – about boy statues and girl statues. I don't know why I didn't think of it before, but the final piece of the jigsaw has fallen into place.'

CHAPTER TWENTY-THREE

Ethelred

'When Hilary Joyner's body was found,' I said, 'I thought, as did the police, that it must be an accident. Of course, almost everyone there could have killed him. As we eventually worked out, nobody was actually in the sight of the others for the whole time. For a while I thought that Professor Cox and Dr Tomlinson could vouch for each other, but later they both said that the other had been out of their view for long enough to commit the murder. Nobody accused Tertius Sly of being close to the well, then he said he'd been close enough to see Henry Polgreen there. I'd seen Henry too – or maybe Iris. Increasingly almost everyone seemed to have had an opportunity. The problem was that nobody really had a motive.

'For example, while it is true that, after the argument that he and Elsie had had on the train, Joyner might have considered murdering her, she had no reason to kill him.

'Similarly, Tertius Sly might have had a grudge against a

number of people, but Joyner was, in effect, his only ally in his campaign to resume excavations. Despised though he was within the village generally, Joyner treated him seriously.'

I paused and allowed Sly to look daggers at me, but this was no time for mincing my words. Iris had already put Sly right on how the village saw him.

'We know that Joyner was aware that Professor Cox was negotiating with Mr Sammartini to sell the Madonna illegally to the Stephenson Museum. According to Fay, Joyner could have informed the university authorities and ruined Cox. But at that stage no sale had been agreed with Hadleyburg. Professor Cox had done nothing more than seek the opinion of the Ashmolean Museum on a statue that had been discovered in an ice house in Sussex. That was scarcely a sacking offence.

'Henry Polgreen and Hilary Joyner were, of course, on opposite sides in the long argument over renewed excavations at the Abbey. Tertius Sly specifically accused Henry of killing Dr Joyner to prevent his support for excavations that might reveal that Henry had stolen items from the site. But Henry Polgreen's only excavations were to establish that Barclay-Wood did indeed dig up the statues himself. His objections to a further dig were purely professional. He had nothing to fear personally or any reason to want Hilary Joyner dead. I thought at one stage that I might have seen Henry's white jacket ahead of me in the garden, very close to the well. I think now that it was Iris. As it happens, I was not the only one to make that sort of mistake.

'Of course, Iris might have been the killer. She knows the garden better than anyone and could have sneaked

274

back to the well. But I do not think that she would have wanted to commit a murder in this way and repeat the traumatic circumstances that led to the death of Walter Sly, her grandfather and her grandmother. Nor did she need to kill anyone. The museum was always going to deny she had sold anything to them – unless the police obliged them to reveal the source in the course of an investigation into a bigger crime. A murder investigation would have made it more likely that the sale would come to light, rather than less likely.

'Which is where I come to you, Fay. You are the sort of woman that my mother should have warned me about and didn't. Fortunately, I have an agent who takes care of stuff like that. But other men have not been so fortunate. You ensured that Anthony Cox would tell you of his plans and would cut you in on the deal. Later you flattered Tertius Sly into helping you. But they were not your only partners, were they? Before that you had been working with Hilary Joyner. You knew he was planning to steal the statue, because you'd already told him when it would be safe to do so. You alone, out of all of us, knew that he almost certainly had the statue with him when he travelled down here. But he was about to double-cross you, wasn't he? He had no intention of sharing the proceeds or anything else with you. He didn't want to sell the statue quietly. He wanted it found in a blaze of publicity that would sell his book – preferably he wanted both statues found. We now know he hid the Madonna here, where you would not be able to find it, while he continued his search for the second statue. You appeared to be angry with Anthony Cox that afternoon at the Priory. But actually your irritation was

275

directed at Dr Joyner, who refused to tell you where the loot was hidden.'

'You think you're very clever, don't you?' said Fay.

'Yes,' said Elsie. 'It's one of his more annoying habits. Really, you'd have got bored with him very quickly. Especially somewhere as small as Antigua.'

'St Lucia's a bit bigger,' said Fay.

'Nevertheless,' I said, 'It's all true isn't it, Fay?'

'What if it is?' she demanded. 'Joyner had the statue. I didn't. But I had other ways of getting what I wanted. I didn't need to kill him. Quite the reverse. I'd have talked him round. You men are all so vain. It's pathetic, really. His death has been very inconvenient for me, and you know it. So, why are you dragging it out like this? Is it because you're annoyed that I ditched you for Tertius Sly?'

'Yes,' said Elsie. 'He is. Annoyed and jealous. I'd have nothing more to do with him, Fay. You are so well out of that one. Much better to stick to that nice Mr Sly. You were made for each other.'

'So, she didn't do it,' said Sammartini. 'What about me? Do I get a clean bill of health too?'

'I've just made a phone call to the police,' I said. 'You didn't arrive in London until the day after the murder.'

'What about me?' asked Aaron.

'You're only the intern,' said Elsie. 'You don't get to kill people. The murderer is never the intern.'

'Sorry,' said Aaron. 'I didn't mean as the killer. I know I didn't do it. I mean, weren't you going to ask me if I'd worked out who it was?'

'Do you know?' asked Elsie.

'Of course,' he said. 'Ethelred has established that none

276

of you had any motive for killing Hilary Joyner. Some of you may have disliked him. He might have caused some of you a little embarrassment. But it would have not been worth the risk of murdering him, with the very strong risk of being found out. Nevertheless, one of you did kill him. And the white jacket is one big clue. And, like Ethelred, I noted Elsie's remark that, in the gloom, one statue looked very much like another – you probably couldn't have even told which statue was male and which female. In the gloom by the well, one person in a white jacket would have looked very much like another.

'Hilary Joyner was not the only person in a white jacket that afternoon. Henry Polgreen was also wearing one. So was Iris Munnings. Iris Munnings was also of a similar height to Dr Joyner. Both were wearing panama hats. For anyone coming into the glade from the very strong sunlight outside, Hilary Joyner hunched over the well would have looked very much like Iris Munnings hunched over the well. It would be easy to confuse the two, at least for a moment. Long enough to strike the person over the head with a brick . . . wouldn't it, Mr Sly?'

'I don't know what you mean,' said Sly.

'He's right, though,' said Elsie. 'That's exactly what must have happened. I don't like to take all of the credit myself, but Aaron is, after all, my intern.'

'Somebody else with no experience of the real world,' sneered Sly.

'But nevertheless, with a cynicism and lack of trust honed by years of reading classic detective fiction and a month working for Elsie,' I said. 'We know that you'd just had an argument with Iris, in which she told you in no uncertain terms how you were seen by the village. And you were not pleased. I saw the same flash of hatred from you when I said the same thing a moment ago – that was the final confirmation I needed. And when you get angry you get very angry, don't you? After all, you'd already had one warning for a road rage incident. You didn't intend to kill Hilary Joyner – your one friend in your campaign against Henry Polgreen – but that's what you did. Afterwards, you looked more upset than anyone about his death. Not because you'd lost a friend, but because you'd killed him and expected that somebody might have seen you. Later still, you kept asking me whether the police thought that it was an accident. You even went so far as to accuse Henry Polgreen in the hope of drawing attention from yourself.'

'To think I supported your application to join the committee,' said Sly. 'And that I might have made you secretary in due course. You're just like the rest of them. Iris's grandfather killed my grandfather. He pushed him down the well. But the judge who found him not guilty was part of the same middle-class mafia that you all belong to. Yes, I argued with Iris. I came after her and saw what I believed was her white jacket by the well. So, I thought, why not? You'll never get a better chance. And, if it had been her that went down the well, she would have deserved it.'

'That sounds like a confession to me,' said Iris.

'You wish!' said Sly. 'If you try to tell the police that, I'll say that it's a conspiracy. I have something on all of you, and Ethelred has told you exactly what those things are. Not enough for any of you to kill Joyner, perhaps, but enough for you all to want to stitch me up if that's what it took to keep me quiet about your dirty deals. That's exactly what I'll tell the police. Lots of witnesses who are quite clearly biased against me. You've no forensic evidence at all. That's the joke that I'm really going to enjoy – you all know the truth but there will be nothing any of you can do about it. If you had thought of recording this, you might have had a chance. But you didn't. So, you're not as clever as you think, for all your university education. I'm in the clear.'

There was a cough behind us. We turned to see Joe there. He'd responded quickly to my call. He'd probably been there a while now, quietly in the background. He looked at Sly and pointed to his own chest.

'Body cam,' he said. 'You're nicked.'

CHAPTER TWENTY-FOUR

Ethelred

'So, what do we do now, Iris?' I said, after almost everyone had gone. 'It's a very fine piece of silver that you have there. It's not one of the statues that the King claimed back in the 1540s. It certainly never belonged to the Knights of St John. There's no proof it was ever anywhere other than your ice house. The complications of disposing of it are nothing like those of disposing of the real Maltese Madonna. As Sammartini pointed out, you just have the red herring in Barclay-Wood's story – the false trail that the Abbot created for the King and the one that's confused all of us, including Joyner, in our own searches. Unlike the Maltese Madonna, I think that you could sort out the ownership of the Maltese herring fairly easily. Whether it's judged a treasure trove and goes to a museum, or whether you get to sell it yourself, you won't do badly.'

'I don't think I'll let Sammartini have it,' said Iris, 'whatever happens.'

'He wouldn't appreciate it?' I said.

'He's already on his way to the railway station. He's off to Penzance. He reckons Cornwallis may have sold one statue to raise capital, but the other could still be somewhere in the garden of that expensive house. If it is, Sammartini plans to strike a deal with whoever owns the house now.'

'So, where would you like it to go?'

Iris picked up the statue and looked at it with affection.

'Not Byzantine, but English,' she said. 'Almost certainly unique. It deserves to be somewhere that it's loved. Shame about the curse, of course.'

'But it isn't cursed,' I said. 'Not this one. I'm not sure any of the statues were cursed, actually. When you think about it, if both of the gold statues made it to Sussex, then neither can have been sold to the Turks as the knight's ransom. There was no betrayal to merit several hundred years of misfortune. So the whole curse story is likely to be pure invention on Barclay-Wood's part.'

'Well, you certainly can't deny they were bad luck for most of their owners, including Barclay-Wood himself.'

'Not Cornwallis,' I said.

'True. But there's no proof he took the statues – only that he'd worked out what they were. I admire Aaron's detective work, but he's still guessing about how Cornwallis made his money. It may have been entirely legit.'

'You're right,' I said. 'For all we know Barclay-Wood may have sold the real Madonna back in 1940. Or he may have hidden it in your garden – he was obviously thinking of doing so. Or maybe it went off as scrap metal with everything else that was cleared from the church and vicarage.'

'Well, I'm certainly not looking for it. Truly, Ethelred,

for all your scepticism, my family has had more than enough unfortunate events while we've had this one. You know my parents were killed in a car crash?'

'I've wondered what happened to them. I'm very sorry. But objects – like this or like the Maltese Madonna – are just that: objects. They have no power to do anything. Unless we let them. I've had it in my own garden and all that happened was that one of my roses died. They do that sometimes, however well you take care of them. Apuldram Roses replaced it free of charge.'

'Well, I'm going to give the statue to a museum, anyway,' she said. 'Also free of charge. I want no part of it, and I want none of the rest of you to have any part of it either. It's not worth the risk.'

'And the house? How will you pay for repairs?'

'I'll struggle on for a while. I fear I'll have to let Pia go. But even then I can't see how I pay for builders. Maybe I can sell off part of the garden for development. Then one day I'll sell the house too. It's always been a bit big for me on my own. I'm going to resign from the Abbey committee, by the way. I can hardly stay on once my role in the sale of the pyx and chalice and the rest of it becomes public.'

'It may not. Joe says that he didn't get the body cam switched on until Sly was confessing to murder. He clearly missed any earlier stuff that might have incriminated you. I don't know what Sly's defence is going to consist of, but it can't be that Joyner's killing was in some way justified by your exporting goods without a licence, and he'll have difficulty proving it if he does argue that. The Stephenson Museum isn't going to admit anything, and Fay abandoned Sly the moment he admitted to murder. She went back to

Oxford in Cox's car. They're quite pally again. I don't think she'll give evidence against anyone.'

'But I know I did it. You don't fancy being treasurer, I suppose? Or secretary. Sly was disqualified from office, under the rule he recently made up, the moment he was arrested.'

'No,' I said. 'I don't want to be on the committee or involved with the Madonna in any way at all. Money corrupts. That's why I'm lucky to be a writer.'

It is seldom that I return to dine at my old College without my thoughts turning to death. It is not the coffin-dark panelling. Nor is it the faces of former Principals, staring down, gowned, laced and bewigged, from the walls. It is that I feel the ghosts of past fellows, passing to and fro amongst the living, and among them the ghost of Dr Hilary Joyner. There is a picture of him now on the wall, with a small brass plate recording the years he was a Fellow of the College, and sometime Deputy Principal and Tutor for Admissions. He is spoken of as one of those people who humbly devoted their careers to the college and to teaching undergraduates, rather than seeking fame through ground-breaking research or publications or television work. A new Fellowship in history has been named after him. It is currently occupied by Dr Fay Tomlinson. It is as well that there are now three history fellowships, since Professor Cox's television work keeps him away from Oxford seven or eight months of the year, filming in Europe and China and India, signing copies of the book of the TV series in Canada, Australia and South Africa, giving guest lectures in Hawaii and Bali. Trailers for the third series of *Cox's*

History of the World are appearing on BBC Two as I write. He still takes occasional tutorials on Henry VIII and the Dissolution of the Monasteries. It is, he says, a period of great interest to him. One in which the British character was made what it is today.

'Have we met before?' asked the old lady beside me.

'A couple of years ago,' I said.

'Are you famous?'

'No,' I said.

'Didn't think so,' she said with a sigh. 'They never sit me next to anyone interesting.'

'The Principal's secretary likes my books,' I said. 'That's why I get seated at High Table.'

She nodded sympathetically. 'I'm going to be eighty-nine next year,' she said. 'Would you like to see some pictures of my grandchildren?'

'Thank you,' I said. 'I'd like that very much.'

AUTHOR'S NOTE AND ACKNOWLEDGEMENTS

None of my characters (as they say) resembles a real person in any way whatsoever. If you don't believe me, check out a few real people. Similarly, my West Wittering grows less and less like the real West Wittering with every book. It has no priory, nor has it ever had one, though the Bishops of Chichester had a country house there for a while. Likewise, Sidlesham (a nice enough place) never had an abbey of any sort. There is consequently no abbey preservation committee. The descriptions of the dunes, the marshes and rosebeds are, however, as accurate as I can possibly make them. Hell, you deserve that much.

Horrocks Greengrocers (who sometimes stock my books) and Apuldram Roses (who do guarantee their plants just as I describe) are also real and both are recommended for their excellent service. Just say that I sent you.

Hadleyburg, strictly speaking, does not exist, though fans of Mark Twain will have immediately noted references to his short story 'The Man Who Corrupted Hadleyburg'. Similarly, I cannot deny making one or two nods in the direction of Dashiell Hammett's *The Maltese Falcon*, an undoubted masterpiece of detective fiction. When I do stuff like that it's called *homage*, not plagiarism, which is something other people do.

For all of the aforementioned reasons, and many more, I remain grateful to Susie Dunlop, Kelly Smith and all at Allison & Busby for continuing to publish this series and to David Wardle for his excellent artwork that may have suckered you into buying the book. (Well done, David Wardle, I say.) In view of what the book says about agents, it may surprise you that I have found any willing to associate with me. They are, however, more tolerant than you might imagine – certainly more tolerant than you might assume from the agent who narrates some of this story. Unless he has taken exception to any of Elsie's activities between my writing this and your reading it, I am delighted to be represented by the talented and immensely popular Mr David Headley at DHH, to whom I must, again, express my thanks for his help with this book and others. And finally, I must thank my wife, Ann, whom I love dearly and who would assure you that, when I depict writers as being vague, irritating and impractical, I am perhaps, after all, not so far from unflinching realism as I may have claimed.

L. C. TYLER has won awards for his writing, including a CWA Dagger and the Last Laugh Award (twice) for the best comic crime novel of the year. He has also twice been shortlisted in the US for an Edgar Allan Poe Award. He is a former chair of the Crime Writers' Association and an Honorary Fellow of the Royal College of Paediatrics and Child Health, of which he was Chief Executive for twelve years prior to becoming a full-time writer. L. C. Tyler has lived all over the world, but most recently in London and Sussex.

lctyler.com
@lenctyler